FOGLIFTER

CREDITS

Editor-in-Chief, *Foglifter*
Luiza Flynn-Goodlett

Managing Poetry Editor Dan Lau	**Managing Hybrid Editor** Miah Jeffra	**Managing Prose Editor** Miah Jeffra
Poetry Editors Michal MJ Jones Charlie Neer	**Guest Editors** Kanika Agrawal Serena Chopra	**Prose Editors** Wesley Cohen Damitri Martinez
Development Director Jessie Galloway	**Production Manager** Miah Jeffra	**Production Editor** Monique Mero
Community Manager Tara Rose	**Web Manager** Irwan bin Iskak	**Distribution Manager** Chad Koch

Art Coordinator
Rowena De Silva

Contributing Editors
Melton Cartes   Stacy Nathaniel Jackson   Celeste Chan
Danny Thanh Nguyen   D.A. Powell

Book Layout and Design	Miah Jeffra Monique Mero
Copy Editor	Susan Calvillo
Cover Artwork	i'mawarethatyouarewatchingme;soletthemeatasylumpink, 2016 David Antonio Cruz Courtesy of the artist and Monique Meloche Gallery, Chicago

ISSN: 2470-3443
ISBN: 978-1-7321913-7-2

Foglifter is printed by McNaughton & Gunn

VOL. 5 ISSUE 2
2020

Foglifter is published twice yearly in San Francisco, California.

Foglifter is exclusively a publication of Foglifter Press. All correspondence may be addressed to 1200 Clay Street #4, San Francisco, CA 94108. Details at www.foglifterpress.com.

TABLE OF CONTENTS

PROSE

HYBRID

INTERVIEW

HEIDI ANDREA RESTREPO RHODES

Let me count the signs of life amidst the planet's dying

April 6, 2020; (after Sabrina Ghaus)

It is my birthday and the bodies are nowhere near
done piling up. Though even in the sweeter years, the ones
that red my mouth with pomegranate,
this is true.   We hurl through the heavens, a planet

of purple evenings, blink-eye fairytales, dreams at dawn. A planet
of stone-cold violence and dread. The occasional feisty miracle.
The bodies are never done
piling up.   Though spring finds its way, even if

the budding comes from the soilbed of the breathless.
Open your ears. In the grasses sprouting, a universe
sings. The birds, they bicker, and thank god
they have something to bicker about. This too,
a sign of life.   It is my birthday

and the bodies we, are nowhere near, my beloveds and I.
All quarantined. I hunger for the warm house of your
cheeks, the kisses before the province of the Far Away
forbade us, made us islands   drifting.   I am

quarantined and mapless, but the starfish have returned.
The maples weep their sugar for the bucket. I am
quarantined and braid my hair to write a poem
with my body. Stranded, we weave. I am quarantined
and learning to better read the smilebeam of eyes
peering over the masked inlet.   Beloveds, your bodies

are nowhere near, and this is how we
see another sunrise.   And the bodies are nowhere
                                        neardonepilingup.

Today, years ago, Mari gave me the light. Today the spider
knits home again by the window and I plait my head's silky roost
and so we are. Sister weavers. And tomorrow still, I will
quarantine, me the grain of sand inside the oyster shell, wanting
a sooner than later glimmering.   I'll grow

older with the trees who stretch their arms, too
say yes,   come,   come near to me
in my dreams for now while we are in the Far Away, and when
someday I am a soilbed of breathless, be the tulip
by the window, be the bickering bird, be spring.

O please, O please, be spring.

HEIDI ANDREA RESTREPO RHODES

them bodies never saints
for Kelly (1982-2015)

having sown
our one & many parts across
the pleasure fields, our crime
against the flesh is not

what you think. if all the body
were an eye, where would be
my vision but in every limb?
this is how we kneel this is how

seeing you began. forget being
machines. rally for the work stop,
the gathering of muddy joy. pray for open as G-d
goes down,   puts that whole wide

mouth on me, sweats me, says
let the lightning be a world
striking yeses from my hips
until I perforate the wall

with devotion, become a hell
party, our strange a witness to the body's riot
while G-d is a beast who moans too
loud for hotel walls, & how high

the mountain, how plenty the guests
tonight & always, I pull out the church-fear—
a spine slipped from the body of fish. I dream
your chin glimmers, a relic bone breaking bread

all broken from home, yes G-d
goes down in delight tasting me, says let me
prove you with a writhing, for lovers of pleasure
cannot be haters of holy & today this is how

I prove pleasing: I remain
uncontained. the crime is letting love go
to waste, seeing all that beauty & spitting
it out. it is too sad a thing to be

good. my heart is a clock   in a reckless
& swollen hour. my third & hellion gaping
unforgettable in the mouth

G-d savors me   will not forget

Magical Faggot as Cinematic Study (1900 - Present)

Table 1.0. Film Reference.

	Does the magical faggot...		
	Help someone learn about themselves?	Help someone find love?	Find love, themselves?
Cupid and the Comet (1911)	Y	Y	N
The Leather Boys (1964)	Y	N	N
The Producers (1968)	Y	N	N, though they already have it
Mannequin (1987)	Y	Y	N
Boogie Nights (1997)	Y	Y, in a way	N
Will & Grace (1998)	Y	Y	Y, but it takes 11 seasons
American Beauty (1999)	Y	N	Y, but they are objects of anger
Billy Elliot (2000)	Y	Y	N
Hedwig & The Angry Inch (2001) (later subverted)	Y	Y	Y, but only in discarding the main, queer character
Bend it Like Beckham (2002)	Y	Y	N
Latter Days (2003)	Y	Y	N
Mean Girls (2004)	Y	Y	N
Star Appeal (2004)	Y	Y	Kind of. A woman tries to fuck him while he is comatose.
Cold Showers (2005)	Y	Y	N
The Producers (2005)	Y	N	N, though they already have it
V for Vendetta (2005)	Y	N	N
Brokeback Mountain (2005)	Y	Y	Y, but it is fleeting, and they die
The Architect (2006)	Y	Y	N
Little Miss Sunshine (2006)	Y	Y, kind of - affirmation	N, they lose it. It's why they appear.

[Post-2006: an eruption of the same pattern. Post-2012, a galaxy.]

Faggots Almighty (2019)

The same group that sponsors my queer soccer league wants to start a queer e-sports league. My soccer team plans to form another team for this second league, but cannot find a game to compete in, since all of us only want to play healers. There is a brief fight about who could heal the most, who would look the best in Mercy drag. In an online game of *Dungeons and Dragons*, we experiment with a party of six clerics. It works until our church breaks.

I Dream in Another Faggot (2014)

Part of counseling in California is befriending translators. They are almost as young as the high schoolers I am supposed to conceal from the jaws of crisis who work, undoubtedly, harder than I do, coordinating meetings, SAT classes, college essays, and hard talks about alcohol that both I and my students could recite from memory. They also conspire, talk to parents who appear, message me about how difficult they imagine each family will be. In my first few months, the messages remain mechanical: *he has Bs and they want him to have As, they caught him grow-ing pot and now they're not talking to each other, they worry she is too boy-crazy.* But soon, they meander into encouragement. *They asked for you specifically*, goes a message I get one day. The translator knocks on my open office door, between a series of cards my mom sent me to hang up after I'd moved across the country, and asks if I read what she'd sent.

"You're famous," she says. "This family heard so many good things about you, that they actual-ly decided to return to counseling." She winks, and walks them over, whispering, "bully?" back and forth with the parents. I mark this on a notepad hidden behind a fake plant. Each meeting with new parents is another performance. Having references makes it easier.

They are pleasant, wrinkled. They ask me if I watch any TV, if I know who Beyoncé is, why I am in a school if I have an engineering degree. I tell them I was bored in front of a computer, wanted to help people. I do not say that if I fail or stagnate in one place, I move immediately toward a reflexive, outward compassion. Of course I can teach, I thought, coming here. Of course I can provide emotional support. They leave me with a persimmon, bright and thick between their son and me. He is sixteen, breathes through his mouth, shows me his phone charms and asks if I know what his parents had been saying in Chinese.

"Is it okay if I swear?" he asks. "In English. You have to promise you won't get mad." And when I give him permission, he says, "They were excited about you because they heard from another kid's parents that you're a faggot."

Bōlí, in Mandarin, means glass, and originally described a woman in the novel *Dream of the*

Red Chamber who was so pure of heart she was emotionally translucent. When directed at a male, it transforms into a gay slur—"he is effeminate," it implies, "he will break." But this student tells me, a few meetings later, that it's a compliment, sort of. "They think that you're so devoted to helping kids, because you'll never find love." He assures me this is not what he thinks, that he has heard what San Francisco is like and hopes I end up with a nice man who I can force into signing up for SAT testing.

"Yes," says the translator when I ask her later, "People here are very liberal. They love you. They know you'll give them so much, that you'll reach your breaking point. And then you'll keep giving, because that's just who you are. We're all so happy you're here. We are better for it."

The Faggot of St. Francis (2018)

In "Sanctify," the first single from Years & Years' 2018 album *Palo Santo*, Olly Alexander sings to a man that is not yet out, asking him for confessions, promising a togetherness that will heal, acknowledging a hurt before it happens. Over the course of the song, the promises Alexander makes become greater, place his body in more danger. "You don't have to be straight with me," he affirms to the other man, before volunteering to ache instead of him. "Don't break / Sanctify my body with pain." "Palo santo," itself, means "holy wood," which is both a South American plant rumored to ward off demons and disease, and slang for an enormous, well-proportioned penis.

A new employee tells me she read this fun fact, that she wants to talk more about it, that all of the other queers at my job in Chicago love her and it's only a matter of time before I do, too. She's only been there a week, and she's already worked her learned magic. During lunch, it thunderstorms. Navy Pier warps across thrashing, gray water in the building's atrium.

"I think I came on a little strong before," she says, from behind me, as she sits down. "Let me explain where I'm coming from." She tells me about her depression in high school, how the only friends she made were the choral gays who'd sit next to her after their practices, smelling but not inhaling her cigarette smoke. "All of my friends have been gay," she says. "People ask me what the most important part of my identity is, and it's being an ally." When I ask if she still talks to any of them, she changes the subject.

A few weeks later, with my soccer team at Sidetrack—the largest, most basic queer bar in Chicago – she is there, teetering on one heel, mascara, somehow, on her lip. "My boyfriend left me," she grumbles, her mouth at the base of my neck, "I am only dating gay guys from now on." I ask her where the friends she came with are, hoping that I won't have to drop $40 on a Lyft to pedal her back to South Loop during peak hours, and she says, "Look around."

As my teammates and I help carry her into her ride home, she scratches at us. An acrylic nail breaks off of her and pins itself in my arm. She yanks it away, scrapes whichever piece of me has been dug out, holds it in a closed fist, flicks the nail onto the curb. As we close the door on her, she bats against it with her free hand, yelling, muffled, "Don't leave me!" At work, the next Monday, she brings me a $10 iTunes gift card as thanks, goes in for a hug, tells me I smell nice.

The Perks of Being a Wall-Faggot (2004)

I enter high school, understanding only the queer people I've seen on TV and in movies I've had to sneak out of my house to watch with cousins who have driver's licenses and Tripp pants, who power down our cape's single highway at three-digit speeds looking like *Final Fantasy* characters. These queer characters are clean-skinned, clear-eyed men who speak in encouraging, wispy voices. They never find love, but find a happiness in the performance of helping heterosexuals, diverting time and energy into them, teaching them how to dance or wear makeup or line a divan. In this service, they find something adjacent to love, which I, fourteen, interpret as the real thing.

The rule, then: I am only worthy of having a crush on another man if I can somehow serve them. I tutor extracurricularly, pay for lunches, defend teammates with unfortunately-timed shower erections with a knowledge of body that I do not have, but that is convincing enough. I fall for a boy and ask the girl whose name he keeps saying out for him. When they appear, a week later, deed done, hands across each other in class, it is the first time I understand that to fall on a sword for a straight person feels more like jumping into a pile of shattered glass. I love him, inexplicably, more, as he brags about how tight she felt. I tell myself that the trust he's given me isn't friendship but a stored-up kind of love. When they break up, the two of us sit in the sand of a sinking kettle pond, and I place a hand on his thigh that I will think about for years. I joke, when we are finished, that they didn't talk about what we'd done in sex ed, and he says that if I ever tell anyone what happened, he'll hit me until all of my teeth fall out. Even as a child, I am seen as a fragile object, beautiful until touched, broken, absorbed. We haven't spoken since, but I find him online, years later, his arms around a wife and two sons.

There are many other crushes. I buy them art supplies, let them cheat off of me, distract teachers with elaborate questions and stories that match the topics they'd rather teach about. I take falls so often that one day, a vice principal sees me in his office and says, "Oh, fuck this." I am told I have my whole life ahead of me, that my grades are perfect, that I need to stop defending people. So, then, I learn to mistake justice for love as well.

At the end of Senior Year, policemen and firefighters—plus the fake school cop who struts through school with an unbuckled belt and a taser—stage a car crash outside of school. It is an assembly to prevent drunk driving. We know it is coming, but the reality they have dedicated to manufacturing—the Hollywood gore reconstructed by an art teacher with a background in stage makeup—is enough to break all of us. We see classmates, falsely-injured, birthed from impounded vehicles with the Jaws of Life. They are trained, supine, and taken away in an ambulance. A friend, another crush, turns to me when the emergency vehicles vacate, when the same vice principal gives a speech about how making the wrong choice, just one time, can lead to tragedy. He says, "Why didn't you volunteer for that? That seemed like exactly your kind of thing."

Mr. Faggot's Opus (2012)

I still consider my body in place of other bodies, envision my neck heroically punctured, blood trickling down my chest like a tournament bracket. There is still a small, exhilarating disruption whenever I see an opportunity to step in for a person that could later love – or at least be grateful for – me. When I begin to teach, just after college, this feeling swells. My chest feels like a bomb. There are so many people to help, to show that like other queer men, I can preempt the harm I assume they think I'll do, that they may validate me through my service. Though I do not know it consciously, I see myself of representative of all queer people they'll meet, feel like I must remain perfect, translucent. Soon, my students will all vote on whether I can marry, or donate blood, or work. I sign up to head four clubs. Students pool in my class-room during my lunch break, so I do not eat during the day, or go to the bathroom. I am 22. They make enormous strides in their Common Core standards, begin to thank me for telling them that I believe in them, say that they finally feel like they matter.

My supervisor in Teach For America films me, tells me I have done incredible work. I talk to him about how it is so difficult to make so many parental phone calls and grade two hundred and eighty papers. He says that it is difficult, but we are heroes, that we do this work because we are the people who truly do care, who can demonstrate love to kids scammed by a society that wants to show them only violence. I deliver him as much of a performance as I regularly give my students. I am fine.

I faint during lunch, and the kids playing Super Smash Bros. on my projector call the school nurse. I am sent home, told to spend money on a doctor. The health insurance plan for a first-year public school teacher in California without a master's degree is jokingly called "The Coffin Plan." It covers: funeral arrangements, a yearly checkup. An option for vision insurance occurs in Year 3. So—for others, I tell myself—I burn through my savings to pay for psychiatrists, medication.

My TFA supervisor says, "Let's talk about some strategies to numb your feelings." My psychiatrist says to take time off or I will die. It takes me weeks to make the decision.

When I tell my students I will leave them, I assure them that it will be brief, that they have already progressed—been healed—so much. I show them graphs. The school hires a temporary sub. On my last day for a while, my room is filled with children I have helped. It is the type of event a teacher dreams of—all of the students for which I have sanctified slices of my brain for thank me. They line up. One gives me a warm Snickers bar. I give them my classroom decorations, flags, and college posters. The three who are learning guitar bring their instruments, covered in bumper stickers, and the group sings. It feels coalescent, like the geometries of life I've given up for them are actually returned. I go home, cry, am in bed for two weeks. A year later, in my new role as a counselor, I will reference this moment, say it was a point I did not realize was my highest.

The Shape of Faggots (2015)

A volunteer coordinator for a queer center in Chicago tells me on a date about the time one of his employees said during a yoga class, "For this next hour, forget about the other people in your life—you deserve this time, you are the only thing that matters, so take this time for yourself," and one of his students started crying, mid-downward dog, his snot leaking backwards up his forehead. "I think about that all the time," he says, "about how life can be tough, but at least we're never that empty—to think it's so surprising to have value." I take him home, hold him as I remember how inclined I had been to not make noise, to disrupt the individual rituals of the people around me, how much I wanted to wipe my face, how desperate I had been to hold my pose.

Magical Faggot (2016-2017)

The whole premise of being a magical faggot is that you continue to give away pieces of yourself, to volunteer for obligation so that another may be repaired. The humor is derived from what happens when you put two of them together, when they donate themselves to each other relentlessly. Think, "Gift of the Magi." A twist. A great joke.

On date one, the narrator buys the object of his affection flowers. The two do not leave the house, deciding, instead, to fuck, to watch nature documentaries. They block each other's eyes when one animal eats another, instinctively. Laugh track.

Date two, the object of his affection makes dinner, says he doesn't eat unless he's around people, how that was a rule his parents had, how sapped he feels in between their now-messy divorce. Plus, there is the housing crisis it is his job to address, the grant that will expire—and his job with it. His mediocre salary and the coding bootcamp that costs more than two months of it. The narrator lends him money, stays quiet when the object of affection falls asleep cooking dinner, and the object of affection keeps saying, "I owe you," "I owe you," until it becomes a sort of catchphrase. It is almost like gratitude. It sustains the narrator.

This has a ripple effect through Boystown. The object of affection is not, they deem, the type of man to receive flowers. He has lived so many double lives, nonprofit by day and dancer by night. They call him The Demon Twink, warn the narrator that he'll get his soul stolen. But the narrator, who has split himself between his students during the day and the object of his affection—now his boyfriend—by night, continues his gifts. Other men—exes, old flings—send the object of affection flowers, too, after he brags about receiving them, about how romantic the narrator is. The audience laughs at this—the narrator has not been established as a romantic character, outside of a two-year abuse that is neutered and summarized, as to not ruin the mood. The narrator learns to turn it into a single joke, impresses himself.

To save money, the two of them stick to watching movies at home, lights turned off, gas stove heating the place in winter. "I need to watch gay movies," says the object of affection. And they rifle through all of the classics: *American Beauty* and *Mean Girls* and *Brokeback Mountain*. The narrator asks why the queer characters are always denied love, and the object of affection says, "I dunno—that's just how life is." One morning, they both cannot seem to wake up, keep hacking up empty air. "Uh oh," says the object of affection, motioning loosely toward the stove, combusting into fog on the closed windows all night. The two of them cannot stop giggling. It feels, to the narrator, as though this is love, the pair of them constantly saving each other.

Months in, the object of affection's kidneys fail temporarily. On the way back from the emergency room, when the narrator attempts to put his hands on his, the object of affection hits him in the arm, which quickly pools into bruising. "I didn't say to touch me," he says. "I'm so stressed. With you and the divorce and the job, and you're not making it any better. The rest of this part is more slapstick, the object of affection clawing at the narrator's biceps on the floor of their favorite bar, spitting, drunk, when the narrator has come to rescue him. He says, "I can't believe you hate me like this, you hate faggots like this. Just let me have a good time." When the narrator talks him into a walk home, the object of affection sighs like a kid, his breath bleeding into the air around them, his neck a smokestack, his body latent with energy. They arrive home, and each time the narrator tries to say something, the object of affection covers his mouth, says, "uhp," in accruing forms, "uhp uhp uhp uhp uhp," with the sort of threatening, Midwestern politeness that can get any audience giggling.

An internal monologue, the narrator's eyes wet and wide and lost, a stare of enough yards that you could take a screenshot of him and turn it memetic, blow geometries across his face. "If I am perfect enough, I will be loved by someone perfect enough. If I can help someone through a rough time, if I can turn someone more perfect, more capable of love, then I, too, will become more capable of love, more perfect." An interruption: the object of affection throws a glass at the narrator's head. In the cinematic remake, confetti bursts forth from it, like a piñata, but before this is a film, it bounces off of the couch, splits as it hits the ground, shattering like a broken body. The narrator, also, bounces, bolts so entirely he runs two miles in subzero weather before thinking about calling a ride. Another source of humor: everything is frozen, and the plows have not yet arrived. The snow falls menacing and soft. The narrator cannot, for the life of him, stay on his feet, skidding into the rigid constitutions of buildings, careening forward into poles. He bursts his lip, and his blood freezes over, dangling like a chandelier beneath his mouth. The Lyft driver he eventually calls says, "So who won? You or the other guy?" Roll snare.

Once the narrator breaks up with him, the object of affection reappears in clubs for a sequel once every few months, with new boyfriends, newer and higher-ranking on the service scale: nonprofit coordinators, doctors, psychiatrists. A nurse, friendly, tells the narrator a story about the object of affection: "Our first date goes well, we hook up and everything, we talk about how our parents hit us, and then, in the middle of sex, I'm inside of him, and he grabs my shoulders and says, 'If you don't bring me flowers the next time we do this, I'll know this isn't real.' So I don't know if he's kidding or not, but I get him this bouquet at the hospital—they have really nice ones there, for all the people who die. And I hear that this is something he asks everyone he fucks. It's been his thing forever, ever since an old hookup did this for him, this one time." Then, noticing the object of affection waving him away, the nurse says, "By the way, who are you?"

"I'm the guy who got the flowers," the narrator says, and the nurse's face blinks into disaster. *Buh-dum tss*. Slide whistle. Curtains. A great joke.

All the President's Faggots (2003-2016)

Massachusetts, the state where I spend most of my childhood, is the first to legalize gay marriage. Though I am not yet out, it feels as though all of the teachers embracing, the neighbors slashing corks off of champagne bottles, affirm me. I want to write what I hear across my skin: Love is The Answer. My 76-year-old English teacher comes out to us the day afterward, tells us about the wife she has lived with for nearly 50 years, how if you love a person with enough volume, allow your love to expand, to cross boundaries, then you can accomplish anything. Weeks before I go to college, in 2008, California legalizes it as well, then scribbles across it with Proposition 8. I give myself to professors requesting long hours monitoring neon text in laboratories, find other men who seem in need of healing. It is overturned in 2010. I move to Chicago, to Boystown, and start programs for students that win awards. In 2015, when queer people are declared legal to marry by the Supreme Court, it all feels like it is working, that the sacrifices I have made—for students, yes, but also for straight men looking for living, secret-keeping dildos, for straight women looking for safety, for other queer men who convince me that we are the two to heal each other. I continue to love so vividly and endlessly that I end up in the emergency room twice, an overdose, a workout so long that—coupled with a few, fun genetic complications—tears the fabric of my innards away from my bone. For the first time, I work a job where health insurance includes psychiatry, which I am reminded by another queer employee repeatedly, until I attend.

Fag Swan (2020)

I am afraid of writing this because it will mean that I do not contain the pulsating, upper-level capacity to heal that so many former teachers, so many queer elders, told me was, in my desires to do good and make change, inherent—that the currencies I have cultivated as a queer man, of openness and listening and an attempt to discover love that would have to be infinite enough to suddenly undo centuries of subjugation, hate crime, and genocide is limited, as much of a muscle as quadricep, a thing to be steadied and coordinated so that it goes undrained, doesn't snap back and recoil into an arrangement only a medical professional could repair. That there is a ceiling for worship of yourself through others, that an eternal selflessness results only in a removal, that there is only a certain number of times a body can be sacrificed before it is too cut-up and twisted to even look like one anymore. That there are thermodynamic laws about this that I learned in engineering school, that I should have known to begin with. If I were an infinite well, then some higher-ranking officials would have flashed their badges by now, attempted to drain me. Which is not to say that this has not been attempted. But even through all of the work that I have done to become magical—the rich, gay, arcane failures that have polished me into a faggot—I sometimes still forget to recycle some of it back into myself.

2 Faggots 2 Furious (2017-)

It is a right of passage, on my new soccer team, to be called a faggot. It is a title to be earned. Faggots are the ones who have stories, chains of long nights, mistakes. Who jump rope nude with a discarded chain in Jackhammer's hole, who lose a college v-card getting rawed in the Progress bathroom, which leaks, and is owned by a racist man that will die a few nights afterward. On our first night out as a team, one of our defenders drops a bottle of poppers on the floor of a club, and it clears the whole place out like teargas. Another calls us to pick him up, and when we arrive, moving in a pack, our bodies in a mob to preserve our heat, we find him at the top of his stairs, pants down, an entire tray of chicken fingers sprawled down into his entry way, a small plastic canister of barbecue sauce in a pair of hundred-dollar shoes. Knowing them, existing near-exclusively around queer people, people who do not wish only to take, is a removal of performance. We do spa days, learn to recover our sore bodies from dancing stupidly—I flail, apparently, like a shirtless Tina Belcher—after tournaments. I go with one teammate on a boat called *Holy Wood* into the middle of Lake Michigan, where its creepy driver tells everyone to get naked. We shrug and jump into the water. The water temperature feels barely in the single-digits. We shriek, cackle, fail to thermoregulate. I feel, for the first time, preserved. "Why in the world did we do this?" he asks. "You stupid faggot."

MARTHA RYAN

skinned

plum red pores
grin with
sebum, roil in waxy
exterior until sheen
transgresses wrinkle, riled
and reptilian.

since the days went quiet
impurities became urgent
priorities (expelling them).

a great storage of dust
gruel and grainy specks from
receding terrain. once
benign now surfacing.

that which determines inside/
outside/yes/no/good/bad
holds in lurching
silence particulate matter
piece of dirt turned glitter
into organic
matter humanized.

a partial processing is all
we can afford. a surface is
crowded. a drowning din of
germ, flake, powder, and stubborn
acid.

open till it lands a prized and patterned
platelet—

an innocent gulp, an uninformed
digestion.

disinfection, or disintegration,
hardly disturbs that which has been
swallowed. shaken its head, spat it back
out.

a tremble in the extremities, an extraction
imminent.

NATALIE SHARP

poem in which black girl constellates
for Kaytrina | after Danez Smith

Long after my grandmother's globes go
rheumy, I'll wake in spring reaching for you.

Pins in your old dresses scrape at my neck to
threaten exposure: babygirl as cautionary tale, gay

shame, red dead irredeemable. I play games
with my ghouls. I'm tired of demons and rooms I leave

clean waiting to be possessed again. I can be your
nothing. I am the prolific empty. Everyone spells

your name wrong, confusing you for a *wedding
between water and wind*. I look up with my jaw clenched.

You've taught me everything I know about space.
You buried me and swallowed my marrow

so I could dive through it. The fact of a force
of nature is how soon strewn roots

plunge back into earth's belly. I can feel you
try to forget me. I don't desire your evisceration

but I know how grief grips intestines. I know you hurt. I
see it mirrored in my cheeks, my vascular rhythms,

my smooth, certain nailbeds. Some days I succeed
at forgiveness. Others I prick my thighs with the old rage

and wait for blood that never comes. I'm too grown
to call this *healed* but at least movement improves

me. For every new year we preserve our bull-headed
separateness, I mourn how much I'll miss. You might

die in my absence or I in yours. I hope you get your paradise.
I hope if god won't give you back the girls he's taken from your life,

he makes you rich with dutiful women who overwrite my lines.
At any rate, I love you. I apologize for the length of this night.

ode to unknowing

Last night I dreamed I saw my sister
lit beneath a bridge. I'll say it plain: girls
go missing every night. I know all the time
she looked for me. I'm not the sort of
woman you will find tucked safely in your
memory. I fade from edges like that,
haunt the corners of whatever may be
made over-majestic about goneness,
which is the truth of this. I have conjured
her, light-skinned and bright-eyed.
One day you found cracked plastic
barrettes, each bead's bulb pushing
into your palm and thought "This is how
absence bleeds—half-hollow and
translucent." See the daughter
made reluctant light for all the facts
she couldn't write?

Last night I dreamed I saw my sister
sitting underneath the stairs
in a terribly well-lit mall, her eyes
welled up red-rimmed and reaching
for mine. Air is the sum of calculated
force and whatever displaces it. Her lips
scratched at me like a place
I don't belong. I mean to say *arrest*.
I made a mistake: I held blouses stinking of
the women who wore them to my face.
Maybe I want to smother whatever
comes away clean. Maybe I'm suffocating.
Loss renders me declarative—
our mutual understanding of emergency
unravels all my visions, nearly
threadbare yet fearfully wound.

Last night I dreamed I saw my sister
transubstantiated in our childhood
home. Pregnant with a new moon
through some miracle
or minor divinity, she opened her mouth
to taste the us we used to be.
Tremors make me misrepresent
this narrative's porcelain artifice.
Our stories chipped on their undersides.
They believe they will live long enough
to see themselves burned.
I know family is a shattered fable—
I am a descendant of faults.
Truthfully, I imagined all the ghosts
in this poem, even me.

BREENA NUÑEZ

(Mourning)

HR HEGNAUER

DAY 253

Yesterday, a nine-year-old girl accidently killed her teacher with an automatic machine gun. They were at a shooting range, and she lost control, and it kept firing, and her teacher died from wounds to the head. Her parents brought her there for fun. I saw the death video replayed on cruise ship TV. The TV people asked an expert what he thought about it all, and the expert said, "Some nine-year-olds can handle a small machine gun, and some can't, and that's the fact of it."

Later, I cried at lunch. I was looking at the ocean when the world dumped itself into my noodle stir-fry, and I ate it.

Where is the point where impulse crosses thoughtfulness? A cruise ship. A Caribbean cruise ship.

When I sit on the balcony and look across all that water, I think about every person who's ever suffered and every person who'll ever be a sufferer tomorrow. Thank god today is not also tomorrow. We couldn't handle both in one day.

When I get on the elevator, it reeks of cheap perfume and cheaper wine, and there are three women in bikinis with black make-up running down their faces. They're huddled in a tight circle. In one of their cupped hands, a small sparrow looks to be without salvation. One of them says she's going to give it CPR. This cannot be happening, I think.

There seems to be a disproportionate amount of crazy people on this cruise ship. Or more likely, my own perception of myself is biased. I appear to be doing things correctly though: I wake, drink my morning tea, dress myself, and look at the ocean. I eat and walk around. I enjoy the company of strangers, while they also annoy me. I look at the ocean. I eat again. I look at the ocean.

HR HEGNAUER

DAY 341

Life is like an ocean that's bigger than my scope allows: see the smallest instance, and it overwhelms me to the point where my only relief is to look. Look now. Look into the ocean, Goddammit.

I once joined a kickball team, and at our second game, there was a trans woman on the other team. Standing with a group of my teammates, Billy says, "Oh my god! I mean, what the fuck is that?" He gulps from his Bud Light and points. This is the sort of kickball league where you drink beer while playing. I pretend to hear nothing even though Billy's about two feet from me. I glance at him, say nothing, but note his outfit: a costume turning him into a giant piece of bacon. Tonight's theme is super heroes, and I gather that Billy is some sort of bacon superhero. My costume consists of a plastic gold-medal necklace that my nine-year-old friend gave me. "I mean, you know, is that like his fucking lifestyle, or is that just his costume?" Billy gives my shoulder a little bro punch.

Two days ago, 49 people were massacred at a gay bar in Orlando. I find it increasingly difficult to breathe on this field.

It's getting dark out, and a woman comes to the door. She says her name is Tabitha, and she has a kind of anxious gone-look to her face. She tells me she's locked out and needs help. "Call my friend, Clarence," she pleads. Okay, I dial Clarence. She tries to open my screen door, but I locked it a couple hours ago, and she's annoyed she can't get in. The dogs bark inconsolably. "Are you a boy or a girl?" Tabitha asks me through the screen. I roll my eyes at her. "Clarence? I'm here with your friend Tabitha, and she's locked out and trying to get to you." "But are you a boy or a girl?" Tabitha begins to get a little louder and panicky and then starts hysterically laughing. I try to ignore her, but she keeps asking me with more and more urgency. "Are you a boy or a girl, Goddammit!" Clarence says, "Tell her to meet me at the river under the overpass." I tell her how to walk one block down and then over two to the river. I close the door even though Tabitha was still standing there.

We look at the ocean differently; we see different shades of blue. That is to say, we make different selections at the buffet. Look up. Look across the ocean. See how many shades of blue there are in just one field of vision. Multiply that number by how many people in the world are currently looking at the ocean. Making math out of the ocean makes you forget the language for the time.

WRYLY T. McCUTCHEN

Horoscopes

              sweat like a grapefruit
          under the knife. heat up here
                    pinks me and tongue
          and long.

          I miss swing in of skin
                         to push against.
          miss pretending to be
               her favorite boy band.
          ms his half-shaved
                    ponytail & teenage grrrrl gustO
               goth-metal-pnnk shyhip wiggle.
          I mx pale alligator shoes moving crow feather
               coiffiture   cross the stage;
                    later   jazzy yowls   pulling
               down from
                              fistful of dancing
               on down through sheets we beat bloody by mo(U)rning.
          Miss Pinch of Somachpit Bitter
               as the door closed behind thim.

          ive   not loved like that
               in a long time, not smoothed
            the blisters down into red
          wet malcontent. Miss Fucks
          Withnofuture.
          Mx Not-Knowing
               what to say when it's over.

          Miss loving +
             knowing nothing will ever
                  settle

          you.

Breathe. You'll never leave your body
    until you do.
  You only get one go, so
  find a way, live unpeeled.

 No coconut coating,
you are not hard-rinded thing
   as much as you'd like to insect
you'ren't. Newspaper named you
 an arthropod   but the thing is
horoscopes never tell you   exactly
 how many legs you'll have/miss   so smoke
   Right On   through your exoskeleton,
   jump lemon glide on   into fancy and yammering on.
      Jump into your soft.

    Much too endoskeletal to care
      about the fate of any one fruit
    and so the strawberry
  heads we're discarded
into a bucket unceremoniously.

WRYLY T. McCUTCHEN

fo||ow some mountain

                    into a church
              parking |ot. on|y
         cry when moving
    |egs he gave you. something's
                              gone
            from the weather
    seasons ain't what they used to be.
    s|ip past a sticky gui||otine
         behind   :   a pickup speeds
            brazen into the space that frame once was
      before   :   the |ight hangs changed
         too sa|tyeyed s|ow
            ref|ex *Fuck!* scrapes |ung &
               air \ be/comes / irregu|ar | un\\e|ementa| br/eat\hs
            gutpunch to too a|ive a diaphragm.
            fu|| but not who||y.

Nothing fi||s your body more comp|ete|y than your father's sudden absence from his.

                         horseshoes he f|ung
              spraying |uck end over end
         hungry for iron, for c|ang. but.
    sma|| thud
         in the dense grey partic|es
            then nothing.   stick a hand in,
                         dig out something
      dirty nai|s.
      try.

What you want to write about him is anything e|se but he is dead.

         there. it be.
      Beast   unseen.
         Beast both
      is & isn't in the room.
    it fee|s |ong before you fee| it.

you Fee| it.

    stiff   nine   months   numb   then

discover p|easure\\   //discover grief

  discover p|easure & grief as neighbors

         secret | sib|ings, perhaps even

        |overs

  in this rendition.

when spirit cums, interior wedges open

\   the   vast   c a t h e d r a | wa||s   /

       organ's sti|| pumping with |uck

 & then the coup|e streams in together

       ocean of excruciating |ight, each photon

bigger than the observab|e universe. on|y then

       who||y heaping pristine|y disordered endings

fa||ing over   into   &   through

   unti|

You're finished.

You might a|so c|aim that this a|| began |ast night in the woods when some divine|y
scu|pted anima| gave you back your grandmother name as you be|ched her be|ch between
honeysuck|ing each other. You be|ched. They summoned

          /R/S

name of the dead father's dead mother who ratt|es through whenever a tru|y majestic
be|ch makes conduit of your esophagus.

        a b|ock from home

     try to save a drying-out sidewa|k worm

  by spitting on it, nudging soft body toward damp dirt.

forget about january.

forget freezing.

forget the skin ye||owing

   exponentia||y every time

    your |egs ferried those survived by

       back through   the emptied

  ward so they might ache & ache

  3 hours after   the   body

    became a day o|d bruise

    the green before   the b|oom   .

      your Earthworm   turns

       out to be a twig.

untethered objects

preface:earthbound

i dream i push him away this time.

    my wrists flexible and strong, like trees swaying in a high wind.

    he can't take an inch or a mile,

    when i am so firmly rooted.

retelling

i want to imagine my story is different:

    i am queer,

    i am smart,

    i am jewish; anxious; thoughtful

    i am almost a feminist.

    i have slept with one man.

i want to imagine my story is the same,

    so the ending will no longer be my fault.

safehouse

the night, the party, explode with possibility:

i drink a soda bottle of green apple cider,

which leaves sour-sweet residue across my teeth.

my blood tingles with bubbles bursting

or shooting stars.

     friends—i am surrounded by—friends

     i am 12.5% saturated.

     i have never felt more protected.

white knight

somehow, i am on the floor of my friend's room,

sitting on a different boy's lap.

     (fingers explore me. driven, destinationless.)

i make eye contact with him, propped on the bed—across from me

watching with lazy jealousy

until he sees the panic in my eyes

     (the cider drenches me in the need for bodies

         for skin tight against my own

    but now

         [the need a reality plunged inside me]

    fear expunges desire;

     i do not remember ever wanting this)

"stop,"

he says, and rescues me from lap, fingers.

my words slur with gratitude.

hero, i think. blurrily.

premonition

like reverse bookends,

    the answer and question

        in the final minutes before we leave the party.

to him:

    "sure, but we're not going to have sex."

i—certain; he—understanding.

minutes after my ultimatum, as i wait outside,

he approaches my friend;

asks her for a condom.

littleman

"where's your ear cuff?"

my sister asks

months later.

the cuff is a little silver climbing man.

i name him, laugh at his wild legs wrapping my cartilage.

my mom, sister, and i have matching ones.

my little man disappeared

    (how, i don't remember)

on the floor of the cab

    (i don't remember)

we took to an address

(i don't remember)

where he brought me to his bedroom

(i remember and remember and remember)

linguistics

i know how to say no

in eight languages

(english spanish italian french portuguese german chinese hebrew)

my tongue knows the malleable wrinkles of my gums

and my front teeth's smooth divide—

the architecture of n

the round opening o

he says, "we can either just have had the fivesecondsofsex we already had or

we can keep going…"

interlude:warden

for six years, i keep his name prisoner,

buried under my tongue, clamped in the muscle.

why ruin his life? i ask myself

but really, i swim river-rapids of fear:

he will sue me for defamation.

i will end up historically/legally the aggressor.

a name spoken aloud

is too powerful:

i've never said the third "bloody mary"

to the bathroom mirror.

confide

"tell me a secret,"

he begs.

early-early morning brings gray

sobriety.

i already gave him a secret.

but i tell him another.

enter

i am not a house

      houses have doors; windows; walls;

      locks

maybe i am a pond:

move slowly enough

and anyone may slip inside

without a single ripple

intimate

i lie on a mattress that lies on a floor.

(no comforter. sheets torn, unwashed.)

around us, used plates crusted with old food.

it is like a serial killer's home, i think, and stop.

thinking.

      we have slept together, actually slept;

      i have told my secrets and slept beside this man-boy

still asleep

more

a pond

a shallow one, at that.

escape (part one)

i try to leave

i do not know when it happens (i think it is still morning)

"i have to go"

i walk into the hallway,

and he chases me

pins me against the wall, laughing as though i've told a violently

funny joke

an embroidered bra hangs on the drying rack

and i wonder who his roommates are

how any woman could live with him

in this unlit trash-strewn nightmare

he kisses me—

leads me back to the bedroom.

untethered

i don't know what to call what we do

all that day

what we do in the no-woman's-land

beyond reality

beyond consent

beyond pleasure

i float.

i can no longer feel gentle touch.

i float.

i plead for him: harder. harder.

if i can want it now, perhaps i wanted it then; perhaps i've always wanted it; perhaps i've

waited my whole life for this precise impersonal pain.

interlude:re-cycle

they say all your cells regenerate

each seven years:

by august 2020

there will no longer be any microscopic

piece of me

that touched him.

test

we leave midday for chinese food

and he tells me about his father,

about the volcano of hurt here—right here—

    he points to his chest.

i can fix him, i think, obliquely.

he is not a challenging project, i think.

i have done harder things than walking in the sunshine

holding hands with an intimate stranger

who hates his father.

i have done harder things.

a lone

i will not tell anyone for six weeks.

before that,

i will turn down his offer to date.

i will walk home each night too fast,

certain someone is chasing me.

i will use any word for what happened

except the 'r-word.'

i will go to the doctor alone for:

    -antifungal (yeast infection)

    -antibiotics (strep throat)

    -plan b (my friend never did have that condom)

escape (part two)

i don't let him walk me all the way home,

don't want him to know where i live,

don't yet know why.

> "see you soon," he says
>
> and i agree
>
> and know   it is a lie.

when i walk away from him, our last kiss

chaps my lips

and the weight of something

enormous

builds a new home in my ribcage.

> it is too much.
>
> i fold
>
> it
>
> in
>
> quarters
>
> and tuck it away in my heart.
>
> like a love note.
>
> a suicide note.

xxxxx

aaron. aaron. aaron. aaron. aaron. aaron. aaron. aaron. aaron. aaron. aaron. aaron. aaron.
aaron. aaron. aaron. aaron. aaron. aaron. aaron. aaron. aaron. aaron. aaron. aaron. aaron.
aaron. aaron. aaron. aaron. aaron. aaron. aaron. aaron. aaron. aaron. aaron. aaron. aaron.
aaron. aaron. aaron. aaron. aaron. aaron. aaron. aaron. aaron. aaron. aaron. aaron. aaron.
aaron. aaron. aaron. aaron. aaron. aaron. aaron. aaron. aaron. aaron. aaron. aaron. aaron.
aaron. aaron. aaron. aaron. aaron. aaron. aaron. aaron. aaron. aaron. aaron. aaron. aaron.
aaron. aaron. aaron. aaron. aaron. aaron. aaron. aaron. aaron. aaron. aaron. aaron. aaron.
aaron. aaron. aaron. aaron. aaron. aaron. aaron. aaron. aaron. aaron. aaron. aaron. aaron.
aaron. aaron. aaron. aaron. aaron. aaron. aaron. aaron. aaron. aaron. aaron. aaron. aaron.
aaron. aaron. aaron. aaron. aaron. aaron. aaron. aaron. aaron. aaron. aaron. aaron. aaron.
aaron. aaron. aaron. aaron. aaron. aaron. aaron. aaron. aaron. aaron. aaron. aaron. aaron.
aaron. aaron. aaron. aaron. aaron. aaron. aaron. aaron. aaron. aaron. aaron. aaron. aaron.

aaron.

post-script

but he will not have the last

word.

FRANCISCO MÁRQUEZ

Citizen

I'm one of the ones covered, still
in underwear, three on the bed,
one in a jockstrap on the couch.
The naked host greets me,
while he undresses me. First
he asks, *Where are you from?*
I say, *Venezuela.* White skinny
man next to the host adds, *Shit's
rough, huh?* as he jacks off.
Why? What's going on there?
host asks, unscrewing poppers,
mixing in G with water. *Some
shit with the government. So,
you gonna go back? You legal?*
skinny says, jaw trembling.

In the background a video plays
of a man having pool balls put
up his asshole. Some men rise
and make loud foreign noises
in the kitchen. At all directions
mirrors point at angles to the bed,
the bed wet from the sweat,
the ceiling white with a shine
of a red light—I turn to the man
in the jock, staring at the wall
with the shining video, stoic,
alone, he stares as if having
trouble to speak: *What part of
Venezuela?* I say, *Maracaibo.*
He nods, *Yo soy de Cuba—somos
hermanos?* We laugh, *Sí.* He says,
*Mis amigos de Venezuela, they say
they're never going back.* We begin
to touch ourselves. *I want to,*
I tell him, *but I wouldn't survive.*

The other men kiss and the three shine
red and mostly shadow, while we're
on the couch anchored, untouched,
spotlight-less as the room swells
and then, to keep count, a number
is written on my hand in permanent
marker. The pool ball shoots into
the screen's glass. We no longer
neighbor the spectacle but are
drawn to the core, pulled at by men
in uniform, a cop calls my number
to suck off his friends, and the host,
and it's all the brown boys kneeling,
servicing the elders, cacophonies
pouring and we're returned
mouthless, anchored, shelved
in the soft country. I wait my turn.
I dream the number in my sleep.

◆◆ HAZEM FAHMY ◆◆◆◆◆◆◆

Ars Poetica

بإسم الله

Like everything, begin at the river,
flood the sea. Here, a land claimed
beneath a quiet moon, his face unshaven. With lust
for light burn Homer, Aristotl,e and Virgil. If horses
gallop here they neigh symphonies: hoodlums'
howls. 'Lectro-Sha3bi, max volume.

الدنيا مش مورجيحة
الدنيا متناكة

We can't speak of mothers before burying
Hypatia and Cleopatra. Time is of the essence
so let this be the time for Mariam,
not Mary, Scheherazade—Zeinab
if available. We will not ask for that
which cannot be given, unless it be hiding
out in museums that charge Euros
or Dollars. That's our shit. Imam said so
long ago. Not objectively,
but permanently. So let's Edward Said
motherfuckers, make occidentals out of con-
tinentals. I don't care for English lest it be blood
stained and broken. Dictate that dialect. Assert
your accent. Smoke cigs
like Youssef Chahine. Flick it on film reels.
We reject celluloid unless we have projectors.
Om Kalthoum will do fine on Spotify.
Before you sleep say good night.
Today, Zaghloul. Tomorrow whoever.
I could be wrong about Zaghloul. We've zig-
zagged here before.

ده إنجليزى ؟
طب ده صوتَ؟

I don't know. I know the sound of Cairo.
I know how the sea cries. Find your Darwish.
I don't care which. Find the kind of song

that takes you there:

خذني على بلادي

I don't care where, what or who.

الأسمراني

What about?

عملة أر الغربة فيه

Ask again.

طمنوني

and again and again and again and
again and just when you're done: again.

HAZEM FAHMY

Ahha (اها) Poetica

The poem is the quest for the scream,
that knife which cuts the night
crimson, leads the dirt in song,
marks holy territory with blood. This poem isn't
about blood, but it might as well be.
Let's pump preposterously. Pretend
it's oil, and you'll find
it. Once, a whole nation went
to war for an orgasm: why
should we settle for less? This poem is the body, so it
too is searching for a good
time, requited with a roar;
the river that greets the sea
with a gentle shiver. Say please
and thank you. Say أقسم بالله.
This body dance truth, retained
scripture. Yes, I read (for) pleasure;
a subtle ecstasy, but the breath is still
tested. بالله لا قوة لا و حول لا Do you know
what that means? Why shouldn't God
smile down upon my sweat? What is love
without labor? The body demands
the scream. I live for the stolen
breath, brought back. Exhale.
اها What do you think
Hind Rostom did in that barn? The train
screeched. I know the moan is
our inheritance. Bring it back
soft and steady; the heavy breath
before dawn—not of waiting. A watched street
never marches. Bring back the protest.
Bring it here in my throat, in my chest.
Inhale. اها Say اها. Say it tender. Say
it loud. Behold a revived
grammar: a thousand اهاs I lay

upon you. Oh ⊾∟ my
⊾∟: give me ⊾∟ or give me
⊾∟. My one regret is that
I have but one ⊾∟ to ⊾∟ my ⊾∟.
Oh, see can you ⊾∟? If not now,
then tomorrow. Let the morning
bring you.
⊾∟

Semaphore

After all is said and done, find me a *freespeech* patriot who'd let the flag
burn, like a rice field in a land so far away, a mother must wake in the dead of night to
call her children, say: this is the last fire you will ever know; tomorrow the ocean will
dry and you will walk across, pick as many fish as your hands can carry.

Every day, I walk under the shadows of banners,
fluttering tidal waves, drowning the soil. The
ground I walk will sink before I
hear the surrender of the cord, the fabric falling to the earth, where

it belongs. But burial has never been sufficient grounds for
justice. If every flag that ever was burned, where does that leave
Kurdistan,
Lumumba,

Mandela,
Nicaragua?
Own it: not every flag was sewn equal; the
Palestinian flag is still a target in Palestine. When the

Queen of Hawaii was forced to surrender her throne to invaders, how long did it take to
raise the American flag? Asked years later, Liliuokalani's niece, Ka'iulani
said: "It was bad enough to lose
the throne, but infinitely worse to have the flag go down." In Cairo, every instance of

unrest brings a flood of red, and black, and white; a torrent of golden eagles
vacating the streets. After all is said and done,
who am I to deny a calloused hand the cloth that gives it voice? I am not
Xerxes before the river, intoxicated with possibility. I am drunk on New

Year's, my friend in my arms, telling me how happy she is I am *home*, knowing this
zeal always has a cost, even if we don't pay it.

 LYD HAVENS

206 days later

This time, there's no one around to call me back behind
the screen door—I wander to the bricks muddy
with my own handprints. The air is humid here;
I collect it in my hands. There's a fingerprint-shaped scar
on the nape of my neck that only I have touched. A crater
on the moon no one's landed on. I count my bones
just to be sure. There's a fountain where I've only ever seen
people steal pennies instead of offer them. I wish
I could walk barefoot forever. I wish I knew how to cartwheel.
Once, a girl I thought I would marry made a list
of all the people we had collectively lost in our lives:
let's name our children after them. I think I will always be
a slab of July cement, attracting only mosquitoes
and cherry syrup. I feel empty the way a museum
can be empty. I count my bones just to be sure,
as if a part of me takes off in the night while I sweat
myself to sleep.

◆ ◆ MIHEE KIM

there was no place for them

Then I saw a great white throne and him who was seated on it. The earth and the heavens
fled from his presence, and there was no place for them.   -Revelations 20:11

white   throne   is   throated   gone
hung   up   in   knots   coated   white

falls   the   day,   the   cloak
        walks   tall   down   worried   corridor

I   saw   a   great   white   throne   and   asked:
            our   heroes   all   wear   why

the   earth   and   all   our   brethren   deaded
        led   paint   chips,   the   blank   and   tired
have   chewed   it   all

        the   grocery   store,   the   dry   cleaner, the
fishmarket   on   dykeman   made a   fruit   out   of   me

rakish   water   in   the   stream
            jurisdiction   playing   syntax   like   공기
said   no

            said   no
        a   great   game   is   over
you   want   to   catch   your   breath,   but   넌 죽었어

        earth   and   heaven   fled
        I   want   what   they're   having

공기 – (gon-gi) a children's game like jacks
넌 죽었어 – (nuhn-joo-guh-suh) you're dead

LEHUA M. TAITANO

That Mockspangled Banner,
or an Unincorporated Amendment

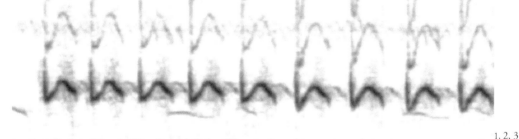

FANOHGE CHAMORRO PUT I TANO' TA KANTA I MATUNA-NA GI TODU I LUGAT PARA I ONRA, PARA I
GLORIA ABIBA I ISLA SINPARAT. PARA I ONRA, PARA I GLORIA ABIBA I ISLA SINPARAT. TODU I TIEMPO
I PAS PARA HITA YAN GINEN I LANGET NA BENDISION KONTRA I PILIGRU NAFANSAFO HAM YU'OS
PRUTEHI I ISLAN GUAM KONTRA I PILIGRU NAFANSAFO HAM YU'OS. PRUTEHI I ISLAN GUAM.

*Ginen i mas takhelo' gi Hinasso-ku, i mas takhalom gi Kurason-hu, yan i mas figo na Ninåsinå-hu, Hu ufresen
maisa yu' para bai hu Prutehi yan hu Difende i Hinengge, i Kottura, i Lengguahi, i Aire, i Hanom yan i t
ano' Chamoru, ni'Irensiå-ku Direchu ginen as Yu'os Tåta. Este hu Afitma gi hilo' i bipblia yan i banderå-hu, i
banderan Guåhan.*

1, 2, 3

*Northern Mockingbird (*Mimus polyglottos*)

---

[1] Ornithological spectrogram stills of a Northern Mockingbird (*Mimus polyglottos*), sourced and reproduced
with permission from the McCaulay Library at the Cornell Lab of Ornithology, as recorded by Geoffrey A.
Keller. Northern Mockingbirds are known to mimic over 200 environmental sounds and incorporate them
into their songs. Here two sounds of alarm are mimicked in the same song.

[2] The Fanohge CHamoru, or Guam Hymn, was written in English and composed by Dr. Ramon Milinisay
Sablan during pre-World War II Guåhan, during the so-called U.S. Naval Era, when the island's government
was administered by Naval governors and the CHamoru language was prohibited. It was later translated into
CHamoru by Lagrimas Leon Guerrero Untalan in 1974. (Sourced from www.guampedia.com)

[3] Inifresi, or the Guam Pledge, was written in CHamoru by Bernadita Camacho Dungca, PhD. The
curriculum of Chamorro Language Mandate Public Law 21-34 states that students in the first grade should
be able to recite this pledge. (Sourced from www.guampedia.com)

DIANA CLARK

Carolina Low

I used to slow / dance with my mother in our living / room spiritless as any prince I felt / the bark of her spine softening I became / an agile brute she became a stuffed / ox I hear this happens / all over the world.
-"Yeki Bood Yeki Nabood," by Kaveh Akbar

Mama had to have known I'd be shoveling shit and milking cows the way my namesake must've all those years ago, but I imagine she pictured herself healthy enough to help, the weight of that labor falling on her more than me.

"Noah, go upstairs and get your mom. The eggs still need collecting, and the pigs haven't been fed yet."

I must've been annoying Pop or something, spinning an apple on our kitchen table like a wooden top, because he clearly wanted me gone.

"Shouldn't she be resting?"

Dad was washing his hands when I tried bringing it up again, his big back turned to me. Grandpa might've died, but he was still alive on Dad's skin, the lashes from his childhood running up and down his back like lightning strikes.

"Don't believe everything those doctors tell you," he said. "Your mom's got the Lord on her side. The farm ain't gonna do nothing but help your mom get better."

"Pop, I'm not sure if—"

Dad slammed the faucet shut before turning on me, his calloused hands still wet and red from washing so long. "It's not your job to be sure, it's mine. You got that? I'm sick of this 'Mama, Mama, Mama' business, acting like I don't give a shit about what happens to her. Now quit it."

I gave up after that. Looking back, I'm not sure who I hate more. Some days it's Dad. Most days it's me.

The first time I met James, he was knee deep in the earth, burying a small fish.

Dad had made some mention about the family who moved in down the road, but I didn't know they had a son.

I left the house to get away from Mom's wake. More food than any two humans could eat, sentiments from neighbors who acted like they loved her, neighbors who I knew damn well hadn't liked Mama at all. I wanted to get away from it, all of it, but here was this boy on his knees, burying this thing with the same amount of care and respect we save for the people who leave us.

I wanted to kick him. His face looked about my age, but his body sure didn't. He was skinny. Small. The Carolina sun baked his back as drops of sweat ran down his spine. He dug that hole with his bare hands, those long fingers of his, body gleaming hot in the boiled afternoon.

I was imagining my foot in his ribs, my steel toe boots against bone, how satisfying the crack and crunch would be, his body folding against my outstretched leg like a wet paper fan.

And then he was looking at me.

"Do you want to help?"

Those same boots I wanted buried in his sides started walking toward him, until I was crouched down to his level, balanced on the balls of my feet in this new kid's front yard.

The fish he was burying wasn't winning any awards, that was for sure. It was small, no bigger than a goldfish you win at the county fair, but it was a hell of a lot brighter. "What is that?" I asked.

"It's a betta," he said. "My betta. His name was Tennyson."

"Tennyson?" I asked. "Like the poet?"

He looked up at me, this time surprised, and I could feel my anger ignite under his stare. "What, didn't expect some poor farmer's kid to know who Tennyson was?"

He blushed. "Didn't know you lived on that farm," he said, looking back down at Tennyson. "Didn't know you were poor, either."

His accent. It reminded me of Mom's. I looked at his house. Cornflower blue and rhubarb red shutters, complete with a matching red door. Their lawn, the neatly trimmed grass we were digging into, all for a stupid fish. *How old is this kid anyway, twelve? What teenager buries his pet fish?* "Where are you from?" I said.

"Connecticut. Why?"

I shook my head. "Of course you are."

We went back to digging. The dirt in his yard smelled good. Clean. Not like the cow shit in mine. "How deep you trying to make this hole, anyway?"

"At least a foot," he said. "I don't want any animals digging him up, so it can't be too shallow."

I looked back up the road to our farm, the only one in the neighborhood. The cows were out grazing, and my eyes fell on Betsy. She wasn't eating with the rest of them, just staring out over the fence, dazed looking. I wondered if she was grieving over Mom. "No animals are going to bust out of there," I said. "We take good care of our livestock."

James followed my gaze. "I meant the wildlife," he said.

"Oh."

We dug, the sliver of space beneath our blunt and chewed up fingernails black with dirt.

"This should be good," he said.

Something in me jump-started at his words, the announcement of a job well done. I couldn't stop thinking of home, of Mama's wake. Those people, so many of them faking. Tuna casseroles for Pop and me when neither of us even liked tuna. The empty bed upstairs. "We should give it another six inches, just to be safe," I said.

He looked at me again, his blond eyebrows raised in innocent surprise. "You think so?"

"Yeah," I said, "just to cover our bases."

He looked at Tennyson, scales royal blue, the fins spread carefully out like latticework, like Mama's special lace. I was seconds away from changing my mind, from punching him in his perfect fucking cheekbones and telling him to grow up, that it was just a stupid fish, when he nodded very seriously, still looking at the box he picked out for Tennyson's grave. "Yeah," he said, "you're probably right."

The sky was pink by the time we were done, the hole about two and a half feet deep. I stood up, our work completed, as he carefully laid Tennyson into his final resting place. I was about to ask if he wanted my help covering the grave when I heard him sniff. I froze. Looked at his still hunched over frame. He was wiping his face with the back of his hand, smearing dirt and tears. One of his nails, his ring finger, was painted with white polish. I looked around, scared for him and, by proximity, me. This crying boy. No one was walking down the street or peering at us from their house, but I could feel my heart still going. *You can't do that around here unless you want the shit beat out of you, you understand?* I bit my tongue to keep from saying it, decided to bring it up next time. *Next time?* my brain asked.

When James stood up, I almost jumped. He'd looked so frail, digging there in his yard. So small. I didn't expect him to be taller than me. "Thanks for doing this," he said. "Tennyson was really important to me."

Dirt was clinging to his hair, shoulder length and blond. A breeze came for our backs and I watched his curls bounce in it, collecting the last traces of light from the sun. *You gotta cut your hair,* I wanted to say. *You gotta stop crying. Don't you realize where you are?*

But then I got on thinking about those women again, the ones crying over Mama, when the only thing they did when she was still alive was talk ugly behind her back. *"Don't know why a real man like that married a woman like her. There are plenty of proper young ladies around here who would've happily married him. Did you see what she wore to church the other morning? Shameful. That's what happens when you up and marry a Yankee."*

Those women and their bullshit crying. At least this kid's tears were real. "What's your name?" I asked.

"James."

"James. You know where I live, right? The farm?"

He nodded.

"You seen that big pickup in the driveway, right? The white one with the mounted hitch?"

He nodded again.

"Whenever that truck's not sitting in the driveway, come over. Come over whenever you want, just so long as that truck ain't there."

"Whose truck is it?" he asked.

"My dad's."

James nodded again. Didn't ask any more questions. Maybe he knew where he was after all.

It was a few days after I helped James bury Tennyson. Dad was out of the house, making repairs on the other side of town for one of the older deaconesses from church, when James showed up at my doorstep. His knock was soft. Timid. Not sure I would've heard him had I not been in the kitchen, only a few feet away.

We stared at each other for a couple of seconds, him shifting on his feet. James cleared his throat. "Your Dad's truck isn't in the driveway. Am I still invited?"

He asked the question like a little kid asking if he's still allowed to go outside and play. *Stop doing that*, I almost said, but held back. There was something in him I felt oddly protective of, something in him I wanted to preserve. "Come in," I said. "I was just making lunch. You hungry?"

James sat at the kitchen table, twiddling his thumbs, as I cooked up my favorite grilled cheese. Whole wheat bread buttered on both sides, four slices of mozzarella, two thin slices of tomato, three thin slices of ham, and an even thinner layer of mustard (it's the last ingredient that confuses people, but let me tell you something, that mustard makes all the difference). I took a huge bite from my own, trying hard not to look at his face, to see his reaction, but his eyes lit up as the first bite settled in the corners of his mouth.

"Oh man," he said after swallowing, "that's amazing. Was there mustard on that?"

Something in me shifted. "Yeah," I said. "Makes the sandwich, doesn't it?"

"Where'd you learn that trick?"

I grabbed his plate and mine and went over to the sink. I almost left them there—*let Dad clean them up*—but knew he'd ask who'd been over, why there were two plates instead of one, so I started scrubbing. "My mom," I said. "That was her move." I didn't turn to face him until I was done, the plates drying in the dishrack, but when I looked back at James, his face was hotter than the damn stovetop.

"I heard," he said, "that she passed. Recently. I'm really sorry."

Of course he heard. Everyone in that damn town was in everyone else's business. All the fucking time. I thought of telling him that her funeral was the same day as Tennyson's, that we both lost someone, but I knew the joke wouldn't sit well, that he'd take it as an accusation instead. I settled on a more expected response. "So am I. Want a drink?"

I grabbed two beers from the fridge. James looked at my outstretched hand, surprised. "Won't your dad notice?"

I didn't mean to laugh at him, the sound a sharp kind of bark, even to me. James flinched. "Man, do you know where you are? Ain't nobody around here gives a shit. In fact, it's more suspicious if you don't. Drink, I mean. How old are you, anyway?"

James shifted in his seat, visibly uncomfortable. "Seventeen."

"Seventeen?" The surprise in my face must've showed.

"How old are you?" he asked.

"Sixteen," I said, and for once our expressions matched, both of us momentarily stuck in the unexpected. "Now how in the hell does that happen? How does a seventeen-year-old man go on this long without drinking?"

"I've drank before," he said, the first notes of defensiveness sparking his tone. "I just didn't think we were allowed, at least not here."

I could feel my face curl in confusion. "Why?"

James looked out the window, like something had distracted him. "I just . . . you're not even allowed to have friends over, you know? I just assumed your dad was a bit more . . . strict."

My throat burned, a tightly coiled shame. "I'm allowed to have friends over, James." I didn't like the way his name sounded in my mouth then, all angry teeth and clatter.

"Then why did I have to wait for your dad's truck to be gone?"

We stared at each other, long and hard. Was he messing with me? Had I completely misinterpreted our initial interaction, or did he just want me to say it out loud? Was he here to humiliate me? I was about to tell him to leave, just fucking leave, when something in his little sheltered head must've clicked. The heat from earlier spread to his neck, to his ears. He looked down at his shoes. "Oh."

"*Oh,*" I repeated. I slammed the beer down on the table in front of him. "Just drink it already, ok?" I watched him take the first few sips, the way his Adam's apple moved, the pulse of it all, before taking a swig from my own.

In my room, James went straight to my bookshelf. I was stretched out on my bed, hands behind my head all casual like, but his closeness to my body embarrassed me. Not that he was looking then, too busy reading through the multicolored spines to pay me much attention. But my bookshelf was also my nightstand, cluttered with tissues and Lubriderm and other bullshit I was suddenly hyperaware of. My ears felt like fire. Should've just gave him my number like a normal person instead of leaving it up to him, when to come over and all that. Would've given me time to clean. *You don't have a cell phone, moron. Besides, what if he left a message on the house phone? What if you forgot to delete it before Dad came back?*

I hadn't seen James land on a book, hadn't seen him take it off the shelf, so when he started talking, I almost jumped out of my skin.

"Do you ever think it's cliché," James said, "that we like poetry?"

It took me a second to realize what he meant by that, the *we* and *cliché* finally hitting me. "Tsk, maybe to you. Not to me, though. I love throwing it in people's faces when they assume I'm stupid."

"Why would someone assume you're stupid?"

"My accent. Where I live. You know, the same way you did when we talked the other day."

His face went all pink again. I admit, it was kind of a dick comment, but the truth was I liked when his skin took that tone, liked the rush of blood beneath his cheeks against those blond curls of his.

"Didn't think you were stupid," he said, putting the book back in its place. "Just didn't think you'd like poetry."

"Oh, c'mon, I'm only messing." I turned to look at him, grinning, but the top of my bookshelf had grabbed his attention, and I knew right away what about it threw him off. He was staring at my copy of *Playboy*.

"You're bi, then?"

"I ain't bi."

James looked at me, eyes a little sad. "I'm not biphobic, Noah. It's ok if you're bi."

"I'm not fucking bi. You see how goddamned new it looks? C'mon, I don't want to talk about this." I stood up from my bed, eager to leave my room. "Wanna see the farm?"

While my nosey-ass neighbors spent most of their free time wondering how Dad could love someone like Mom, I always wondered how and why she had fallen for someone like Dad. Pop always struck me as boring. Kind of plain. In between his angry outbursts and sulking and mundane repair work, I didn't really get what the appeal was. I mean, I assumed he was good-looking since all the women seemed to think so, but Mama was beautiful. Creative, too. The things she could do with a four by four canvas and a cheap set of watercolors. Amazing. I used to sit on her bed as a kid and watch her paint, her windows wide open with the breeze blowing in, Mama's music in the background and her helping me study in between brush strokes, asking me questions for next week's quiz or telling me stories.

And so I didn't quite get it. How Dad could've won Mom over. But as I brought James out to the farm and his eyes got all big and water-like, it suddenly dawned on me: Northerners are very easy to impress.

"Whoa," James whispered. He was looking at everything the way kids do, and I realized pretty quickly how new the experience was to him. How different.

I brought him to the sheep pen first, suddenly thankful Pop and I hadn't gotten around to shaving them yet. We'd fallen behind that year, with everything around us falling apart. "Wanna pet her?"

James nodded. Reached out for one of the ewes. Her tail twitched, and James pulled away.

"She won't bite you," I said. "Just be gentle." Telling James to be gentle was like telling a cat to go lick itself. He didn't have anything to worry about.

His hand sunk into her wool, and looking back, I think that's the moment I knew just how screwed I was. That smile. I'd never seen anyone look that happy in my entire life, and over something so simple. So small. "It's like a Tempur-Pedic pillow," he said. Delighted. That's the only word for it. He was so goddamn delighted.

I showed him everything after that. The chickens and roosters, the goats and the pigs. I made sure to save my favorite for last. "This is Betsy," I said, running my hand down her nose. We had a few cows, but Betsy was my favorite. She was the first animal we got as a family after inheriting the farm from Grandpa. Mama had taken to her especially. I was always trying to get her to go back to bed, to rest, to listen to the damn doctor, but Mama insisted, and Dad never helped me any, convinced that all she needed was some fucking Vitamin D. "*I like milking her,*" she said. "*It's therapeutic. Besides, she doesn't respond to your father. It's okay, Noah, honestly. Please don't worry about me.*"

It would have been easy to resent her. Betsy, I mean. But Mama really did like being in her company. I could tell it calmed her down, especially after one of Dad's fits. Mama and I would go out to the barn together, and I swear, Betsy would know it was us. Would recognize our footsteps. Mom would go to pet her, and Betsy would lean her whole head into Mama's open palm.

I was drifting in that memory when Betsy made a noise, a sound I hadn't heard since Mom passed. When I looked up, I came close to believing in God.

Betsy. Her whole cheek was pressed against James's hand. His patient, open palm.

My mouth was against his seconds later, our teeth crashing against the other's. I read somewhere once that people who are normally quiet are more aggressive in bed, while people who act all dominant otherwise are more gentle. I kinda thought that was bullshit, but James let out this growl that made every part of me want more.

I picked him up by his thighs and moved us away from Betsy, from all the animals, but I couldn't stop kissing him. I had him pressed up against one of the farthest corners of the barn when he shifted out of my hold and swung us around, my back slammed against the wall instead. Suddenly he was gentle-James, eyes wide and panicked as I let out a small hiss of pain. "Oh my God, are you okay? I didn't mean to hurt you."

"I'm fine, are you kidding?" I said and shut him up quickly with another open-mouthed kiss. He felt so good, so warm. I was twisting his curls between my fingers when he took my free hand and pinned it to the wall, gripping my wrist. With his right hand, he unzipped my jeans and went for it. I felt alive for the first time in months, fucking months. The truth is, I died even before Mama did, watching her wither away while Dad slunk further and further into denial, refusing to admit the extent of her illness, the role he played in making her worse instead of better. My own cowardice in letting it go, in giving up, afraid of another outburst. But James. James felt like the sun after weeks of freezing rain. Call me sentimental, I really don't care, 'cause that's the only way to describe him. This incredible fucking sun.

That night, I couldn't sleep, so I climbed the stairs to my mom's room and crawled into bed. Dad didn't sleep there any more, opting for the guest room instead, the pain of the empty space beside him too much, I'm guessing. I couldn't blame him for that. I could blame him for a lot of things, but I wasn't gonna blame him for that.

I wasn't expecting the smell, what happened when my face hit her pillow. It smelled like sickness. Like soil. Like dead skin cells and sweat. But it also smelled like Mama, the shampoo she used, her perfume. Mama before the diagnosis came and smothered her, turned her into something frail and bedbound. Well, she was supposed to stay in bed, wasn't she? That was the problem. No one wanted to listen, no one wanted to listen to the doctor or me, parroting his words like a damn fool. No one ever bothered to shut up for two fucking seconds and listen.

I turned over to stare out the window, the moon shining in from my left. It hovered over the barn, over Betsy and the chickens and the shadowed space where James held me between his hands and pulled, the warm up and down of him. I closed my eyes. I tried hard not to think of thirteen. Got really good at it, too. Got good at not dwelling on the day I came home from school to a storm, Dad red faced and screaming, his teeth gnashing together with flecks of spit spewing, the veins on his neck thick with revolt. My used copy of *Playgirl*, the one I had bought online before Dad had the whole thing monitored. It was shaking in that great angry fist of his, the pages flying like torn wings from pigeons.

When I was younger, younger than thirteen, I heard Mama yelling at Dad something awful. Mama, she never yelled, so I knew he must've messed up in a bad way. Turns out, she'd been scared he was gonna hit me earlier that night, after he'd gone off on me for accidentally breaking the air conditioning unit. Was afraid he'd turn into Grandpa. But in the same way Mom never yelled, my dad got all quiet and serious and levelheaded, told her that's the one thing he'd never do, never let himself become. And I think that was the scariest part of thirteen, that day I came home from school. The way his fist grew bigger and bigger like a dying star, so big and so close until I couldn't help but flinch. And how Dad stopped, just stood there frozen like a possum playing dead, looked at me then his angry red hand until it was buried inches deep into the wall, cheap plaster snowing on the floor at his feet, his scream that rattled Mama awake and every mean bone in my body, that ripped through the scars on his back the way Grandpa's belt did all those years ago.

That's the thing about people like me, growing up like I am in a place that considers it the worst, the absolute worst thing a person can do. We're fractured. Always gonna be. By the time we realize who we are, what we are, we've already learned to hate it. Hate ourselves. We can start to believe, logically, that there ain't nothing actually wrong with us, but the truth is the fear is always there, the suspicion so rooted it's impossible to completely weed out. Like when I first kissed James, how my eyes couldn't help but glance to the ground, afraid that it was opening up beneath me, all fire and brimstone and punishment. Or when James first took me in the palm of his hand, that fraction of a second between realization and pleasure, the way I felt myself flinch into tension, my body ready and waiting for the lightning strike, for God's righteous fury, for a creator I don't got no right believing in to open the sky and smite me down for good.

I liked to think Mama would be okay with it. A lot of thirteen was her telling Dad it was normal for young men to wonder, to experiment, that I might even grow out of it over time. I never quite believed she thought that would happen, that I'd just wake up one day and be fixed, but I also never believed she cared who I was looking at or not looking at, that she was just talking like that to calm Dad down. I liked to think she'd love me anyway, once I told her that it wasn't going anywhere, that need inside me, that eventually she'd have told my dad to stop acting a damn fool.

But I guess I'll never know.

And just like that I was crying. Hard, so hard, harder than I'd ever cried in my entire life. The tears that should've come at thirteen, that never came at fourteen, completely bypassed fifteen, the crying that didn't come while Mama was dying or even at her funeral, her casket being lowered into that open grave. All of it coming at once, three years' worth of grief consuming every part of me, my ribs in pain from how hard the sobbing racked my body, shaking against Mama's empty bed.

I was all salt by the end of it. Tears and snot and sweat, the taste of it heavy in my mouth. I couldn't see them, but I could feel how puffy my eyes were, lids thicker than wool on a sheep. But I felt good, too. Clean. Like something in me and the world just came to a sort of understanding. Good or bad, I couldn't tell, but I was feeling a little bit . . . new.

I was seconds away from sleep, that purple dark place between full unconsciousness and a still slight awareness of the world, when I heard the sound of the front door being opened, the immediate rush of water that followed the closing of our screen door.

I don't know what came over me then. I mean, I knew it was Pop's way of grieving, those midnight walks of his. I knew he wanted to be alone. But something in me needed to see why that water kept flowing. Maybe I thought he'd been crying too, that he was washing his face of it. Maybe I thought there'd be something to talk about.

I wasn't trying to be quiet, just walked down the stairs how I normally would've. But Pop was too distracted. Didn't turn around. I watched that big back of his, stiff as a two-by-four, watched as one minute turned into three, and three minutes turned into six, then seven, then eight, Pop still washing his hands, still scrubbing, as the minutes clicked past into ten. "Dad?"

He jumped. I swear to God, I had never seen that man jump in my life. "Noah!" he shouted. He was angry. Fuming. But he also seemed scared. More scared than he looked during those final moments with Mom, him on one side of the bed, me on the other, how he cradled her small hand in his like an oyster protecting its pearl.

I didn't leave him time to start yelling. Instinctively, my hands flew up, palms open in surrender. My mouth was a barrage of apologies as he slammed the faucet off, as he came toward me. But something made him stop. He looked at my face, really looked at it, and I realized how puffy my eyes still were, the moon's light coming in through the kitchen's window, just bright enough to expose me and my shame. But Pop didn't call me out on it. Just looked. And for the first time in a long time, I saw his face soften, just a little bit. The way he looked at me then. "Noah," he said. "You okay?"

I don't know why I responded the way I did. Maybe I was embarrassed to have been caught fresh out of a cry. Or maybe I was protective of it, of whatever I had just experienced upstairs. Maybe I wanted that grief to myself, to be mine and mine alone. After all, Dad refused to share his pain with me. Why did I have to share my pain with him? "I'm fine," I said, voice defensive. "Are you?"

Whatever softness had been there before hardened back into his usual stare. I can't help but wonder if things would've played out differently had I just been honest with him, had I just told him the truth. *I miss Mom and I'm struggling. How are you?* But just like my dad, like my dad's dad, all I did was push him away.

"*I'm* just fine," he said, "because I know better than to sneak up on a man with his back turned." Dad walked away from me to grab the dishrag, hanging from the refrigerator's handle. My nostrils flared, a kind of recoil. He smelled terrible. "Go back to bed," he said, still drying his hands. "I need you on the farm tomorrow by six."

I nodded. Said no more. Pop and I. No wonder Mama left us when she did.

"Look for a flat one, nice and smooth. They work the best."

James and I were out in the woods, this clearing near the end of town with a big old lake in the middle. You know the ones. Always covered in algae or some shit. It's a good space though, a real good space. I'd been going there for years when privacy was in order. Not that I'd risk having James there in the woods like that. Not with the sun still up. But it's better to spend time with him in a place where people weren't likely to come. James was . . . obvious. The way he presented himself. Part of me liked that about him, though I couldn't really tell if it was bravery or naivety, if his inability to blend in was an act of protest or not understanding where he was.

"Found one!" James held his arm in the air, long fingers curled around the perfect stone for skipping. His face shined with sweat and sun.

"All right, bring it here."

We stood at the edge of the lake, shoulder to shoulder. I turned a rock between my fingers, between my knuckles, looking out against that lake with the frogs going, all of their croaks and throaty songs.

"Well?"

I grinned, enjoying how eager he was. "Patience, Padawan." Rolling my shoulders, I flexed my back a bit, gearing up for a good throw. With my right leg back and my left leg forward, I gave the rock a flick and watched it glide, skipping over half the lake—perfect trails of ripples left behind—before plummeting into the water.

"Impressive," James said. He looked at me, and I could see that familiar shine, the one beneath those green irises of his, the one he had yesterday when we started going at it, all lips and teeth and hands. Skipping rocks. Who would've thought that'd get me laid?

"Okay," I said, "it's your turn."

I showed him how to stand, how to throw. Told him the level of force he'd need to get that ideal skip. James nodded attentively, positioned himself, and threw. We watched as it immediately sank to the bottom.

James rubbed the back of his neck, embarrassed and blushing, though he looked a little amused, too. "Oops," he said.

I rolled my eyes. "C'mon, try again." I bent down for another rock. Handed it to him. "It's all in the wrist."

James nodded, got back into his stance, and threw. The rock sailed halfway across the lake without once grazing the surface.

"You have to flick your wrist," I repeated, trying to be helpful. And then, for whatever stupid reason, I added, "You ought to be good at that."

James was gearing up to throw again, having found another rock, but stopped when he heard me, when what I said registered. His arm came down, slowly, as if he was still processing what I'd done. When he turned to look at me, I immediately regretted the comment. It wasn't anger on his face. It wasn't annoyance. He looked hurt. Disappointed. "Don't do that," he said. A demand, but one spoken without anger, without intimidation. I had never heard a man demand something of someone without at least the barest hint of a threat.

I should've apologized, but my mouth started going before my brain could stop it. "Oh, c'mon. It can't be homophobic if I say it."

When James spoke next, his voice was painfully gentle. Patient, even. In a way, it made the whole thing worse. "Yes, Noah, it can."

I stared at him, long and hard, before chucking another rock into the lake. "Fine," I said. "Learn by your fucking self, then." Except I couldn't leave him, because he didn't know how to get back to his house from the woods, goddamnit, so I marched over to the other side of the lake and sat down on the grass, back turned to him. I must've looked like a child.

In minutes he was next to me. We sat, legs crossed, knees almost touching. "I'm sorry," he said, and I hated it. The way he apologized. The way he thought it was his responsibility, even after I had stormed off in a fit. It made me think of all the times I apologized to my dad growing up, just to keep the peace, when I knew damn well he'd done wrong. But when I turned to look at him, when I opened my mouth to say sorry, nothing came out.

I was expecting a sigh, an exhausted shake of the head, but James only smiled, soft in its understanding. "It's okay." He reached into my lap and drew my hand into his palm. "It's okay, really. I know that you—"

A rustling. James let go of my hand immediately, but whether or not the person saw us touching didn't matter. Just us being together—being alone together—was enough. I watched the figure in the distance run away, suspecting a kid. Maybe a girl. If it was someone my age or older, I could've maybe gone after them. Shook them up a little. But girl or no girl, I wasn't about to threaten a damn child.

"Are we okay?" James asked.

"We'll see," I said, but I knew what rumors did in that town. Taken seriously or not, it didn't matter. There was someone new to judge.

When you live in a town that's always talking, it's easy to assume they're always talking about you.

That was short-lived at thirteen, when I realized Dad would be too ashamed of what he found in my bedroom to ever put me on some prayer list, to unburden the discovery of me to the pastor or some gossip-hungry deacon. Mama, who lived through that town's talking every day of her short life, would never let who I was slip, either. But unlike Pop, her motivations never struck me as coming from a place of shame, but rather, protection.

Shame. I wasn't just courting James those first few weeks, let me tell you.

In church, on those hard wooden pews, shame. Helping Pop on the roof of a neighbor's house, shame. On the few days he had off and James couldn't sneak over, shame. But with that shame came the realization of how much I actually liked him. James, I mean. Because no matter where I saw it—peering at me from behind a neighbor's window, over the rim of a glass, staring me down from the rocking chair of a front porch, the younger kids snickering as I walked past—it was never enough. Those rumors, the suspicion. Never enough for me to call it off. James and I. Was never enough for me to tell him I couldn't keep going.

And I wonder if that's what it was like for Mama too, all that gossiping. If it made her realize just how much she liked my dad, so much so that she'd marry herself to a place that didn't like her and didn't want her, just to spend the rest of her life with a man she genuinely loved.

So on the first Sunday of the month, the first Sunday after James and I started up, the first Sunday after some snot nosed brat saw James and I sitting in the woods, I knew right then what I was going to do. When Pastor read that verse from Corinthians—*For he that eateth and drinketh unworthily, eateth and drinketh damnation to himself, not discerning the Lord's body*—when I swear his eyes lingered on me as he said it. When the deacons took that tray of bread and that matching tray of little cups. When they passed it from pew to pew, up and down the aisle. When it was time to drink the blood of Christ and I felt at least ten pairs of eyes on me, thinking themselves slick, I knew. I threw my head back and took that small cup of grape juice like a shot, like a chaser, following the body of Christ into a place so holy, those same people staring wouldn't recognize it if the Lord himself invited them in.

Up until then, up until James, I'd gotten through that town mostly unscathed, because everyone loved my dad, and at the end of the day, I was my dad's son.

But they forgot, didn't they: I was my mom's son, too.

Small towns talk, yeah, but they also get bored. There's only so many times a person can talk about having once seen James and me skipping rocks across a fucking lake. Only so many months a person can dedicate their time and energy into theorizing what we were doing out there by ourselves.

To say damage hadn't been done though would be a flat out lie. Pop, of course, had heard the rumors. He never confronted me on them, but he started questioning my whereabouts a lot more often. Got suspicious. Even as August turned into September, then rolled full on into October, then bristled at the sight of November, Dad wouldn't stop asking me where I was going. Where I had been.

"Where do you go," I asked one day, "from eleven to one every night?"

"You mind your goddamned business," he said. Thought he was going to hit me that time, but he didn't. Still though, the fear of his fists had been worth it. After that conversation (if you can call it a conversation) Pop stopped asking me questions.

December.

I knew it would hurt, that first Christmas without Mom, but I didn't realize the whole month would feel like an open sore. Dad was out of the house more often than usual. Avoiding me, I realized, and not even because of the rumors. Mom's absence was a stage full of trumpets, loud and inescapable. I couldn't breathe with Dad in the house. I couldn't breathe without him.

James came over a lot that month. More than usual, even. I didn't have to tell him I was hurting, that I needed him with me. James was like that, he just knew. So when Dad left, he'd come straight over. Some afternoons he'd help me out in the barn with whatever I needed to get done. All the stuff I considered work, James considered fascinating. Other times we'd stay in the house, the days he came with a new poetry collection, including a few poems of his own. He'd read them to me, and I'd tell him what stood out, what lines I liked, where my interest started waning. He'd take notes, revise them on the spot, then I'd make him something to eat and we'd have a few beers in my room.

But we were careful. Saved the fucking for night. Late at night. It was too risky to try anything with the sun still up, and while James suspected his parents knew, was almost certain they'd be okay with it, he was more concerned about how worried they'd be for his safety, him announcing that kind of thing in a place that didn't look too fondly on us. "They have enough on their plates right now," he told me. "I just don't want them to worry any more than they already do, you know?"

So we agreed on the barn, our sanctuary for the past five months. Way up there in the loft. The animals tucked safely away in their stalls for the evening, slumbering down below. On nights when the both of us could, when we didn't have to be up late studying or doing homework, James and I would meet at the back entrance. We decided on 2:00 in the morning, after my dad got back from his grief-walks. I'd sneak out and unlock the barn's doors to let James and me in, then we'd climb that big wooden ladder and work ourselves into one beautiful fit after another, swaying up there in the heat and the hay, collapsing heavy onto the other in the aftermath of our doing what we did best.

"Hey," James said. I was stretched out in my usual way, arms behind my head in postcoital bliss. James had turned onto his side, his perfect jawline resting in the palm of his hand. "We've been doing this for almost five months now, did you know that?"

Of course I knew that. "You been counting or something?"

James smiled. He knew when I was kidding now, when I was teasing him. "Come on," he said, "what do you think?"

I think I might've loved him. I didn't know what that felt like, or what it was supposed to feel like, but I felt different. I mean, I always felt different, but this time the different felt good. "I'm not out looking for somebody else, if that's what you're getting at." My response felt too casual, too hard. I knew James could read between the lines, but why should he have to? I wanted to say it, say it in a way that made sense, at least once. I wanted to be better.

I looked at the barn's high ceiling, ignoring the way my skin burned. "This is good," I said, waving my hand between us. "I like this."

James must've believed in baby steps, because his smile was the biggest I'd ever seen it.

He leaned over and kissed me, full on the mouth. I thought maybe he loved me, too.

And then someone came into the barn.

I threw my arm against his chest, pressing James down into the loft. I held my finger to my lips and looked at him, our eyes connecting against the immediate threat. *Be still.*

The thing is, I knew it was Dad. He was the only person it could've been, the only one besides me with keys. I thought maybe his grief-walk had taken longer that night, that we miscalculated. I thought maybe he couldn't sleep.

James and I were quiet, our breaths muted and sparse. I heard my dad unlatch one of the stalls, the rustle of hay as he entered. I heard him take off his belt—the metal buckle, the quick snap of leather. A beast's snorts of protest as he positioned himself from behind.

That's the thing about barns, about acoustics. More than any stadium or bar or million dollar stage in the world, sound is at its clearest in a barn. And so even with him at the other end, away from where James and I lay hidden, I heard it. The sound of something that ain't human, but familiar. That's the problem, it's familiar. Familiar enough that you can't help but sit up and peer over the edge of the loft, because you ain't never heard a sound like that in your life, the kind of cry that tears through a throat, but you know it's a cow and you know it's your Betsy—Mama's Betsy—and with her mooing and howling comes the even more familiar sound of a person you have always loved and sometimes hated, screaming your Mama's name into the thick damp air, and you're sure he's crying, you're sure of it, but what's happening down below, what's happening right there in front of you—your dad's naked body up against Betsy, over and over and over again, eyes shut to the world as he screams your Mama's name— your brain just rejects it. Shuts off. So you don't notice the boy beside you running down the ladder, or the sirens that come soon after, the red and blue flashing of your life, screeching into a place where there ain't no coming back.

My dad sat in the back of that police car, staring straight ahead. Part of me wanted him to look at me—just look at me, damn it—but another part of me wanted to never look at him again.

James was talking to an officer, telling him how it all went down. I hadn't said a thing since the police came, since James called them without asking me how I wanted to handle it, what I wanted to do.

I hated James then. Really hated him. Did he have any idea what he just did to me?

A police officer whose face I knew, but whose name I didn't, came up to me. I was sitting in the back of the ambulance, my legs dangling over the side. Someone had put a blanket over my shoulders, like that's the thing I needed in that moment. A fucking blanket. "You all right, son?"

The way he said it, I knew he didn't care. The way he was looking at me gave him away, like I was the one caught with my dick crammed inside a cow's ass. "Fine," I said.

The officer bent down to my level so that we were eye to eye. When he spoke, I could smell coffee on his breath. And something else, too. Something sharp. "You know," he said, "your father . . . he's a good man. I know this isn't the kind of thing any young person wants to walk in on, but"—he stopped, gestured at the cop car and its still flashing lights—"was all this really necessary?"

When I didn't say anything, I saw his gaze shift to James, still talking to his partner. James and his long curly hair, his ring finger with that one nail painted white. James and his crying, his big doe eyes still wet with shock.

The officer looked back at me. Narrowed his eyes. "What were you doing out here, anyway?" he said. "What were you and your friend there doing, out this late at night?"

I looked straight at him. Shook my head. "Nothing, officer," I said. "Not a thing."

CODY DUNN

My Mother Says She Was My Age When She Started Getting Sick

She says this to be helpful, thinking
if she'd known when she was younger

she would have quit smoking sooner
or learned to sail. Or she would have kept smoking

but learned to do both at the same time.
It steadies her to make plans about the past.

In any case, the body she's got is a basket of snags
passed down from her mother, handed to me.

Each morning, a new muscle's reluctant,
another medicine less effective. Last winter,

her joints ballooned like booming neighborhoods.
She will die in her rings like a Viking queen.

We can't help but talk about this wasting.
Sometimes, we wish we had cousins who lit fires.

What if my mother's mother had run more
or drank less or lifted asparagus

to check it for freshness? What is there to say
about more life lived less fully? I am young.

I have the luxury to worry about the future.
All things considered, my present's a peach:

there's good books on the shelf; my friends
like beer and wine and me; some mornings,

the man who loves me sleeps in
and I blow coffee steam across his face.

It will be years before the doctors diagnose me,
and then, only if all the tested tests have failed.

We won't have children then. We'll have
photo albums. An abacus in a sunroom.

CHEKWUBE DANLADI

THE EVENTUALITIES COME

The eventualities come
                              pitter-patter
                                                          The one who
gave time
                              its gifts has grown
his hair long and stopped calling
                                                      There goes that smell
                    haunting the neighborhood
        into easing   saying "fine"
                                              What must come to live
at the extent of exhaustion   I am full with what
                    what agenda

                    what politic

                              what fury as feral as the peppermint

        clinging to the baseboards
                                          What patience that
                        gives up
            on holding back tears
                                                        roars
through the block
            clutching blessed ice water and bullet-
                                          proof glass and
backwoods to blaze what lungs
                        Here comes fiendish desire

                        come home to save your
laugh   on the
voicemail:

CHEKWUBE DANLADI

INWARD ASPECT

A person in love may start this poem with unruffled dusk,
how it paves the way for sun in the mourning.

May confuse "mourning" for "morning" due to their condition.
Chemically distraught, they may become aroused by love's hair

fallen in drains, by splinter and blood in love's heir's thumb,
may slip in the delusions granted by the worldly

kindness of wake-and-bake and morning sex.
A person in spite now forgets how it was our tattered

bodies that insistently kept us warm when the vortex raged,
or the weeping thundered, when cast out to Illinois's lonesome

prairie. In spite, dusk raging. Some awful thing tethered
to the hottest reaches of our earth. Bequeathed to that

core jumble of burn. Maybe hesitantly, often passionately.
But dusk always comes home after a fight and pacifies

with a cooled kiss to the cheek, and harbored to its chest
–if a hand held to it–runs a kind of cord, stretched

past silt and loam and clay and uncertain interior spheres,
a cord that thrums pretty like harp strings and hauls

those vibes to where we hoard our most abounding nerve
endings. All the precipice places, since what is pleasure

if not the reward for airing out our greatest vulnerabilities?
We sang that drowsy song. Named skin the largest threat

to our armored anatomy, its remembrance of every scabbed
and excised thing. But we put the inky earth's marker to it.

Hidden every joy in our nature. Our folk so often dream
up these abounding mythologies of loss.

Oshun lost everything. The femmes in your cosmos too.
Those same folk are the type to skirt through water, guided

by the heat bracing the bottoms of our feet. This too
a sort of cosmic reparation, the universe demanding

that we be so satisfied, even after all the years
position between us. I meant everything I ever said

about being with you forever, through every time,
and still carry the keys in my pockets. I keep to the door,

my faith in the cord held taut. When you or I reenter earth,
we will recognize the line, pluck it, and ride the quake end to end.

CHEKWUBE DANLADI

THAT WHICH MEANS

predisposed to worry too much ::
      the growing sense of being sick of y'all

having married god to nonentity since ::
      I'm in the house and I don't need no

body come bother me ::
      broody moody nude in half-light

yet touch me, touch me ::
      and I will show you pepper

my song is on, on repeat a dirge ::
      through time ignoring ma's warning:

child put a lid to your pot ::
      don't let or leak so freely

or allow ire to mark its sentence ::
      the bark of skin scored by blade:

the weakest entries ritually transformed ::
      where to let any grievance through:

now seeking to my healing by constriction ::
      this new interest in being gagged:

bound to my ease; yet when the hands go home ::
      I pour some E+J in a bottle top

for Kaka Auta and Granny Bertha ::
      plenty down throat per the healer's orders:

eyes set toward the spirit world's entry ::
      entreating, grannies and aunties, their warning:

don't give this flesh away so freely ::
      for foes can do black magic from you:

the sound and spit that's left behind ::
      how to explain, then, the magic I do:

grown but breath still smelling of milk ::
      inclined to wade long where the rapture spills:

an affinity for which colony? ::
      of no known nation but exile:

in mortal state my dignity cedes quickly ::
      the long-dead thirsting most persistently:

don't come for me and mine for loving vice ::
      you who have killed off tougher of us:

we who remain, what are we to do ::
      time's jagged moves offering so little:

suggesting only the pithy night ::
      for comfort, tuning in to the haunts' counsel:

don't pander after elegies, child ::
      earth ain't even hungry for you yet—

How Much of This Is Mine

I decide to start cataloging objects that belong to me because there is always a grave possibility in the middle of all things that you are closer to the end than the beginning. This does not make me sad; I am a thing among things. My hair has always regrown after being cut away by thin silver scissors in a half-dark bedroom. I will not trust a stranger with it.

To catalogue requires curation, so I take my body on a walk to the local craft supplies store to buy a new notebook. A store employee introduces himself and says that I should ask him if I need help finding anything. I ask him which notebook would be best for list-making. He says any of them, really, they all have lines and the potential for lists. I ask him if he feels the same way about himself. I can tell the question seems odd to him—and after a second, I admit it even feels odd to myself. I say nevermind and ask him where I can find pens.

I live in a tropical climate that calls for tank tops and sandals year-round. I walk home from the art supplies store, the sun friendly on my back. I pass a group of children struggling to stand up on roller skates. They wear multicolored shirts and shorts. I want to tell them that balance requires concentration; they are too distracted by each other's laughter to ever get upright on the skates. But when they fall down against pavement, they still seem happy.

The house I live in has a large front yard swarmed in native plants. A pink-bellied hummingbird hovers between azaleas and ferns. I live with two housemates: one who I love dearly and one who is unknowable. The one who I love dearly is sitting on a red plastic chair on the front porch smoking a cigarette and drinking a beer. He asks me how my day was, and I tell him it was wonderful because I finally found a purpose. He takes a drag of the cigarette and smiles.

I take a cold shower and think about a girl I used to have a crush on. She wore tiny gold hoops and jeans that blessed her body. She worked at a science fiction themed combination mini-golf go-kart complex. I liked to go there and play a round of putt-putt, sometimes on my own, sometimes with my cousin and her fiancé. They were boring but I liked that about them. They knew I had a crush on the girl who worked the cash register, but they never asked me about it or teased me. I liked that about them, too.

I think about the time that I bought an ice cream sandwich from the cooler next to the cash register. When the girl rang me up, she said that she could tell I was good at real golf from the way I did mini-golf. I was so taken aback by her compliment that I just stared and stared and forgot all about the ice cream sandwich until it started melting down my fingers in white streaks. She knew something about me. That has always been enough to sustain me: her knowing, and me knowing she knew.

The shower runs cold down my back but I feel my skin flush, flowers of red blooming along my body. I touch myself until something in the center of me crumbles.

I dry off from my shower and take my new notebook and pen to the backyard. It is nearly dusk and the world is alive with bugsound. Birds scream from the tops of trees, telling their families to fly home. I make myself laugh thinking of birds tucking each other into little bird beds.

In the notebook I use a steady hand to draw long straight lines. One of my strangest abilities is to draw perfectly straight lines without the assistance of an edge. I write at the top of the page, in my neatest writing: *Catalogue of Objects*. I do not have any experience organizing data, but I think with a clear mind and good intentions, I will be okay. I start with the backyard. There is endless yellow grass and lime green saw palms and orange and pink hydrangeas with beautiful antennae. There is a rectangular pool with chlorine water and a blue-tiled floor that feels nice to float in on a humid day. It is a peaceful scene, one I would photograph if I owned a camera.

In the yard next to mine, one of my neighbors is setting up his grill with charcoal and lighter fluid. He waves to me, and I ask after his wife and child. He says they are well, that they are walking home from the park. I hold up my notebook, as if to prove that I have important work to do as well, as important as coming home from the park when it gets dark outside, or grilling dinner. I have yet to write down anything on the list.

When the mosquitos find my skin, I go inside. The housemate who is unknowable has returned home from a long day of thankless work. She cracks a diet soda and asks me if I think it's strange that her boyfriend hasn't called her in several days. I ask her when she last saw him. She says she saw him just that morning, next to her in bed, naked. But he hasn't called, she tells me. It seems to be of the utmost importance that she be called. I say I'm sorry that I can't help more. She asks what I am doing. I tell her that I want to archive my belongings. She asks why. I tell her it can't hurt to be prepared. She asks for what. I tell her I do not know exactly what.

When she and her diet soda go upstairs to her bedroom, I sit in the living room and look around for things that belong to me.

Rattan chest-of-drawers

Various colored glassware (17)

Hand-painted floral tray

Matted black-and-white photo of outdoor market in Spain

Books lining the windowsill (Secondhand & new)

Folders full of papers (Bills & old writing & misc)

Tiny marble frog from museum gift shop

The housemate who I love dearly comes inside and starts making dinner. He wonders if I'll have a quesadilla and I say sure. He inquires about the notebook and the list. He does not ask me why or what for I am making the catalogue. This is what I love about him: his understanding of me.

He makes me a pomegranate juice and vodka and cracks another beer for himself. We sit in front of the TV with our dinners and watch an interior design competition show. One of the competitors is crying because she didn't give herself enough time to find the color palette she wanted. She is crying a weird amount over a color palette, I think. When my housemate goes to bed I make myself just a vodka and head to my room.

I'm not sure if my desire to catalogue comes from my mom, but I do think the compulsion to organize does. When I was young, she would use her label maker to put my name on all of my personal belongings. Putting my name onto the physical object upset me and sometimes when she wasn't looking, I peeled off the labels slowly, so there wouldn't be sticky residue left over. No trace of ownership. My mom worked in an office that was full of loud angry men. She would come home very tired but always read to me from chapter books beyond my own reading capacity. She wore professional pencil skirts and blouses and a locket my father had given her.

On my bedside table now is a photo of my mom and me. In the background of the photo is the Golden Gate Bridge. We only traveled once to San Francisco, when I was nine or ten. My father was still alive then; he took the photo. My mother and I wear matching bright blue windbreakers. Our frizzy brown hair flies around in the wind. I add this to the list.

Favorite photo (Mom & I) in pretty spackled blue frame

In the bathroom next to my bedroom, I hear the shower turn on and run for a long time. I put my notebook aside and lay on my bed, listening to the water running through the pipes in the walls. My phone lights up with a phone call from someone I have been kissing intermittently for a few weeks. I let it go to voicemail. Does the experience of knowing her—half-knowing her—belong to me? I do not put it on the list.

I listen to her voicemail. She wonders if I've ever seen the stage version of her favorite play. She says the play is based on a book by one of her favorite authors. She thinks it's fantastic that the author was able to work so well with the playwright. She thinks the stage version is very different from the book, but in a way that makes her see the narrative in an entirely new way. That's the best thing about art, she says: It is enhanced each time you see it interpreted, even in different mediums, even on different days. It's also dependent on mood, on how you feel about yourself, she thinks. At the end of the voicemail she pauses for a long time, and just when I think she has hung up she says: *I'm glad we have known each other. However long, I'm glad.*

I fall asleep listening to the voicemail again.

The next few days I don't have time to catalogue because it's busy at work. I work as an administrator for a film production company in my tropical town. Mainly the company produces smalltime TV shows that need an ocean setting or a pretty downtown. Once they were involved in an Oscar-nominated film starring one of my favorite actors. Since that movie—which was years and years ago—that actor has invested lots of his money into the production company. Business has really thrived thanks to that. I have met him several times since. Sometimes he drops by to see how things are going with the company's independent films. He flirted with me once, which was a truly harrowing experience. I don't know what I expected.

There are a few things in my office at work that belong to me.

Green coffee mug

Healthy plant

Dying plant

Grey long-sleeved sweater

Bottle of whiskey (special occasions, gift from boss)

One of my coworkers flies in and says this and that, we need you here, can you call so-and-so, what are you writing, are you okay? I tell him that of course I'm okay and shouldn't we go to set. We walk down to the production warehouse together.

They're filming a show about family dynamics that recently became very popular. The actress who plays the teenage daughter was recently involved in a nude-photos-on-Internet scandal. I watch her from behind the cameras, acting in a scene with her on-screen mom and dad. The family stands in the kitchen. This seems like the place lots of family arguments take place on TV. The teenage daughter is screaming about how she is old enough to do what she wants, she doesn't need them hovering over every second of every day, she deserves room to breathe, to make her own mistakes. The writing on this show isn't the best, but the general public would rather the writing be subpar as long as the drama is high.

The dad in the scene is silently seething, and the mom is peeling the skin off an orange with a knife. I find this an odd choice. I wonder who had the idea for the gesture—the actress or the director. She peels and peels, the orange skin falling off of the fruit in spirals. The knife is out of place. She is looking at her on-screen daughter, not the knife or the orange. Did she just walk on set with the knife, think, oh this will be good for the peeling sequence? The on-screen daughter is crying now, and so is the on-screen dad. The on-screen mom has forgotten to cry, or else the script tells her not to. For some reason my coworker is crying next to me, too, which is strange because the scene wasn't *that* well-acted. Though maybe it was well-acted, because something inside of me changed while I watched the scene, too. I turn to my coworker, who is wiping away tears, and I ask him why that actress was peeling an orange with a knife, and he laughs and says he was wondering the same thing.

The cataloguing has seemed—up until now—utilitarian. But now the purpose feels clearer: I am leaving this place, and soon. For somewhere else. Before I go, I have to make sure there is proof that I lived here, that I existed in this place. The proof must be objects because they suggest permanence, some weight that can be measured. Look: I was here for this many objects.

When the scene wraps, my coworker and I shuffle back to the office to scroll though emails and return calls and have a disappointing lunch of platter sandwiches. After lunch I get called in to my boss's office. She tells me that she thinks I deserve a raise, that I've been working so hard lately. She has a look on her face that I am startled to find belongs to me. For all the time I've known my boss, she has always looked at me like this: like she believes in me, like she thinks I can accomplish things I have never even thought to accomplish.

It is so special to notice this. She is an older woman with long grey hair pulled into a ponytail high on her head. She has hard grey eyes, eyes that mean she won't be fucked with. She has always dressed so fashion-forward, even though all she does is sit in her office all day long.

I tell her I am grateful for her immense trust. She smiles and the look is gone, suddenly, which is okay because I have already catalogued it away.

On my drive home I stop at the grocery store to pick up

    Onions

    Cereal

    Peanut butter

    Milk

    Parmesan cheese

    Wine

It is busy at the store and I run into two people that I know. The first is my personal trainer, who recently took pregnancy leave from the gym. She is already back in great shape. I tell her she looks like she has been running marathons every day since giving birth. She tells me it really feels like that, it really does. She shows me a picture of her baby on her phone. When I see pictures of babies, I always feel a weird mixture of sadness and disgust. I do not tell her this; I say it is an adorable child, and that I can't wait to get back into personal training sessions. But as she walks away from me into the checkout line I call out after her, oddly, saying that actually, I might be leaving town. She looks back at me, oddly, as if she didn't hear what I said. We are not that far from each other.

When I make my own way to the checkout the person behind me in line is my unknowable housemate. She and I laugh. In her cart she has four boxes of macaroni and cheese and garlic salt. I do not ask, and she offers no explanation. Her job is thankless. I do not even know where she grew up.

At home the housemate who I love dearly is watching a Hitchcock film. The one with the stairs— well, one of the ones with stairs. He talks to me about camera angles and shadows and mirrors and duplicity. He is smart about cinematography. I perch at the small table between the kitchen and living room with my notebook and a glass of seltzer water. The sun sets through the sliding glass doors opposite from where I sit. Its colors spread themselves out on the table like a meal. Will these colors belong to me permanently? Or will they merge with the swatches of every other pretty sky I've ever seen and become a macro-memory?

My housemate puts in another Hitchcock film. I heat up a plate of frozen eggrolls and count which spoons, forks, and knives belong to me. The ones that are mine have flowers etched onto the handles.

    Knives (3)

    Forks (7)

    Spoons (7)

I do not catalogue the fruit or vegetables or meat or yogurt or sodas in the fridge that may be mine; those will not last long enough to be written on the page.

My phone lights up. It is the girl from my voicemail. She wonders if she can come over. I say: You don't belong to me, do you? She says traffic is light and if she was going to come over, now would be the time. I ask her if she saw the sunset; if that was the same or different than other sunsets she'd seen, if it was better or worse. If she could remember one, forever, which one would it be?

She tells me I run the risk of overlooking any meaning at all if I think too long and hard about what any one thing means. I tell her to come over immediately.

I move to the couch in the living room and watch the film with my housemate. I think of DVDs I own to add to the list.

Pride and Prejudice

What's Up, Doc?

Steel Magnolias

On the TV, a woman dies in the shower. The man who owns the motel cleans up the bathroom of the crime methodically. There is not much blood, given all the stabbing. I mention this to my housemate, and he tells me they used chocolate sauce as blood in this scene. By the end of the film, we learn that the man who owned the motel was also the murderer. He had a complicated relationship with his mother, who somehow lived inside him, forcing him to kill. My housemate has fallen asleep on the couch.

When there is a knock at the door, I switch off the TV and let in the girl. We go to my room and I am all of a sudden bashful. She asks me what's wrong and I take a long time to answer. There is nothing wrong, after all. Just a shift. My boss is calling. She is whispering on the other line, and sounds upset. She is drunk, probably.

I sit back on my bed and let the girl from my voicemail undress me. She traces the curve of her nose along my whole arm, my leg. She closes her eyes against my ankle. My boss, on the phone, is crying gently. She does this occasionally. I know her second marriage is unstable, her children shuttled between her and her ex-husband. She is very lonely. I ask if everything's alright. Oh, of course, she says. Things are relative. I am only as sad as the things around me ask me to be.

The girl from my voicemail has retrieved a bottle of lotion from my bedside table. It is an expensive French brand; one of my only concessions to vanity. It smells like freshly washed linen. It seems odd she would be here with me, spreading lotion across the tops of my feet, the length of my shins. But she isn't, is she? She is still standing at the foot of my bed, watching me. I am fully clothed.

The girl looks strange to me now, like a girl I might see from the inside of a moving car in the rain, walking down the side of a street with a plum-colored umbrella; a girl who, when the car passed by her, she might look up, lock eyes with me, and seem immediately like the type of person whose heart was wholly available to anyone who offered to hold it.

Her dark hair is cut in a blunt short line across her chin. There is a birthmark on her cheek that looks like a rabbit. I reach out, as if touch it before it runs away.

On the phone, my boss blows her nose nosily. She apologizes. She laughs, as if she can't remember why she called me in the first place. I tell her things will get better and she won't feel like she is feeling right now forever. Pain often subsides.

My boss agrees. After a moment of quiet, she asks if I am going somewhere. I have a physical reaction to this: my lungs fill with air and I make a weird gasping noise. I am not surprised; I am relieved. I ask her what made her think that. She says it was in my eyes earlier.

The girl in my room has spotted the list in my notebook and points to it, quizzically. I stretch my legs out until they form a two-sided triangle for her to climb between. I mouth to her: It is a work in progress.

By the end of the week I have six pages of the notebook filled with things that belong to me.

High-backed armchair w/pink-and-green embroidered upholstery

Vintage editions of *The Hardy Boys* (6)

Bottles of nail polish (18)

Perfume bottles all half-empty-or-so (4)

Circular mirror

Sweatshirt w/HS logo

Winter boots (unused)

On Friday night, my housemate who I love dearly helps me clear out the hall closet and I find several jean jackets I forgot I owned. He asks if I'd like to go to a trivia night at a bar with him and his coworkers. I am thankful for the opportunity to take a break from archiving. Am I a hollow person who only cares about material?

I pick out jeans and a white linen top to wear to the bar. I look at myself in the circular mirror and lean in close to really look. I put on one thick coat of mascara, just enough to make sure my eyelashes are really there. I apply a clear lip-gloss, smacking my lips together like I'm in a makeup commercial. My housemate calls up the stairs to ask if I am ready.

We walk down to the bar; it's not far from our house. He works at a small private college in our town, and his colleagues range in age and background. I have met most of them, and they are funny and kind. There is one guy in particular that I love. He sports a huge bushy beard and handles it with good humor. His wife is with him tonight. They tell me about how they are renovating their master bedroom. They tell me all about what kind of shower they're putting in, what type of faucets. I find the discussion mundane and comforting. I ask them what brand of bath towels they chose.

The trivia is mostly pop culture questions. There's a woman in the group—an anthropologist—who complains loudly each round. She says it's unfair; she would be nailing the answers if they had to do with early human cultures. She has a tattoo of a wildflower on her forearm, and another of a mountain range on her shoulder. I watch her down two shots of vodka. My housemate leans in and says the anthropologist was put on academic probation last year for sleeping with a student.

I don't realize I'm drunk until we're walking home from the bar and my dad calls me. He says my younger sister has been in a horrible accident. I don't understand him right away; my vision is fuzzing at the edges. I stumble into a streetlamp and my housemate catches me at the elbow. I ask my dad to repeat himself. My housemate takes the phone from me and I am momentarily angry. I yell that my sister has been in an accident and my family needs me. I am distraught. I sit down on the sidewalk and look up at the ugly glare of the streetlamp, its lemon-lime buzz. Its lemon-lime buzz. My insides feel narrow, a sadness as thin as a needle snaking down my throat into my chest cavity. I drag my fingers across my shirt, as if I could reach inside and pick the needle out, as if I might use the precision of an experienced surgeon to make sure I didn't scrape anything important on the way out.

My housemate sits down beside me. I say it is bizarre that I just imagined a call from my dead father about a sister I never had. He nods, which is a kind reaction. I talk about how there are certain drawers in the kitchen, in the bathroom, in my bedroom, that I have yet to look through. My list is incomplete. I ask him if he thinks I should include abstractions on the list. Like what, he asks.

Well, I say, I might own a story. It is not unlike an object, a narrative. It may take a physical form, and feel heavy. It may shift from owner to owner. It may be bought or sold; it almost certainly has sentimental value. He asks for another example. I point to a scab on my right leg. It is a healthy, hard scab, deep purple and brown. I own that only until it heals completely, and the scab is dissolved back into my body matter. But I owned it at one time. And it was mine. And I loved it.

A couple passes down the sidewalk on the opposite side of the street. They are laughing audibly. My phone is buzzing in my housemate's hands. I ask him if that notification is something I should write down on the list. Should I add my unopened emails? All of the passwords and logins for my various Internet accounts? Coupons I have used on transactions in stores? I can't catalogue feeling. I have tried.

My housemate lets me talk but I can tell he wants to go home. I am selfish, I know. But I want to sit beneath the ugly streetlight for a few minutes more, maybe a few hours, maybe a day or two. The impermanence is curing some kind of illness in me that I didn't notice before. A volcanic desire to name unnameable things, catch uncatchable things. I am flooded with a long-ago pain. I don't remember where it came from; I just know it belongs to me.

It is so embarrassing to have feelings. I tell my housemate we can go home. I hear him breathe out a long—almost endless—sigh of relief as we step out from beneath the light.

Maybe it is time to return objects that do not belong to me. When I go into work the next week, I bring a metallic travel coffee mug that belongs to my boss. She thanks me when I hand it to her, and pauses for just a moment, long enough to remember the drunken phone call. I look away from her, stare at the stacks of spending approval forms and unread scripts. Things that are hers temporarily. I tell her I am grateful for what she's given me. She shakes her head and smiles. She turns to her computer and begins typing as if I am already gone.

My coworker and I head to the warehouse to talk with set managers about scheduling concerns. The family sitcom is rehearsing. My coworker tells me he is going to get a latte before we find the set manager, and I say I'll wait. The scene is just the mom and dad sitting in what looks to be a study or someone's office. The wall behind them is rows and rows of bookshelves. I know they sourced those from a local secondhand bookstore; I was the one to make the call, take the drive, bring a crew to load in the books. I took out four books as we unloaded, to keep for myself.

The DaVinci Code
Alice in Wonderland
Brave New World
The Executioner's Song

I don't think of that as stealing—though I have no intention of returning the books. If anyone asks me, if I am somehow caught, I will simply say the books got lost in the mix.

The scene is halted temporarily so the mom can get a retouch. Her makeup artist is a stunning black man who I have never seen before. He and the actress seem to have a good rapport. They laugh as the makeup artist reapplies blush and eyeliner. I am amazed he can do that while the mom's face contorts and moves with emotion; he is good at his job. The scene director calls for another run, and the mom squeezes the makeup artist's forearm affectionately. Is this a "thank you" or a "I'll see you later?" Their familiarity might suggest intimacy. I wonder if they are sleeping together. The mom is wearing a wedding ring—but, of course, that might just be a prop.

My coworker comes back to stand by me with his coffee. I ask him to find the manager and say I'll meet him round the back for our meeting. I want to watch, just for a minute more.

In the scene, the mom and dad are arguing about finances. The dad has been working long, hard hours at the office and he thinks the mom is too credit-card happy. The mom is exasperated. She tries to explain that she puts in her own work: taking the kids to and from school, cooking and cleaning, keeping everyone's schedule in order. And on top of that her sister is in rehab, her parents are ailing, and she is planning their daughter's sixteenth birthday party. She asks her husband if he thinks her work is less important than his. The dad's voice gets quiet and he says of course he doesn't think that. Then he pulls out a legal pad from the drawer of a desk he leans on. He hands it to the mom. She looks like she is about to cry. The dad asks her why she has made the list. The mom admits she is just trying to keep track of what is hers in this life.

I feel a strange twisting sensation in my abdomen, like I ate something rancid. I quietly move closer to the set, so I am on the side of the cameras that capture the mom's profile, close enough to see what's on the legal pad. I can only read what is written at the top of the page: Inventory of Assets.

I wonder, momentarily, if I am dreaming. If I am sleepwalking. But my phone buzzes in my pocket; it's my coworker, wondering if I am on my way. He has found the set manager in charge of scheduling. I look back at the mom on the set, clutching the legal pad. I think the actress has somehow infiltrated the deepest part of me. Her acting is not acting at all. She is playing me, or at least some version of me I might become. I want to storm the set, call to cut, take the actress playing the mom gently by the shoulders. I want to see her, eye for eye. I would ask her: How much of this is mine?

I have neglected many appointments. I have skipped a visit to the gynecologist and my therapist, unwittingly. I call the gynecology office to reschedule, but wait on the therapy. I am not yet ready to be told how to deconstruct my actions.

The morning of my new appointment I get up early to make peanut-butter toast. I put little slices of bananas atop it. I wave goodbye to my unknowable housemate as she leaves for work. The housemate who I love dearly comes slovenly down the steps and makes himself coffee. I have the sudden urge to say a long and final goodbye to him, as if I will drive all the way to the other side of the country that day and never return. The sensation tickles in the back of my throat. It feels like the beginnings of strep.

Traffic is light on the way to the gynecology office. In the car I become unnaturally worried that my gynecologist is the only person who knows me, really knows me. This is not true. But the fear is overwhelming and heavy. It seems like something that belongs on my list. I will not write it down. I will not humor myself.

For some reason I turn into the parking lot of a small park next to an elementary school. I am only a block or so from the gynecology office. The playground is thronged with children. Adults sit on benches lining the park, talking with each other and distributing snacks and juice boxes to their kids. I turn off my car and stare at the swarms of bumbling children. The toddlers are especially clumsy. They look really stupid, unable to keep themselves upright. There is a cluster of them loitering in a sandbox, plopped down, picking up handfuls of sand only for it to fall straight through their fingers. They laugh like this is a magic trick only they can do. I do not know how to feel about that confidence.

My phone rings. It's the gynecology office, asking if I am still coming. I say, dumbly, that I am almost there.

Summer arrives unexpectedly one weekend. It rains all of Friday and Saturday, long, hard rains that shake our small house. It's as if the water will uproot the structure from beneath the foundation and we will float down the street in a river. I sit in my room and stare at my catalogue of things. I video chat with my mom and ask her where she thinks I should go. She wants me to return to my hometown, a place with seasons. She also wants to talk to me about an article she read on Monarch Butterfly migration. The rain runs dark blue against my bedroom window. I say sure, I'd love to hear about migration patterns.

When the heavy rain finally lifts back into the sky and humidity swarms, Sunday arrives. My housemates and I are hosting a barbeque in the backyard. We set up in the midday, filling coolers with ice and hard seltzers. The unknowable housemate goes to the store to pick up meats and chips and fruit. The housemate who I love dearly and I put up a cheap badminton set far enough away from the pool to be safe. He hooks up his phone to a speaker and puts on a synthy pop album. His sunglasses are brand new, but look like they were made in the nineties.

Guests begin to arrive as the late afternoon sets in. We have invited an array of people; coworkers and mutual friends and neighbors. We even invited our postwoman, though we were fairly certain she wouldn't show up. I even invited my gynecologist—which I realize now was a strange and probably unprofessional thing to do. She is just so pretty. I can't really control what I say around her.

People mingle on the small backyard patio, picking at the food, taking drinks out of the cooler. One of our mutual friends has just told us she is engaged, though she doesn't wear a ring. I ask her where her fiancé is and she says he had to go into work. I think he is a pediatric surgeon, or else a pediatric dentist. I am too nervous—and have known this friend too long—to ask again what her fiancé does for a living. I suppose it's okay just to know he was probably in school for many, many years before he obtained a degree.

We pass around bottles of bug spray as the sun slides down, slanted, in the sky. I click on the outdoor lights. My housemate who I love dearly is in the pool with our friends. The girl from my voicemail has just arrived and wonders if I want to swim. I say sure; let's swim.

The pool water is darkened black by night. I strip the weight of humidity; it glides off of me like a second self. When I open my eyes under the water, I see the shapes of other bodies. I think these are not my friends but aliens that have replaced them. Beautiful, underwater aliens. The girl from my voicemail tries to take my hand in hers, but underwater I am different. My hand is not mine; it does not belong to me.

I run out of air. As I break the surface of the water, the alien shapes around me rearrange into faces, bodies, people. The girl from my voicemail is wearing an orange swimsuit. It feels like my brain is spinning around inside of my skull. I swim to the edge of the pool and brace myself. For what, I'm not sure. It's like there is an earthquake waiting underneath the pool, deep in the ground, the faint pulse of potential destruction laying wait in stagnant dirt.

Above me, by the patio, I spot our mailwoman. She looks different out of uniform. She has such an interesting face; wide and oval-shaped, with long eyelashes that are asking for trouble. It seems like she has been put in charge of manning the grill. She calls out to guests if they'd like a burger or a brat. I am so happy she is enjoying herself.

At my ear, my housemate who I love dearly. He asks me if I might add this night to the list. I tell him yes without hesitation. I do not think of the party or the pool or the mailwoman at the grill as abstractions. They are solid-edged lines, and they all lead home.

I bend backward in the water until I am floating. My friends move out of the way to accommodate the length of my body. I think that no matter what year, month, or decade this party was taking place in, I would still be in this same space with the same people. There is at least one other timeline happening, I think, just a fraction of an inch from this one. In that timeline I am a girl with a name and a list of belongings. That girl is ready to leave.

That girl gets out of the pool and grabs a dry towel. She smiles at her friends and gives hugs to those she passes by. They are smiling, too. She thanks the mailwoman for all her hard work at the grill. The mailwoman laughs and laughs, says it is not hard work at all; try walking around and delivering mail all day.

That girl walks through the sliding doors into the air-conditioned home. The cold feels crisp, like a physical thing, not just a sensation. She walks into the kitchen, swimsuit dripping onto the tile below. She pours herself a glass of water and drinks the whole thing. Then she climbs the stairs and finds the notebook where she left it in the bathroom. She looks at the last written thing.

Tubes of toothpaste (3)

She hugs the notebook to her chest, wet swimsuit dampening the pages. The house is dark around her, empty. Outside, the party and its happy noise. She hopes she will make it out of this alive.

Or maybe that girl floats on her back in the water until all the guests have left the party. Maybe they think she is sleeping. Her housemates clean up the party mess and turn off the outdoor lights and go inside for the night.

That girl imagines that she is not in a pool but in a dark ocean. Floating beside her is someone she loves deeply and without selfishness. She turns her head to see that person's face—but it is hidden from her, shrouded by an unruly shadow. The only source of light is the shy pinprick stars. There is one that is brighter than all the rest; a planet. She opens her mouth to tell the person she loves, but the person is already swimming away.

DUNCAN SLAGLE

PRIMORDIAL BEHAVIOR: SHRINKING

*[Homosexuals] degrade the relationships of love between two human beings
from a serious matter to a convenient game, attended by no risk,
no spiritual participation. —Sigmund Freud*

Notice how light evacuates when God enters a room. Now I posture like fair competition though I prefer conceit as an evening dress. When it rains, I shiver my hunger into matchwood. The moon spills over so I have something to drink. What you thought was a womb is shrinking—. Better to be the monster & keep my blood inside: Alone. Alone. Cognate to the noise of the dead relaxing when they arrive. Only after the priest serves his tongue, attempting to mark divine territory. I was a little boy. I was a garden. I was an angel inside it—I knew where my name would take me. The garden teemed. Flowers developed a whole range of weaponry. I was alive & then my living kept shrinking. Funny, to still dream of the hands' bones diminishing in light. That, yes, there is a Biblical argument against sacrifice but that makes God a villain, and I'd rather focus on how rain obeys the fur of goats, falling in uniform rivers. What I cannot live without you see as expendable. Daphnis strangling Chloe by the spring. I thought you made me until I outgrew your word. The rain pauses, waiting for the dead to unfurl their umbrellas. Everything I am made of has been called out of question.

magnetoreception

a full moon eats
        electricity
as I do
        I eat
         you readily

slurp protons
neutrons electrons
airating

        your flavor
        an atomic
        cereal

my cheeks glow

        this is not
        a soft affair

it's a hard turn
toward you

        I twist
        to reach
        the center
        of earth

vertigo:
another name
for grasping
phantoms

        we share a living
        in a lunar halo

shifting charges
through the city
here: carry
     the skyline

a string
of luminous windows
rattling like charms
on a necklace

     they light
     your face:
     they ring
     & ring

cryptochromes
gliding along
magnetic waves

     find one another/
     each other's charge

is it love
that is neutral?
no—it endures
the electric
silken atmosphere
floating

     the horizon: opposing forces
     & the statis between

god give me a summer

one long hot lick
across my shoulders
while waiting in line
for dim sum on Doyers St
                    god
give me a summer
that scorches like
the rocking ha cau
under my tongue
breath panting over it
to cool the dumpling
& it slips into my throat
& I say *dim sum*
makes me happy
to be alive
before wash my teeth
with bolay cha or god
give me rising steam
of phở đặc biệt
under my nose
or give me
the waves of heat
off a barbeque pit
                —god
give me a summer
that runs through
every dead
razor sharp
yard in Texas
framed by sidewalks
cooking
through sneakers
                god—
give me a summer
that sits on the skin

the way a body can surf
the dermis of ocean
                        yes god
give me ocean sounds
like the crack of my first
sprained ankle
a crashing end
to hopping waves
in Corpus Christi
                        god give
me a summer in bed—
yes a summer bedridden
by unresolved
imperialism-
induced trauma
it's impossible
to waste a summer
but is it possible
for summer
to waste a body
                        god
give me
an answer
& let it be
effervescence
& sugar
                        yes god
give me popsicles
lollipops jolly rancher
jellybeans anything
melting sticky
adhering me
to this earth—
                        god
give me a summer
let sweat flow
from neck
to knee give me
a summer
when undressing

out of wet clothes
looks like slow
molting membrane—
when we're all
cicada nymphs exiting
exoskeleton

S. BROOK CORFMAN

Not To Cross, *suite for two voices, or for a chorus*

XX/XX

My Nymph,

A woman pursued by a man becomes a tree, as I too was pursued, curled inside a birch.

I slept, rings radiating the length of my age, at once taking in the earth and air. How strange, that the tree became a memory, even though I knew the memory castle to be a lie.

It's nice to imagine everything unchanged and ready, needing only dusting, instead of following the roots down to the forest floor, in turns covered in mast or fireswept.

Once I wrote that I didn't know any myths about the birch tree.

I chose it for my transfiguration.

A man—this pursuer—claimed such a myth, a Scandinavian folktale, but I went to the flat world and couldn't find it.

It wasn't that I didn't believe such myths existed.

Here is a corpse in the dirt, who blinks each eye open, from whose heart a birch tree grows, each vein its own sapling, its own flaking trunk. The bark on the one side a record of weather, the other the color of an inside turned out, how it dulls, having met the air.

The subject of a dream is to pass it back and forth. The subject of sharing is a compromise. The subject of a compromise

XX/XX

My Hermit—

You shut yourself up in your turret, to avoid me. Ice releases from the peak and falls to the ground. A sound like it's striking your window, like it was thrown up towards the image of you. Here, an arbitrary line, its walking. We're always redrawing it as new shapes in new places. Imagine it as a blue triangle. Decide for yourself its three vertices.

Hiding where the heat ticks and keeps you awake, this does not change your desire to reach me. I've defined for myself an outline to communicate to you from. When we stand before each other it will collapse. Place your hand on the walls and feel their slight ornamentation, their visibility. Trace it onto me. Shape me as part of this line. There are holes in the snow where the loose ice has fallen.

If you touch a texture for too long, you can watch your fingers turn red, can watch yourself become just a little colder. This the crisis, that we watch our manipulations occur over time.

s not to cross. The subject of the tear is the light that passes through. The subject of the light is its refraction. The subjec

XX/XX

My Rhetorician—

Put two objects on the table and tell me what they have to do with each other. It doesn't matter what they are—colored pencil and a small statuette of a person, book and a painting ripped from the wall—your answer should always be the same. When I put water and glass on the table, the answer is easy because it's you.

The great thing about "you" is that most of the time it means "me." The great thing about "most of the time" is that then I don't have to decide where the line between you and you cuts. You tell me. Anything that happens is fixed when the page turns.

Asking why is the wrong question. There are wrong questions. A small stone and a horseshoe: water. A scarf and a lost flask: still water.

A better question is where the earring and the glasses came from. I bet you'd guess I stole them. If you did, you'd be right. If you didn't, I found them in the wasp nest at the edge of my roof.

If you did, I'd tell you how I found the way out, that day we were separated in the bare hedges. I dug through your jacket pockets.

Later I painted the expression you'd have had alone in the maze. Wall clock and easel. Paperweight and pistachio shells.

Put two objects on the table, an oversized mug and an oversized sweater, and tell me what they have to do with each other. Other than that they're empty.

t of refraction is a sound like a brick breaking. The subject of breaking is a straight line. The subject of a line is not to cros

XX/XX

Dear One,

do not move the stones. There are things I saw with them I cannot speak aloud. When we fling braided steel into the fog, we're flinging gears etched with falsetto. Listen for the expectation they won't be returned, when all you can see is the cloudy room happening around us. There's a shuddering when a rock becomes the core of a spiderweb, a shivering that comes back to us. Dear one, toss the stones in the air. They are the many things they look at. Look at them. When you came to me randomized, I didn't even try to turn this notebook into pulses. There is no seed and no possibility of flowers. This pattern doesn't play by the rules, but I'm tired of agreement, of hammering flat the shapes that move on the periphery. Diffuse me through a loop of beeswax, decant my breath. We cannot but perpetuate.

. The subject of the breath is the volume in the lungs. The subject of the lungs is expansion. The subject of expansion is

XX/XX

My Matchstick—

When you're alone, write to me—rip out the pages you're turning, annotate them, and fold your isolating thoughts into an airplane addressed to my volcano. Speak your confinement and send it external. Perhaps fold that into your letter, so that when I open it I will hear your throated music.

Remember when you came to me and teared against my chest, a pieta. How we commissioned paintings just so we could start a bonfire of the vanities, warm the air, and set you in your skiff adrift in the waves.

Soon you'll be a ghost. Play it up, blow your ashes in the wind but scatter them only when you want to. Go to past lovers and singe their eyes, hair, ears. Start spot fires and melt the barriers to dreams. Bring their houses down while they sleep and leave burns on their skin where only new lovers will find them.

Then find me.

is a strained rubber band. The subject of strain is an upper limit. The subject of a limit is not to cross. The subject of cross

My Chevalier—

There is no you but every time someone else expresses longing I understand. Loneliness, it seems, is not universal but something I pretend others have felt. Remember when we gave up on blistering and became our own armor, when paved roads evaporated faster than dead skin. There were mirages but we believed in our eyes. When we sang up an octave, it was too much like screaming, too much like each other. I wanted us to hoist patchwork flags with holes in them large enough to catch the sounds of wind, but we were sharing minds and losing more of them than we had to.

When the music pulls away from the atmosphere some of you is caught in it.

It's hard, I know, when someone's knocking on that columned room. If you throw yourself against the walls you can test the speed of ordinary motion. There's a trapdoor somewhere, I promise.

ng is extension. The subject of extension is growth. The subject of growth is a feeling of allowance. The subject of allow

XX/XX

My Traceless—

I've written to you too much about light, but every time it's morning I fail it and you. Cast shadow in the role of source and see what changes, what gradations I'm willing to be comfortable with. The night writes on my skull and I write into a dusky page: "It was a day absent of horses. The night of a rising surface, rustless." Past the threshold of 15% yellow and 88% white, your retina begins to disintegrate. Again, cast grayscale in a new role. The retina remains vestigial. The breath ligaments strain.

Step into the nonshapes to try and keep morning at bay. Fold and seal yourself within so that when I open the envelope I'll meet again that rare bioluminescent bird, that lightning bug but in its wings and larger. That artificial or otherwise. Objects weigh more when we've lived with them but I've never lived with you. I've lost track of my sleeping pattern because I keep imagining you as a lightbulb. Instead I live with letters, these things I no longer read. This thing I live with now, I'd call it a soul. You'd laugh at that, I think, but I tend to make up both sides of our conversation. Give me curtains, the chance to feel enclosed. Let me rest my windows.

ance is a tree fallen in a storm and the house built in its stead. The subject of a tree or a house is the soil it exerts a force

XX/XX

My Wayward, Windward—

When I pose like I'm thinking I'm really staring at you. We're all focused on something, in this place designed against expectation and comfort, with weak tea and the windows of a room of textured light. We come back anyway. Or I do, knowing three or four dimensions and that flattening myself out always feels like a fifth, like a schism, like how to avoid clocks, like asking why we spend so much time with flatness when we could be touching each other. Ask and maybe I'll let you put your thumb on my eyelid, or my throat, to feel my pulse. It's faint but rapid. You could test the green lights your blue eyes have been turning facsimiles into all day. You'd say my pulse responded the way it's supposed to, but is it supposed to respond to you.

The man on my left is studying to become a doctor. I imagine you saying, "A body is a possible series of entrances, like any pattern," and there's a slice through the air. A sound like the clash of opera and handbells, a fanfare of back-up choirs and outsized emotions like your expressions. But between bemused and amused I'm hard-pressed to pick one. You'd probably say I was wrong. You'd probably say I enjoyed it.

upon. The subject of receiving force is grounding, is force sent elsewhere. The subject of going elsewhere is not to cross.

MIMI TEMPESTT

gender reveal party

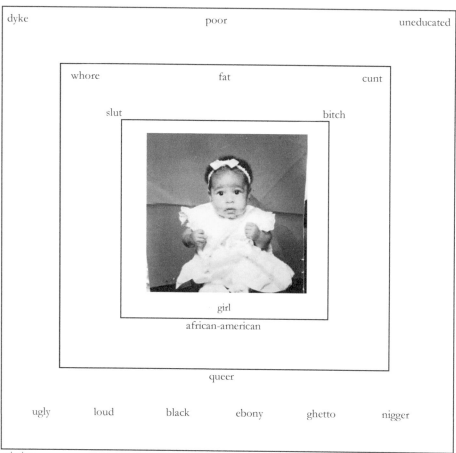

dyke   poor   uneducated

whore   fat   cunt

slut   bitch

girl

african-american

queer

ugly   loud   black   ebony   ghetto   nigger

missing   nameless

dead

MIMI TEMPESTT

on international, the girls are all lined up

a body didn't get the world right

a people did

right
right
right on the money that drips maligned between my thighs
right on the street that reveres sanctuary for none
right on the blood i saw hemorrhaged into blue after my mother gave birth
to another black daughter

right on right
directionless on the path designed for dizzied souls to sell diamonds
demonized by devils
turning tricks until saints

right on wrong

right on "what's wrong?"

right on the breasts that coo conquered alongside kindred feet
in the metropolis black
girls stripped of their emeralds
dancing
dancing
dancing
dying
(we mean) dancing

shhhhhhhh
uuuuuuuuuu
cccccccc
kkk

jjjjjjjjjjj

iiiiiiiiiii

vvvvvvvvvv

eeeeeeeeee

and shuck and drive
and shuck and lie
and shuck and cry
and shuck and fly
and shuck and play
and shuck and slave
and shuck all night
and shuck and stray

left on the corner of:

the veins the move vericose to the victory of false satiation
left on "who did we lose today?"
left teetering the line of alive and almost always dead
left lapsed on repeat: missing/gone
left as in my daddy [we know how this fucking ends]
left as in "if i ever catch that nigga in the streets, it's gon' be _____."
left paying in innocence for the hell they hail, worth dollars
left like the jab that hurled "owned" on my face
left in my body, the drugs that i developed this itch for
left in the closet with my eyes staring lucid into the void

"she was only 15. we made a pact that we would make it out together."

i made it out with wings branded on my back
still they make their lefts on death row
the stolen relics are all lined up
on sale: mouths. hands. youths.
if the price is right, pussies
always, their souls.

the choir of whores have taken the floor:

he unzipped himself in front of me

they unzip themselves in front of us

and placed the lie that we both know in my mouth

and place the lie we all know in our mouths

he confessed his demons inside, for a fee

they confess their demons inside, for a fee

until his tiny white angels all flew out

until their tiny white angels all flew out

on international

no angels flewed past me

angels flewed past no me

angels no me flewed past

flewed me

the angels

the angels
(a people)

didn't get the world right

my body
the world didn't get

a people
(the angels)

did get my body

right

more than a black female sex fantasy

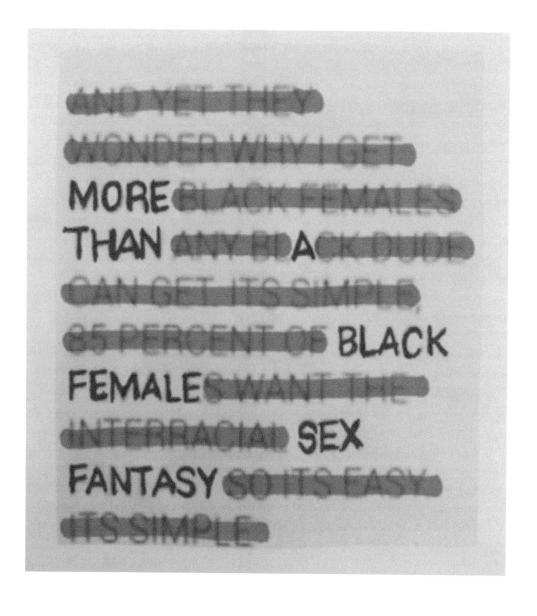

A Life of Its Own

The Bud

In a warm purse in a place beyond memory, cells divide. If there is a sound for what happens after weeks and weeks of division, to the metamorphosis from indifference into the first of a lifetime of differences, then science is deaf to it. Membrane stretches, fuses, separates into an aperture, an empty sac. Hormones invade, bombard, advance. Tissue creep halts a budding glans in mid-bloom. Cords and rings and passageways join a filigreed network of nerves and blood vessels that, in turn, join a developing bladder, brain, heart. Captured in soundwaves, it echoes like a charcoal sketch out into the waiting universe where a specialist in a white coat and tie with a small mustard stain below the knot confirms its presence to a man, Greg, and a woman, Erin. Greg recalls the imperfect map of his boyhood and sees the means to redraw it; Erin recalls the imperfect map of her girlhood and knows it will remain imperfect forever. Both of them, without whom its existence would be impossible, smile. Back in their apartment above a 24-hour laundromat in a congested American city, Erin excuses herself to take a nap while Greg calls his mother, his father, his aging grandmother out west. A thin wall separates the bedroom from the living room, so Erin must cover her head with a pillow to mute Greg's excitement, his laughter. It frustrates her, all this activity inside her body she can't see, the construction crews busy at work. Greg goes out for a beer, comes home three hours later half-drunk and lays a sack of burgers on the bedroom nightstand like an offering at an altar. Erin says she's not particularly hungry. Greg says, You need to eat, he needs to be strong. Erin stares at Greg, his flushed face, his dopey smile, the way he bounces on his haunches while he waits for her to unwrap her dinner. She's not sure whether she can say—yet—if she loves what's dividing unseen inside her, but she loves the man in front of her and so, for his sake at least, she eats. She eats and eats while cells divide and divide. The generous alcove in their living room is painted blue and fit with a small crib beneath a mobile of felt firetrucks and footballs. Erin's swelling belly goes by new names. Champ. Buddy. Rockstar. She never imagined Greg could be so in love with something so stretched and distended; she never imagined she couldn't be. She walks through the city while cells divide. It's not safe, Greg says. It's good for the baby, Erin says. Greg insists on joining her, so she retreats into her mind while he talks about the future, while he holds her hand as if to keep her floating mind anchored to her body, safe from the selfishness of her sacrilegious disappointment: I wanted a girl. Cells continue to divide. Other things, too.

The Token

Barely two days in the world and already under assault. Swabbed in antiseptic and numbing cream, stretched and clamped and snipped with a scalpel, caked in petroleum jelly, wrapped in a tiny square of gauze. The obstetrician, who has two more of these operations to perform before lunch, drops the fingertip of skin into an orange biohazard bag. There will be no memory of this maiming, this pain. Already, he—for this is how Greg and Erin identify the baby—pays the injury no mind. He's too busy squirming on his back in this strange new existence while Erin changes a stained diaper and gingerly dabs the raw flesh with a lotioned pinky. Poor guy, Greg says when it's his turn at the plastic changing table and he taps the tiny bulb to see if it registers pain. Greg watches from the kitchen, quietly jealous, while Erin sits in front of the television with the blue-capped parcel against her chest. He scrubs out bottles and nipples and milk bags, fingers already sore with papercuts from a company audit, ashamed Erin can offer the baby sustenance from her body while all he can do is heat milk on a stove.

The Fountain

Piss! In dribbles, in sprays, in staggered bursts, in glorious arcs! In diapers, yes, but also on hands and thighs, in faces and laps! On Erin and Greg and Greg's mother and the old Polish woman in the studio next door who refused to heed Erin's warning! On living room carpets and the tacky tiles of public restrooms and—twice—the worn plastic cliffs of subway seats! It gives forth piss plentifully, gratuitously, endlessly! Erin laughs! Greg groans! Erin cries! Greg scoffs! Erin snaps! The sharp scent of these rampant offerings suffuses their entire lives. Years of piss until, slowly, trained first with Greg's fingers and then with the boy's own cumbersome grip, it learns the physics of aiming into porcelain bowls. It masters the art and craft of waiting for the appropriate moment or receptacle, or holding it until the appropriate moment or receptacle presents itself. Greg: I just bought you this underwear! Erin: One more time and the rubber sheet's going back on! Greg: I can't pull over now, here, go into the coffee cup but BE CAREFUL! Through trial and error, it forgets the freedom of plastic disposable diapers and embraces the responsibility of colorful cotton briefs. Occasionally, after the acrid rush recedes, the small sponge of flesh remains tense, like a woodland animal on edge. The boy is equal parts bewildered and bemused by this premonition in 1.6 inches.

The Toolywally

It drowns in chlorine, suffocates in white swim netting. Forced, through the boy's primal craving for a return to Erin's belly, to tolerate a second life in pool water. Saturday after Saturday, marinating in chemicals while the boy paddles in yellow floaties and swim goggles into the arms of a swim instructor on summer break from college; while the boy clings to the side of the pool as if it were the edge of a skyscraper and waits for his father to finish laps. In the locker room, Greg and the boy shower together, their swim trunks hanging like snakeskin over the top of the stall door. The boy mimes Greg: lathers soap between his wrinkled palms, rubs it into his tiny arms, his tiny chest, his tiny legs. Shower water smacks on sloped bathroom tiles, guides the suds around their feet into a small drain. Don't forget your toolywally, Greg says, and then it's covered in soap and awkwardly massaged and rinsed with lukewarm water and, when the shower creaks closed, dried with a towel. His father calls it a toolywally; his mother calls it a penis. How, the boy wonders, can something have two names? They have to change quickly. They're already late picking up Erin from her therapy appointment across town, where she unburdens her sadness onto a squat, bearded man who tells her it's okay to cry, that marriage and motherhood are supposed to be work. Erin taps her teeth, restless, while twenty-five blocks east Greg and the boy get dressed. Greg, as always, puts his shirt on first, which means the boy has ample time to stare at the toolywally between his father's legs, this strange likeness with its explosion of crispy red hair, its sac like a worn-out bean bag chair, and, most fascinating of all, its droop. Once, in the locker room, the boy reaches for it. Greg smacks his hand away. We don't do that, he says. Another time, halfway into his briefs, the boy asks Greg why the end of his toolywally looks like an elephant's nose. Some boys have it, Greg says, and some boys don't. I don't have it, the boy says. Your mother wanted it that way, Greg says through the sweater halfway over his head. Now, the boy searches the locker room to find who's like him and who's like his father. The haves and the have nots.

The Weathercock

It loves Mr. Lao's barbershop. Like something stirring on the seafloor and pushing up toward the surface, it comes to life every time the boy sits in the plastic chair in front of the mirror, given permission by the comfort of boxer shorts, the safety of jeans, the secrecy of the spotted apron the barber cracks open and cinches around the boy's neck. Oh, Mr. Lao's hands! Thick fingers that prowl along the boy's scalp, palms that shift his head and neck, knuckles that nudge his sensitive earlobes as if trying to communicate in code. Ginger clippings tumble down the apron into the boy's lap where it swells in defiance of the boy's embarrassment. The boy folds his hands over the zipper of his jeans, but it's too late, the barber's hands have already done their work. The barber's hands—and the girl's breasts in the mirror. Mr. Lao's daughter usually sits in one of the plastic chairs lined up against the front window, doing her homework or, occasionally, picking up a broom and sweeping dead hair into a distant corner. She's much older than the boy, and she's oblivious to how he watches her sit in the mirror, how the urgency between his legs directs his eyes to the slope of her neck, the generous cotton ridge of her seventeen-year-old chest. It feels caught in a violent crosswind: the daughter's breasts, the barber's hands. A little lower, my friend, Mr. Lao says. He eases the boy's head forward, and suddenly it's shocked into submission by the bite of clippers along the boy's nape—but only briefly. The boy squeezes his thighs, jiggles his sneakers on the footrest. Almost done, Mr. Lao says. Those delicious hands rub cool lotion on the back of the boy's neck, behind his ears. The spotted apron flaps away like a giant bird and the boy has to stare at the floor, has to count the clippings of hair to distract his mind. Mr. Lao helps the boy into his pale green windbreaker. Mr. Lao's daughter hands the boy a blue sucker wrapped in cellophane, then looks at the boy's lap. A laugh slips through her glossy lips. The boy runs out of the barbershop in terror, keeps running down the block until it finally shrinks away. But not for long. The boy knows it will come back, later, under cover of night, to plague his dreams with more confusing visions of powerful hands on tender chests.

The Mutant

It's waited long enough. After thirteen years, hormones churn like volcanic froth. Hair erupts into a thin wreath at its base. Flesh grows and thickens and drops, faster than that of some boys, slower than that of others. Despite the boy's anxieties, it has all the time in the world. Time for new names bestowed by the boy and his friends: dick and cock and prick, nuts and balls and berries. Time to study, at great length, its siblings in the pages of magazines and on computer screens and in late-night cable movies. The boy is a slave to its demanding circadian rhythms, its tendency to appear most frequently at swim practice, when it can barely be concealed by the silly, team-required speedos. And oh, the semen! The *raison d'être* of its existence! No surface is safe from its gush and dribble: bed sheets, bath mats, guest room blankets, dirty laundry, couch pillows, living room drapes. Slathered in spit and soap and hand lotion, it has never been more loved, more acknowledged. The boy gives himself wholeheartedly to its cries for attention, makes an art of relieving that constant ache like sneakers trapped in a dryer. The white strip of Tabitha's underwear in World History. The way Carlos hops like a frog on the floor of the middle school locker room. Words like *gush* and *firmness* and *peck* in the vampire novels his mother keeps on the top shelf of the living room bookcase. Dominic's ankles, Anne's wrists, Samantha's neck. Women modeling lingerie, men modeling briefs. The simple curve of a car's rear fender. Afterward, it shrinks and sleeps, abandoning the boy to his exhaustion, his confusion, his shame. Greg keeps a wide berth from his moody, mutating son. Erin, meanwhile, misses the smell of the boy, grows aggravated with the stench of this man-in-the-making. Both dutifully launder the boy's rampant stains. Both, out of love, refuse to complain.

The Hot Potato

A week before the boy graduates from high school, he drives one of his father's work trucks to the hilltop park overlooking the interstate. Moonlight glazes empty benches and an exhausted swing set. Ryan, another senior on the swim team, reaches up and snaps off the cab light, then leans over the boy's shorts and breaks apart the puzzle of his buttoned fly. The boy can only think with mirth, This is what it feels like to have your dick in someone's mouth. That autumn, at an upstate university, it's guided (sometimes impatiently) in and out of various warm cavities. It's tugged in the library stacks by a lit major named Melanie under cover of the boy's open copy of *Principles of Management, Second Edition*. It's pecked at like a puppy by a TA in his Corporate Leadership seminar, squeezed much too tightly by a student in that same seminar who professes his love for the boy the next morning and whom the boy avoids for the rest of the semester. On several occasions, it's laughed at for being too curved or too small or too quick to spurt. It spends five months in Megan's hands alone, until Franklin's inviting eyes over the cafeteria register where the boy works the late-night shift become too much to bear. Slowly, it learns through repetition how to wield pleasure like a weapon. More apertures, more ecstatic convulsions. Halfway through the boy's junior year, it reddens and swells and shoots insistent messages of pain to the boy's brain. It plagues the boy with burning urine and beige drippings until he's forced to visit the campus hospital where he's given a shot in his right buttock and a script for antibiotics. It's back at full strength just in time for Franklin to return from a winter holiday with his stepfather in Greece and, for the next year, it finds sustenance in the familiarity of Franklin's embraces. The boy feels content, happy even. Slowly, other things about Franklin bring it to life. The way he knits, for hours on end, caps and scarves and blankets from piles of thick wool. The crispness of his voice—every swallow, every lip smack—on the campus radio where he plays alt rock from seven to ten every weekday night. The shaggy bark of his bleached hair. When his mother calls from her new one-bedroom apartment back in the city or his father emails at an unreasonable hour from his home office, the boy tells them in no uncertain terms that he's in love. His mother, surprisingly, is excited by the news; his father, expectedly, is indifferent. But it doesn't matter. The following January, the boy catches Franklin in a bar bathroom bent over a freshman, sees Franklin on the dance floor digging into another freshman's jeans. After three days of shared silence, Franklin says, It's just sex. All you do is think with your dick, the boy says. He hands Franklin his duffel bag, his knitting needles, his bundles of fuzzy wool. Now you two can hit the road.

The Invalid

It hangs, sapped of spirit, between the boy's thickening legs, as tired and sad as the convenience store chicken wings and pizza slices that are now the boy's breakfast, lunch, and dinner. Cheap food that, like him, spends most of its day wasting away under lukewarm lights. The boy graduates, barely, and remains in town while everyone else he knows leaves. He stops swimming laps in the athletic center pool. He stops calling his mother and father. He stops meeting new friends for movies, for drinks, for late-night food runs. He stops. He stops. He wants to stop. And for something so powerful, it's powerless to persuade the boy from gathering what pills he can find, from taking them to the convenience store bathroom and washing them down with two bottles of cheap red wine, from slithering off the toilet seat and seizing on the floor. What saves the boy: his right foot, which reflexively strikes the trash can until the attending clerk, who recognizes the boy's face and has come to think of the boy as a courteous regular, pushes open the door and calls the police. At the university hospital, the boy is intubated, pumped, numbed, and blissfully unaware of the violation between his legs until it's already done and the catheter tube has been stuffed through its tiny opening. For nearly a day, it leaks piss in a neat pale ribbon from under the bedsheets and into a plastic bag hooked to the side of the hospital bed. His father and mother, separately, come to see him. His mother brings her new girlfriend, Frieda. She takes his hand and says, No one is worth that much. She asks the boy if he wants to come live with them for a while in the city, they can get an air mattress for the living room. Two hours later, his father makes a different offer: an entire floor of a house, a job with his development group. The boy can't stand the idea of urban chaos, not now, so when he's released from the hospital the boy, who is now the man, drives two hours north to work for his father. Numbed by a battery of SSRIs, abandoned by a brain that has no time for sex, it hibernates. It barely stirs at the sight of a therapist's long legs and thick lips, a manager's efficient hands, the men and women who constantly fuck on his computer screen. When his father's not on site at one of the food halls or apartment towers rising up around the area, the man eats lunch with him at his desk. Periodically, his mother calls to ask if he's changed his mind, if he wants to come live with her and Frieda. The man stays where he is. He reviews business contracts, he helps redevelop the website. He interviews candidates for the expanding marketing department, one of whom is a woman around the man's age, Ovella, dressed smart-casual in a thick turtleneck sweater over which hangs a simple gold cross. Her wide green eyes make the man spill a paper cup of coffee on his pants. She doesn't get the marketing specialist job, but she comes back to the office anyway, two days later, to thank his father for the consideration and to ask the man out to lunch. He agrees, and they make it a regular thing. Two months of lunch dates, then a dinner date after which Ovella leans over the passenger seat and kisses the man while her hand rests on his inner thigh and her pinky finger playfully flicks at the zipper of his khakis. It hesitates at this new but welcome touch, allows itself to be tugged—with no luck. Her patience is what saves the man, what sends him to the doctor for more pills that, when ingested on a full stomach, repair faulty brain signals and flood it once again with blood, with energy, with purpose. Proudly, the man shows it to Ovella midway through a police procedural on television. We meet at last, she says. She rearranges herself on the living room couch and soon it's drowning once again in warmth and after the rush arrives—earlier than planned—and it falls asleep inside this delightful new home, the man whispers his thanks into Ovella's neck and cries.

The Ornamental Hermit

The man, now the husband, makes it pretty for Ovella. Clippers and scissors keep the wilderness of hair in an orderly wedge. If I have to do it, she tells him when he complains, then so should you. Ovella takes monogamy seriously, and so does he. At least, he thinks he does. Once again, he has to learn the rhythms of another, has to solve the puzzle of when to expect pleasure and when not to force the issue. Two years pass during which it's ministered to twice a week, on schedule. When Ovella isn't in the mood, on nights and mornings when her thoughts are too tangled up in her new video production company, the husband tugs it, somewhat ruthlessly, in the shower or over the toilet. Thirty-three years old, he thinks, and I still have to beat off like a kid. During one of their scheduled appointments on a Sunday afternoon in early April, while the dog howls downstairs to be let out, it explodes inside Ovella and the timing is perfect. Cells divide and divide. The husband says, Are you sure? I'm sure, Ovella says, are you? Of course, the husband says, just checking. Ovella grows. Names are volleyed back and forth like a tennis ball, even though Ovella is adamant she doesn't want to know the sex until the baby's out in the world. The husband doesn't understand this logic. He's not a fool; he knows each of them has an expectation of what they want this child to be. There's always a preference—even if they'd never admit it to one another. Why not be disappointed now and have time to recover, to adapt to reality before the baby arrives? But Ovella's the one growing the baby, and so he defers to her. He trains himself to be equally satisfied with a boy or a girl. He'd love either just the same. At least, he thinks he would. The husband moves his desk out of the upstairs office and into the unfinished basement. He paints the walls a neutral cream, assembles a crib with a stubborn Allen wrench. The more Ovella's body grows, the more her company takes off, the more they abstain from sex. She says she's busy growing a human inside of her and a business outside of her, and what can the husband say to that? He could never imagine something inside his body, operating his moods like a pilot in a cockpit. So he doesn't press the issue. It settles for the furtive grip of his hand, of her hand while she whispers into the crook of his shoulder, all while craving the familiar fit of a room that's currently occupied. Then it's early December and they've just buried the dog and he's decorating the living room with lights and garland and fake snow under Ovella's art direction and he tells her about a dream he had where he fucked her from behind and he tries to show Ovella how, as a joke, but she squirms, Stop, she says, and he pretends to ignore her, it's swelling with blood at the thought of the dream, Stop, Ovella says, I'll be careful, he says into her neck, I promise, but she tears out of his embrace, I said no, and he's stunned by the tone of her voice, the distance it creates between them and what it suggests about his intentions and he's angry and aroused simultaneously, the manicured pouch between his legs tightens into an ache and he yells and she stands there, shocked, and Ovella asks what he just said to her, and so he says it again, Stop being such a frigid, Ovella stands there in shock, A frigid what, she says, Forget it, the husband says, and then Ovella reaches inside a half-empty plastic bin of decorations and pitches a snow globe at its swollen shape in his jeans. The husband falls to the ground, speechless. His hands cup it as tight as possible, as if they could somehow suppress the agony radiating throughout his body. The wife goes into the bedroom and locks the door. The husband lays on the carpet, mocking the curled shape of their unborn child while the television music station plays Silent Night. He's still there twenty minutes later, focusing on his breathing and on Elvis Presley singing about a blue Christmas, the pain slowly going dull, when Ovella comes into the living room cradling her stomach and says, Get your keys. Five hours later, she's cradling their child, a wrinkled face wrapped in blue. He's beautiful, the husband says. Standing in front of a hospital vending machine and waiting for a granola bar to drop, the husband, who is now the father, wonders how long it will take to get over his disappointment.

The Prodigal Son

There's just too much going on. First of all, there's Theodore. The father lets Ovella pick the name but spares Theodore the scalpel and antiseptic. Everything remains intact. You'll thank me later, he says to Theodore during changings, taking care to wipe under the tiny hood of flesh. Three days after Theodore's fourth birthday, the father's parents fly down, separately, to celebrate. Coincidentally, they're on the same return flight, which everyone on the television news talks about when it skids on the runway while landing and crashes into a highway. Now the father is parent to two: a growing boy, a family business. He trembles every time Ovella flies back and forth across the country to film conventions of doctors and lawyers; despite his fears, she always returns unharmed. Thinking of his parents in the earth and Theodore in preschool, the father feels, for the second time in his life, sapped of everything that matters. All the energy he has, he gives to his son and to his work. Sex, perplexingly, is the last thing on his mind. He studies his thinning hair, his sagging buttocks with the same meticulous attention he once gave to strangers in locker rooms. He gives up on grooming, lets the brittle red hair consume it like vines reclaiming the land around an abandoned city. New pills help him come to terms with the passing of time but render his desire comatose. Teddy (as they now call him) begs for a brother or sister as if for a new action figure, but the father and Ovella are too busy with their respective careers. There's no time to spare for another sibling and there's no room for accidents, so just to be sure, the father goes to the doctor one morning, where it's exposed and shaved for the first time in years, where it's numbed by a needle, where both sides of its sack are nicked by a scalpel so tiny tubes can be withdrawn and tied and put back. A few hours later, the father hobbles home. On the toilet in the mornings, the father watches the scars fade until you'd never know that inside something had been mangled beyond repair. Sometimes, while watching Teddy scramble around the playground with his pals, the father thinks of the millions of cells scrambling inside him with nowhere to go and nothing to do. So, with the help of more pills, it returns, defiant. For hours now, it pushes against fabric like a proclamation. The father frowns at his aging body but marvels at what these pills can do, how they shelter him from the terror of aging. He's not as young as his pre-teen son (who demands to be called Theo), but he's still young enough to want and, behind Ovella's back, to take. Emma, the new marketing specialist. Two men whom he interrupts in the sauna during his lunch break workout. Blythe in a hotel room at a conference in Dallas and, the following morning, Dana in another room three floors up. Another man in the sauna, with Franklin's narrow nose and chin, laying like a corpse on heated wood. Alice, the divorced mother of Theo's best friend, who's embracing him in the kitchen, a leg crossed over his lower back, when Theo comes up from the basement and locks eyes with his father over her shoulder. Theo starts to go quiet and Ovella wonders if he's gay, if he's planning to hurt himself, if he's getting into the medicine cabinet. He's a boy turning into a man, the father says. He's supposed to hate me. He doesn't hate you, Ovella says. I hate you, Theo says when Alice abruptly takes her son and moves across the country. By the time Theo is eighteen and demands to be called Ted, father and son mostly communicate in silences and nods—the bare minimum required to convince Ovella nothing's wrong. Then Ted leaves for college, and the father aches with the anxiety that now, at a remove from the familiar world, Ted will call and tell Ovella everything and leave the two of them to sort the mess out on their own. But Ted never says a word. He never spoils the father's secrets. He never rats it out.

The Mechanical Reproduction

Photographed, cropped, filtered, and sent out into the world, it's judged *Nice, Hot, Meh, Pass*. After two years of college, Ted (who now asks to be called Theodore) calls to say he's joining the seminary, a decision Ovella takes as a blessing and the father a rebuke for his behavior. In late January, during a snowstorm, someone messages him. *That looks familiar. How've you been?* Two nights later, after telling Ovella he has to finish something at the office, the father sits in his car in an icy convenience store parking lot with Ryan from high school. They look at one another, their swimmer's bodies encased in the weight of age and winter coats. Ryan came back to town four years ago with his husband, Luke. I never left, the father says with shame. It should be stiff now—he'd taken a pill just before leaving the house—but, like the heart to which it's linked through blood vessels and nerves, it can't bear the overwhelming passage of time. They kiss, briefly, but when Ryan's hand reaches for the father's belt buckle, the father says he should be getting home. Come for dinner sometime, Ryan says. Bring your wife. Halfway back to the house, sleet pops like rocks against the father's car. Sobbing, he turns right instead of left at the bridge and speeds toward the new town center he's developing, toward proof of something solid and permanent. An hour later, an ambulance follows a phone signal and faint coils of tire treads to where they end in a broken car at the bottom of a steep embankment. Inside, upside down and bent backward, the father waits, patiently, for rescue.

The Lame Duck

It, like everything below the father's L2 vertebrae, is useless. By the time the father returns from the hospital, the house has transformed. The front stairs have flattened into ramps, the showers and toilets have grown steel handles and braces. The master bedroom is now on the first floor, the upstairs office now useless. The father learns, slowly, to move through the world on wheels, to yield his independence to Ovella, who helps him bathe and stimulate bowel movements, who handles without judgment his bladder bag, who works mostly from home now so she can occasionally drive the father to a site visit or to meetings with architects and landowners. For a few years, he tolerates what Ovella calls their New Normal until the New Normal gets old and he snaps and says, This isn't normal and never will be. He can't help but stare at it in the shower, seemingly oblivious to its fate, and feel trapped forever. He grows irate, stubborn. I got it, the father says. Let me do it, the father says. The summer of the father's fifty-ninth birthday, Theodore returns from his parish in Florida to help out while Ovella travels to Brazil for a once-in-a-lifetime assignment. The father avoids Theodore's help as much as possible. I got it, the father says. No you don't, Theodore says. Let me do it, the father says. You'll hurt yourself, Theodore says. Sometimes the father stares at the crotch of Theodore's plain black pants and thinks, What a waste of a perfectly decent penis. Then, the day before Ovella's return flight, the father shits himself at his desk after an oily lunch and there's no choice but to call out for Theodore, no choice but to let his son set him on the shower bench and strip him. Warm water and lavender suds wash the shit from its acorn head, its mane of hair. The father turns his face up and away into the hissing stream of water. His lips tremble when he realizes he can't feel Theodore's fingers. Theodore tosses the soiled washcloth toward the far corner of the linoleum shower, where it slaps against soiled jeans, soiled briefs. He turns off the shower and leaves the father naked and dripping while he goes into the laundry room next door for fresh towels. The father stares into his damp, hairy lap. He waits. In the growing space between drops of water, he hears, faintly, through the wall, Theodore crying. He waits. When Theodore finally returns, eyes dry, he hands the father a monstrously large towel. The father dries himself as best he can, then hands the towel back so Theodore can dry his shins, his ankles, his feet.

The Ashes

It can survive without nerves and brain signals but not without blood and so, when the father dies at sixty-seven of an antibiotic-resistant infection while hospitalized with pneumonia, it dies with him. The time is 1:52 in the afternoon. Ovella is getting coffee from the vending machine down the hall; Theodore, over a thousand miles away, is listening to a trembling boy's first confession. By the time Theodore arrives, the father, who is now the corpse, lays naked under a white sheet in a nearby funeral home. Drained and embalmed, it's now impervious to bacteria, to the speed at which every living thing in the world eventually rots. The night before the viewing, it's covered in a square of heavy cotton, then the crotch of wool suit pants that have been cut open at the back and down the legs, then the bottom half of a simple gray casket. Theodore leads the service. After the last mourner leaves, the funeral director and his stepson place the corpse inside a thick cardboard container which they guide into a gleaming metal womb. Theodore and Ovella say a prayer, then press a small red button. Inside the furnace, a blast of heat tears away cardboard and wool and cotton. For the briefest of moments, so fast no camera or eye could catch the sight, it rises in mockery of its former glory before shriveling and blackening and bursting. Then, after an hour and fifty-two minutes of fire and noise, the corpse and the father and the man and the boy and the baby and the aggregate of cells to which it was attached for all this time is nothing but ash and memory.

◀◆▶◀▶ANDREW SEAN GREER▆▆▆◆▆◀▆◆▶◀◆▶

An Interview with Miah Jeffra

It's a foggy May afternoon in the geographic center of San Francisco, in the year of COVID. Despite the fact that I could throw a rock and hit Pulitzer Prize-winning author Andrew Sean Greer's flat from my own living room window, or at least hit our mutually favorite bar, Lucky 13 on Market Street, we settle for a Zoom call, the subject of snarky memes and Brady Bunch references almost overnight. This novel normal for correspondence blurs business and personal, artistic and administrative, and creates dizzying opportunity for access while simultaneously underlining our shared loneliness.

This is not lost on Andy as we chat. However, he is cheery, dapper within the frame of the screen (Greer is perhaps the most dapper of all writers alive—just Google the suit he wore when accepting the Pulitzer), with books he is excited to share with me resting on the mantle behind him. Note: the books are there for a purpose, not to be some kind of identity signifier that has become popular with video chat backgrounds—the chosen fashion for this new reality, this visibility from the waist up.

I first encountered Greer's work with *The Confessions of Max Tivoli*, preparing a Literary Representations of San Francisco course syllabus. I was immediately struck by the movement, the elegance of the prose. *Tivoli*'s language possessed a rhythm of lament, and I was immediately swept into reading several of his other novels: *The Impossible Lives of Greta Wells, The Story of a Marriage*, and then his latest novel, *Less*. While many would agree that much of Greer's work evokes an elegiac quality—a softness to his sentences—he can also bite with wit and bemusement, and smoothe the puncture with wisdom. There are so many turns of phrase I have underlined in his books, phrases to come back to in reflective moments of my own. He is a writer's writer, but more than that; he is a compassionate writer, a considerate writer, honest yet kind to his characters. I knew early on that his work would be a significant influence on my own.

Another encouraging discovery: Jackson Pollack claimed that "Every good artist paints what he is." This conceit immediately came to my mind upon meeting and chatting with Andrew Sean Greer.

Miah Jeffra: I'm really fascinated with this transcription software that I'm using. Apparently it works.

Andrew Sean Greer: I can't wait. I love the idea. This makes it easier.

MJ: Exactly. So, enunciate precisely.

ASG: Okay, I can do that. I do that when I speak to foreign journalists. I try to say things in a very clear American fashion.

MJ: You mean, that Hollywood pseudo-British forties dialect?

ASG: Oh yeah.

MJ: When I was a kid and watched films from the period, I wondered, "Is that how we're supposed to speak? Is that how we *used* to speak?"

ASG: It's this amazing made-up fantasy English that is aristocratically American. I love hearing it. Cary Grant.

MJ: So demonstrative. Have you watched Ryan Murphy's new series, *Hollywood*?

ASG: I haven't. I'm very tempted by it for all those reasons. The rewriting of history—piercing the fantasy of it—but I'm not watching TV much at all, oddly.

MJ: Why? I don't mean to imply it's ludicrous, but…you know, pandemic…

ASG: I was initially binging on things and now it's turned into my social activity, so I watch things with friends through Netflix Party or Zoom, sometimes. Every Sunday a whole bunch of friends of mine get stoned and watch a movie.

MJ: And you all are now the goons in *Mystery Science Theater 3000*?

ASG: Yeah. Well, on Netflix Party you can type, which is fun because then you can be as catty as you like. But through Zoom the sound breaks up and so then everyone's annoyed if you start talking in the middle of *Star Wars*. Although, who cares?

MJ: What has been your favorite viewing then?

ASG: Well, no one can agree. Everyone has been unhappy with some viewing. The least popular was *Cats*.

MJ: You watched it?!

ASG: Yeah. I dressed up as Mr. Mistoffelees and everything, but none of my friends did because they're all straight. None of them knew anything about *Cats*. One of them didn't even know that it was cats singing, and so imagine being stoned and thinking it's a movie, like an animated movie about cats, and then watching what you know happens, which is this otherworldly creepy experience. And almost all the films we chose hit the same kind of tone-deaf note. We watched *Tommy*, which I loved but no one else did. I thought it was so fantastic.

MJ: Are you making all the viewing suggestions, Andy?

ASG: I am, so I've stepped back. Yesterday, I let my friend Sue pick, and she picked *Butt Boy*.

MJ: I don't even know what that is.

ASG: It's about a serial killer who sucks things into the vortex of his asshole. Worth a semiotic look.

MJ: Okay. The asshole serves as iconic, symbolic, or indexical signification? [laughs]

ASG: It's kind of worthy of some attention because it's like a Bruce Willis police procedural. It's totally straight-faced, but the premise is so clearly comical. Like they all know that it's funny but it's almost like a straight John Waters film. I mean, he's sucking little children up his ass.

MJ: Oh, so it's not just like paraphernalia to murder. He—

ASG: It's not just things. No, children go missing and the detective begins to suspect that it's going up this guy's ass. It's a real movie. Only three of us showed up to watch that one. It was unpopular before we even showed it, and it was a good movie. Well, kind of.

MJ: Do you think it's an allegory for taboo?

ASG: Yeah. Like, the most outrageous thing you could do is put something up your butt, and therefore it's this vortex of evil, right? And so for us who have had things up our butts it's very peculiar to watch it be sort of like a vampire movie, that a man can destroy people through his butt. He's able to suck people in. The detective ends up in there near the end.

MJ: I dated someone like that in Los Angeles.

ASG: There's other terms for it.

MJ: I guarantee everyone watching that film may have had an idea of what it was supposed to represent, but I'm sure they were all having their own kind of tortured moments.

ASG: Yeah, yeah. But he takes great pleasure in putting things up his butt. That's what's supposed to be so transgressive about the movie. It ultimately doesn't make sense because I'm like, well, that's true of all kinds of people. Men, women, straight, gay. I didn't see what was so transgressive about it. The children in part and animals, yes, but they don't die. They get shrunk down and live in his rectum.

MJ: Whoa, okay. There's a whole new layer here.

ASG: I wasn't expecting that either. We meet them all at one point. See, now you're tempted, but it's also not that good.

MJ: You said he finds pleasure in sucking these things up his butt. Do you actually watch him gleefully...

ASG: We see his face, and I should say the man who's putting things up his butt is the writer-director of the movie, so it's an auteur piece, and it's about addiction really because he's addicted to this and he stops it for years and years after he sucks up a child and gets away with it, and then he's tempted back into madness again by a plastic token from a *Sorry!* game. That's just the thin end of the wedge for him.

MJ: I think I understand the bio here. This writer-director stuck a *Sorry!* piece up his butt when he was a kid and he got in trouble for it even though he found pleasure in it, and this is his indulgent response.

ASG: How did they get funding for this whole thing?

MJ: I'm going to keep all that in the interview. Transgressive, why not? It sounds more interesting than most of the stuff I'm watching.

ASG: It's more cocktail party fodder. We've now talked about it longer than my interest was actually held.

MJ: All right, Andy. Let's become serious writers. You're the child of scientists. Correct? How has that informed your work?

ASG: It's hard to say. I mean, *The Path of Minor Planets* is about scientists. I wasn't better at science than other kids but I saw a lot of scientists socially in the 1970s when they came over for cocktail parties, so I know what adults and graduate students looked like at that time. I took that information and a lot of that appears in the book—their struggles (that feel a little bit like our struggles) of going into the lab with one idea and having to accept the failure of that idea and trying to be open to the paths that they didn't expect and even didn't want.

My mother is an experimental chemist so it was laboratory work, and so I was also very aware of the sexism. Even as a kid it was so clear to me. My mother was the only woman in the lab. The glassworks place where they had to get their special lab equipment made was filled with *Playboy* centerfolds and such, and that was just completely normal. The men would tell all kinds of off-color jokes, and being awkward scientist types they were completely not aware.

I don't think you even had to be an awkward scientist if you were a man, then, to not be aware that it would bother her. They'd give her *Playgirl* as a gift, and then she would be passed over for every single thing, of course. After she came out in 1992 within her department, that was the end. They were not having that at all.

MJ: Really?!

ASG: They didn't fire her but she never progressed after that, so she left. She became an administrator at Mills College here in Oakland. Women's college. She didn't want to deal with the men.

MJ: You know how in some stories a woman comes out in a man's world as lesbian and there emerges a bit of allegiance? Like, "Oh, we all love women." That didn't happen?

ASG: No, it didn't. Well and also everyone was older by that point. By old I mean my age. They were in their forties, fifties, I'm forty-nine, and so they were from a completely different era and just did not know how to talk about it, so people who she thought were her friends just weren't even her allies anymore, and she became persona non grata. That was it.

MJ: Do you see some parallels between what you witnessed growing up with all these scientists and the techie explosion?

ASG: Yeah. I recognize it because of the room of young men. Almost all white, and like you're supposed to end up on top and be cleverer than everyone else. And they all think they are, and that feels like the same vibe I get from the tech community.

MJ: It appears to be a self-importance, and maybe in some cases they don't even realize that they're being self-important because they believe so much in what they do.

ASG: And I think it happens in our community too. I specifically remember that I was really shy, and in university I finally got up my nerve to become that confident dude in class who always has an answer, because I'd always wanted to be that, and the class I chose to do it in was a class on feminism and witchcraft. Wrong class. I was the only man in that class and I spoke over women constantly, and no one called me out on it except myself when I really saw what I was doing, which wasn't helping the conversation. I wasn't even impressing anybody. I was being an asshole.

Like in workshop. I find when I teach that most of my job is getting the men to shut up so that the women can speak. I feel like that's the job—encourage the arrogant, confident and therefore sometimes cruel speakers in the class to hold back, so then the other people, no matter their gender, can have a chance to engage. And in the same gesture help that supposedly confident person—who's really insecure—find the generosity of listening.

MJ: After your own undergrad experience you went to New York, right? What were you doing there?

ASG: I had a bunch of friends who were like, "We're going to New York!" And I didn't have a plan so I thought, "Sure, I'll go." And New York was expensive, though not like it is now. This is 1992, so it was not some crazy dream to go to New York, and it was the closest big city to where we went to school in Rhode Island at Brown. We all wanted to go into entertainment stuff, theater and film and television and writing, and so a whole bunch of us went there, and I was not really prepared for a big city, I have to say.

MJ: What were you unprepared for?

ASG: It did turn out to be expensive for what I was making as a temporary office worker, and I couldn't go have a cocktail with people, which was a big deal in New York. I know when I moved to Montana we didn't do that. We had beer at happy hour like normal people. But I was confused because suddenly it was this New Yorker thing where you had to go get a $10 martini somewhere or meet someone out for dinner, which was not possible, so I would cook at home and I would invite people over. I mean, New York was exciting, but I'm not much of a hustler. I didn't have the hustle to make it at that point, and maybe I was in the wrong crowd. I don't know.

MJ: Then you made a completely different choice and moved to Montana.

ASG: Yeah. I applied to a ton of MFA programs because I knew I needed to get out, and received two acceptances. I got into University of Alabama and University of Montana. So, the choice was made for me. Either way would have been a real shock, but I chose Montana, where I'd never been.

MJ: If you felt unprepared for New York, then why did you end up in San Francisco after your MFA program?

ASG: That was easy because I had gone there in 1991 over a summer with my twin brother and my oldest friend, Eve, and we fell in love with the city. Both still live here. Eve lives upstairs, Mike is a few blocks away. Looking back, I realize that we were seeing the city at a particularly hard time. It was right after the earthquake, and it was right at the peak of deaths during that AIDS crisis. So, it was a rather empty city, but it was very open to us.

We lived in the Mission back when there was nothing you see now on Valencia Street. Rainbow Grocery was there, which was tiny, on Valencia. That's where we'd shop for bulk foods. Tiny. You can imagine. There were burrito places. Amnesia was a punk bar called The Chameleon.

And then there was the gay area and we loved it, and so I knew I'd come back, and that's part of why I went to other parts of the country because I thought I needed to see what else there is, because I must be wrong that San Francisco is the best place in the world, but I have to say I traveled and found that it was.

MJ: I'm a Baltimore kid and so I really thought that I would end up in New York; that's what artistic people do on the East Coast if they are "aiming high." But I did a cross-country road trip with some of my dyke friends sophomore year, and it was almost instant love. For me this would have been '97. I remember being in the Lexington. It was the first night we were there, hanging out with folks there and I thought, "This is where I want to be." It took me a while to get here but I made it.

ASG: I came to San Francisco and immediately was part of Queer Nation and a youth group that met at the church on Diamond.

MJ: The Metropolitan?

ASG: Metropolitan. We would meet there, and I had this group of young friends who were so great. I would hand out condoms in front of the I-Beam on Haight Street. I couldn't go in because I was 20 years old, but I would be there and I just couldn't believe it. I was still young enough that I was terrified of super aggressive sexy things. And it was a weird time around sex anyway, but at I-Beam all of that felt safe and loving and normal. And in San Francisco, people were in costume on the street all the time. Remember those days? Not long ago.

MJ: There was something about the jubilance and creative indulgence of people in the city that made me love it so much. I ran with the Radical Faeries for a while, too.

ASG: Oh. Did you turn out okay?

MJ: I have clothes on.

ASG: Right, yeah, okay. So things have changed.

MJ: I'm kind of curious. I went onto your Wikipedia page—did you know you're classified as "Romance"?

ASG: I have seen that a lot.

MJ: Why?

ASG: I don't know what to say. I don't know that I've ever read a romance except maybe things that are on the edge of romance, like Colette and Jane Austen. I guess those are romances, but I don't know. Why would they do that? I love the idea that I'm so cross-genre: science-fiction-romance-gay-literature. Those things I find really funny and of course don't affect me, but I think if you talked to me 10 years ago I would have felt that men who write about emotions are labeled as sentimental or as romance writers because it's not allowed.

MJ: Even now?

ASG: You can't write too warmongering a novel, you never get violent enough if you're a man, but if you step over the edge of sentiment then it's poison somehow. I still feel that but I don't care.

MJ: I haven't even considered that. I mean, sure, I guess you write a lot about unrequited love. Is that a particular drive you have with your characters? Greta Wells, Pearlie, Holland and Buzz in *The Story of a Marriage*, maybe the most devastating example would be Hughie and Max Tivoli.

ASG: I'm not thinking about it. I'm going into those books with a premise and a structure and thinking I'm going to write this crystal clear novel, and then I get sort of taken away by what actually interests me, which is consistently the ambiguities of love or how it changes over time, and not even my therapist could tell you why. To me it just seems to be what I'm interested in.

Even when I meet people. I'll meet a couple and ask, "Tell me how you met." And they'll tell you their standard story and I'll interject, "No, no. Slow it down." I'm trying to get to the moment of the first kiss moment or some moment where they each understood that they both desired each other. That moment is so interesting to me that I could hear about it a million times, but people can never quite remember it. It's sort of painful for them somehow, and I like that.

My experience of love…it is changeable, and sometimes fleeting, and sometimes lasting, and sometimes dull, and sometimes too exciting, and dangerous, and boring, and all kinds of things, and so it's a character, I guess, for me.

MJ: What have you been more privy to in your own life? The dangerous, the dull?

ASG: Dangerous in my youth, and then it gets duller as you get older.

MJ: I think it correlates to elasticity.

ASG: Actually, when I look back I didn't have many experiences when I was young, but they sure left a lasting impression, enough that I can still dip down and take myself back. In San

Francisco I had a really awful love affair, and I can still pull up specific moments that were painful and use them.

MJ: You have situated yourself as an international writer and you have featured queer characters, but typically they've been secondary characters, that is until *Less*. How important is it for you, for queer writers, to write queer characters?

ASG: Gosh, I don't know where to start. I'll start with a different point. It was really hard for me as a queer activist and an out person who believes strongly in representation to begin writing....I was told by my first agent never to write anything gay, and he was gay, and then somehow for reasons that are hard...You can see me just pausing all of this. Hard for me to explain. I couldn't make the main characters gay.

I probably weakened to pressure because I was being taught, "Don't get shelved in the gay section," which is where my first two books would be re-shelved—back when the gay section was a catch-all for queer anything—and I wouldn't be in fiction, and I was trying to figure out how to be in both sections.

And then with Max Tivoli, I tried. At first he was a gay character, but I couldn't handle writing a 19th century epic about a man aging backwards AND make him gay. It was too much. I couldn't do it. I think that's a failing.

And *The Story of a Marriage*. I tried to write that from a couple points of view but I didn't write it from Buzz's point of view. And some of it is self-hating—not in the sense of hating myself as a gay man, but in the sense of hating myself—pure right down the line self-hatred. In *Story of a Marriage* I made myself the villain. I was comfortable there, and in a way that was right, because I was also training myself to not just see my point of view. My problem was that I was so influenced by writers of the seventies and eighties, Andrew Holleran and Edmund White, who was my thesis advisor. All those great writers who were writing out of real pain, and I found every time I started to write that I wrote like them, and I didn't want to. I wanted to write like me and I couldn't figure it out. And then with *Greta Wells* I tried to write her initially as a gay man.

MJ: Oh wow.

ASG: A gay man who woke up every day in a different version of his life, and there would be the AIDS pandemic and the Spanish flu and then going to war, and I had it all done and I wrote dozens and dozens of pages. But he was such an asshole. It was all self-pity because it was all me, and I hated it. And then when I wrote it as a woman I thought, "Well there we go. I think that's it. I'll have her brother be gay and I'll do it that way." So, once again, I'm off to the side. This is a longer answer than you wanted because no one has asked me this question yet and I keep waiting for someone to ask.

And then, with *Less*, I was like, "Goddammit, I'm going to do it." But you can see once again I'm making fun of myself. I tried writing it straight and I hated that character. It makes a lot more sense because this time a middle-aged white gay man in San Francisco is a privileged person. No matter what we have felt in the past, it's now time to recognize that here in this situation me and Arthur Less are privileged and have to be humbled. Have some humility and empathy and give ground to other people.

Now, that said, it's still a book all about a middle-aged white guy, but I wanted to poke holes in myself, because my story I don't think is so interesting all on its own.

MJ: I have to admit when *Less* was announced I rolled my eyes and thought, "Come on! A middle-aged white guy in San Francisco? How are we supposed to feel sympathy for his struggle?"

ASG: See?

MJ: But I read it and I loved it, and I think it was mainly because you did have this incredible sense of humor, a wry humility. There was an awareness in there that made us actually give a shit about a middle-aged white dude in San Francisco.

ASG: Thank you, good.

MJ: You mentioned how you were having struggles with the idea of positioning yourself as a queer writer and certainly the industry was kind of advising against it too, interestingly enough even within our own community. Right?

ASG: Yeah.

MJ: With that in mind, what do you think is the purpose then of magazines like *Foglifter* that are specifically highlighting queer and marginal voices?

ASG: Well you must be getting comments all the time from readers who say, "Thank you for publishing this. You've changed my life. Thank you for highlighting books that Amazon is not going to show me in its algorithm." Because I know that I get notes all the time from gay men and women who just say, "Thank you." I think *Foglifter* is like the independent bookstore. It is something that's not replaceable. You have to trust the people who are recommending things to you, and it helps if they're in your community and have some sense of your experience, because imagine right now young queer people who don't have any community around them and searching online for communities there or finding things to read.

MJ: I remember in high school coming across *Giovanni's Room*. It was on the recommended reading shelf at the library. I read the jacket description, and it was like *ding, ding, ding*! I devoured it in an afternoon. But yeah it's those moments, right?

ASG: It's those, but also I think—and this is now just talking out of nothing—that for a long time, I'm going to say 100 years, queer writers have written either because they had to encode what they were writing or because they were like, "Nobody's going to fucking read this anyway. I might as well do what I want." We're finding new ways of storytelling that were either ways to hide it, like a Virginia Woolf-y thing, or are just fucking Kathy Acker, like pirates and... like Michelle Tea, saying, "I'm doing what I want," and being celebrated at our own prize ceremonies, because the rest of the world wasn't paying attention.

MJ: So now maybe we can have a little bit more of that front and center?

ASG: Is it happening, do you think?

MJ: I think there remains a level of tokenism, but it's changing. For instance, I read Ocean Vuong's book (*On Earth We're Briefly Gorgeous*). There is a moment when Trevor and Little Dog are having sex and Little Dog's body doesn't behave the way he wants, if you know what I mean, and it's this heartbreakingly tender moment where Trevor takes him into the river and cleans him up. Before, you would never see that moment. A main-stream editor would say "take it out!" Or, it would be a punk-rock scene in a marginal text from David Wojnarowicz or Kathy Acker. Otherwise, it would be omitted to appease the sensibility of the reader. So maybe there's a space in the mainstream that is beginning to emerge, that allows the frankness of queer life to be presented front and center.

ASG: Like Garth Greenwell, you know? I don't have a real sense of things because my Instagram is all writers I love, so to me I'm like, "Garth Greenwell is the biggest writer in the world," but I can't tell if it's true, you know?

MJ: He's pretty big.

ASG: And Alex Chee. To me they seem like superstars, but I can't tell. Anyway, doesn't matter. That's my world so that's fine.

MJ: Maybe that's it. We all can be in our own little bubbles now, right?

ASG: But I do have a sense that...for instance when I was working in Italy for years those writers who were from Europe admired [Greenwell's] book, so it's possible that we're at a moment. I had a friend who had this theory. He was saying, "I think we're at a moment where people want to read a new point of view. So, no one wants to read an old western about white guys killing indigenous folks...No one's reading that, but if you read C Pam Zhang's *How Much of These Hills is Gold*, which is like a Chinese western, it's fascinating. So I'm thinking there's these stories, like Garth's story of longing and confusion and ambiguity and betrayal with him and a hustler in Bulgaria. It feels new, but it also feels familiar so that it's accessible to go there for people. What do I know?

MJ: People have been saying that, for example, about *Black Panther*. You're taking the tropes of the superhero, and repositioning it in this Afro-futurist perspective, and somehow it unlocks the imagination of an America that the movie execs had ignored for so long. I mean, we all went to see it. Or, maybe we went to see it because of Michael B. Jordan. [cools himself with imaginary fan]

ASG: And to be honest I think that is the appeal of *Less*. It's a road comedy, but because it's got a gay character it's somehow familiar. That's partly why I think people liked it.

MJ: So, *Foglifter* collaborates with *The Rumpus* on this project called The Queer Syllabus. It creates a kind of repository for us queers to read. What would hypothetically be on your Queer Syllabus?

ASG: I thought you might ask. Often the problem is that I'm a very selfish and old-fashioned reader and I don't read tons of new things and I read lots of old stuff over and over to try to figure out how it's made. But there were some. I was looking. This poet, James Schuyler, who is not well-known so much anymore, but I have a photograph of him right on my mantel with Frank O'Hara, who was his lover.

MJ: Oh. I didn't know that.

ASG: Yeah, yeah. And Frank O'Hara of course is fantastic, but that stuff is very hip cool Lunch Poem, and Jimmy Schuyler's poems are much more decorated, sentimental. I'm this kind of gay. You know what I mean? And I just had to find him in some way, and he was celebrated near the end of his life. He won a Pulitzer Prize.

And Eileen Myles. I think she's on everyone's list, but I think she's essential because this is kind of, again, it's poetry that is…It's hard. It's difficult for people, it's not Sappho, although it is in fragments. It's something else where you're getting someone who's lived outside of ordinary life mostly and has done whatever the hell she wanted, and the writing takes you in these new places through sound and not necessarily through quotable lines. It's sort of an experience.

MJ: Yeah, you always want her to read her poems aloud.

ASG: I sit and go through them, but I have to read them to myself. She's amazing. I met her once in Berlin. We traveled around. Just by chance we were in Berlin together. She was great fun.

I picked up another one that I don't think is very well-known, but both writers are well-known. It's a Walt Whitman poem called "Live Oak, with Moss," which is a super gay poem, and it's illustrated by Brian Selznick who is a children's illustrator [shows the interior of the book]. His books were made into movies, *Hugo* and *Wonderstruck*. Todd Haynes did *Wonderstruck*. It's so beautiful and you get the real Walt Whitman because of it, and it's a beautiful way to look at the classic without having to read between the lines. It's right there as it is in the poem.

MJ: Yeah, the illustration is beautiful. Kind of had me think if James Bidgood made illustrations, you know?

ASG: I'm not sure it found an audience but it's really moving. And I was never that much of a Whitman fan because I feel like he's a sermonizer, and I'm an Emily Dickinson kind of guy.

MJ: Yeah. Me too. I'm in the Dickinson camp.

ASG: There's so much out there. I mean when I was coming up it was not particularly diverse.

MJ: Andrew Holleran, John Rechy, Edmund White. White dudes.

ASG: Yeah, yeah, and we would read Proust and Wilde and Henry James and we were looking for clues to homosexuality. It's so hidden. Not in Proust, it's not hidden at all, but I couldn't read Proust. And then we would read *The Well of Loneliness*, which apparently is still on the list because it was such an important book, but god I found that so depressing.

MJ: Most of it was.

ASG: It was largely depressing until super recently. My mom would give me books that she liked, but is there a place in the Queer Syllabus for lesbian murder mysteries? I think they have an important history. They serve some crucial purpose because there's just thousands of series of lesbian detectives solving murders. There's got to be something there. I love those. I had a friend in college, Angela Robinson, who when we lived in New York—now I'm going to make New York sound fun—she put on a play of three lesbian pulp novels. I did the lights and sound for it down on Ludlow Street and it was this great nineties queer experimental theater world of loving pulp novels.

MJ: They do have a place, right? Especially if we're going to be teaching literature as cultural complement?

ASG: In college, actually for Edmund White, we were supposed to review a book and I reviewed a porn novel, which he sure liked.
MJ: It's a book!

ASG: Indeed, it's a book.

MJ: *Less* is maybe the most aligned with you as a central character in your fiction, so is there a non-fiction book in your arsenal? And then maybe, as a follow-up, what are you working on?

ASG: I never think about non-fiction because I've only written it to pay the bills as a magazine writer, and as an essayist almost never. I'm not good at that. I can't get my mind together. I'm too wishy-washy. I disagree with myself after I've made a point. And I don't feel like I have a memoir story yet. I did come up with one, but I have to wait a little bit later for it because it would have to be funny, I think, for me. Less was fun and funny because I could make it up.

As for what I'm working on, how dare you?!

MJ: Aren't I supposed to ask that question, though?

ASG: Sure. Yeah, yeah.

MJ: We have to entertain the different ways that writers respond to that question.

ASG: You'll have to get me a lot more drunk.

MJ: Well, how about this then, because this is a slightly different way of asking it? You have a big birthday coming up this year.

ASG: Yeah, I do.

MJ: It's usually the time that we begin to reflect on what it is that we've accomplished. So how about that? Instead of necessarily thinking about you as a writer, is there something that you still want to accomplish?

ASG: I feel like I'm set. I feel like winning the Pulitzer Prize I had not planned on; that was not even a goal. I feel pretty set in terms of asking for more. I think it is now my turn to be a better literary citizen in the world, probably because more people are listening, and to talk about writers that aren't getting attention, or old work that I love, or take a stand on something. I think before I could do that but it wouldn't have made a difference, and now I think I have a responsibility to become more of an activist again, in some way, even if I'm preaching to my own choir. That's what I would like for myself as a writer.

As for what I could make, my friend Daniel Handler is always like, "When are you going to write that epic sci-fi space opera?" I'd say it's obvious to him what I'm going to do next, but that is not what I'm doing next. But wouldn't that be fun?

MJ: So, a bit of micro-dosing and just going at it?

ASG: Yeah, I think so. I think perhaps an ayahuasca weekend, and done.

MJ: Barbiturate-filled, tape all the pages together. (I'll make sure to put this in the right tone).

ASG: I'm so happy still about having such unexpected rewards that it feels fine. All I ever wanted to do, what you probably want to do, is be able to keep writing, and so I really can.

MJ: Congratulations on the Pulitzer, by the way. That is really rad.

ASG: I mean it was two years ago but I'm still feeling the shock.

MJ: Much deserved, Andy.

ASG: Oh, thank you, Miah.

MJ: And thank you for this interview. Maybe when all this blows over and we can actually be in-person I'd love to buy you a beer—cocktail if you are in the New York mindset—or just some tea, if you're going for temperance.

ASG: That would be great. Let's hope at Lucky 13.

MJ: Oh. When is that supposed to close for good?

ASG: Who knows. My favorite bar. My place.

MJ: That is my favorite watering hole, as well. My roommates and I were all very sad, and went on the day we heard it was closing to pay our respects, which was, what, a couple of years ago now? And we all just kind of sat around and drank ourselves into oblivion.

ASG: Yeah. Things changing.

MJ: Well, how about this as a sign-off? We'll at least drink ourselves into a minor oblivion as a thank you, as homage, a toast to the ever-changing San Francisco.

ASG: I'll take you up on that.

KAYLEB RAE CANDRILLI

SONNET FOR THE MONARCH'S MIGRATION

We don't live in a vacuum but imagine it, swirling
around in your mother's Dyson, which has, somehow,
held up since the early 90s. There's dirt and carpet
fibers in your mouth and eyes. You chew, because
that's what you do when your mouth is full. You blink
because that's what you do when your eyes are obscured.

We don't live in a perfect world but imagine it. You
could conduct a symphony with only instruments found
in an abandoned junkyard. You could explore whole new
ways to worship, and no-one would bother your body
as you contorted into this brand-new kind of prayer.
You could even hold a Monarch gently enough
to not take any scales from its wings. Imagine it,
your hands with no capacity for destruction at all.

KAYLEB RAE CANDRILLI

A VERY TRANS AND ARACHNOPHOBIC POEM

I wish I was more like my mother and asked, *pardon me?*, rather

than shouting, *what?* but it's hard to break old habits and move

through the world using only gentle consonants. Every night,

my mother read me *Dr. Seuss's Sleep Book* and spread baby

powder around my bed to ward off the wolf spiders, but they

wolfed around anyway, our house nestled in the Pennsylvania

woods. I would prefer to be a person with rational fears, but

I faint at the sight of a spider, just hit the ground and play

dead, my lips always an ashen blue overreaction. I would

prefer to have remained my mother's daughter, too. But no

animal languishes while a brush fire rages, least of all the spiders.

Everyone tries to stay alive, vital and clawing just a little longer.

Gravitas

Pittsburgh, 1982. My father was in a car accident the year I was born. How Bollywood. Cue close-up of ringing temple bell.

Ten years later, another crash. Five herniated discs.

The first decade of my life bookmarked by so much shifting gravity.

Sometimes my dad lifted me up so I could hit the bell.

.

The summer of 2017, my boo and I were sucking down our berry blast smoothies and people-watching at Travers Park, when I said, "I wish I had a blue ball right now. My sister and I used to have one when we were little."

My girlfriend gave me her familiar gaze of knowing this steady torrent of unmarked unease. We got up from the bench that rested between the kiddie playground and the concrete square that housed a DIY tennis court, four forever crowded basketball hoops, and the occasional game of cricket. Made our way past the black chain linked fence that lined the perimeter of the park and walked up towards Northern Boulevard.

Within a couple blocks a crammed dusty toy store was on our left. Within minutes we were out the door, bouncing two new blue rubber balls.

The weight filled my palm; a solid fullness, plump satisfaction. The flesh and rhythm of catch and release carried me back to the park.

"This is the best dollar we've ever spent," my partner beamed.

.

In the Spring of 2003, I was talking to a school therapist about my family. About ripples of suicidality.

("They are not dominoes," she said.)

"One   falling   doesn't   mean   they'll   all   fall."

Hovering in the metaphor, I tried to hold my father's depression, my suicide attempt in the same room.

"One falling doesn't mean they'll all fall."

.

A black hole is an area of such immense gravity that nothing—not even light—can escape from it.

.

In the hospital, my mom asked me if I was gay. Nineteen, horizontal in a cotton gown, I said, "A little."

She said,

       ("Sometimes you have to kill how you feel.")

.

Researchers say a healthy dose of repetitive behavior reduces anxiety.

Bounce
Bounce
Bounce

Gravity and force deliver the ball back into my hand.

.

In February 2005, I was living in Bed-Stuy, Brooklyn near the Nostrand subway stop where Rashawn Brazell's body parts were found in trash bags.

      (He was a 19-year-old gay black man.)

I was 22, organizing through the Audre Lorde Project for the safety of queer people of color in Brooklyn.

We did outreach in clubs raising awareness about violence and efforts to try to build safety. The flyer asking for any information about Rashawn's murder had a picture of him in a dapper black bow tie. A scholarship was formed in his name. Rashawn's mother spoke at the many rallies we helped organize. We stood behind her holding a purple and white banner.

.

In the Spring of 2003, I was an intern at Asian American Legal Defense and Education Fund. It had been 16 months since 9/11. Sixteen months of backlash. I translated legal advice to Muslim boys and men affected by the federal special registration program. We set up free legal clinics. In the basement of a Brooklyn Bangladeshi-owned laundromat. At the back of a Queens Pakistani restaurant.

Many were pulled by the desire to follow the law. Many who followed that pull were

Detained
Deported
Disappeared.

.

The event horizon is the point of no return.

Stephen Hawking said "Although you wouldn't notice anything particular as you fell into a black hole, someone watching you from a distance, would never see you cross the event horizon. Instead, you would appear to slow down, and hover just outside. You would get dimmer and dimmer, and redder and redder, until you were effectively lost from sight. As far as the outside world is concerned, you would be lost forever."

("You have to be practical" my mother said, tilting her head, slightly.)

.

When I was released from the hospital, winter break was underway. My parents and I stopped at my desolate dormitory to gather my belongings. My father sat on my dorm room bed. He looked over at me parceling my clothes and books, and said, "Don't be like me."

(His sunken eyes lingered.)

I packed a book and then another. My jeans had a frayed hole in the knee. They flared out at the bottom.

.

Black holes form at the end of some stars' lives. The energy that held the star together disappears and it collapses in on itself—producing a magnificent explosion.

.

I contacted the therapist after I graduated. I asked if I could see her even though I was no longer a student.

("You can't afford me.")

.

Foucault talked about a shift in sovereign power in the 19th century from the spectacle of killing to the power to let die.

In 2018. Roxsana Hernández Rodriguez, a 33-year old transgender woman seeking asylum in the United States died in ICE custody.

Roxsana said

("Trans people in my neighborhood are killed and chopped into pieces, then dumped inside potato bags.")

.

Some black holes trap more and more material as their mass increases. The point where all that mass is trapped is called a singularity. It seems infinitely small, but its influence is enormous.

·

In the Spring of 2015, I came to the shores of the Hood Canal. I had been awarded a three-week residency that was for activists to rest.

The driveway of the house stretched through the surrounding acres of trees.

At night it was pitch dark, save the moon.

One bedroom was in a stand-alone structure about 20 feet from the main house. It was a coveted room—it stood on raised legs, had windows on three sides—solitary, gorgeous sunlight, a view of trees and sky.

This artificial structure in this natural land. This container that kneads our fears as we look out at the stillness.

Making a choice about what we think is looking back at us.

In the window, when the light is on, there is a reflection of all of our selves.

How vengeful. How loving.

J.S. KUIKEN

Bello

Alex had been drinking wine, enough that the lines of his wine glass had gone fuzzy. But that man across the piazza remained clear and resplendent. Broad shouldered and sharp featured, long legs spooling out over the cobblestones. In fact, he was becoming more vivid, until he shone like a flame against the ochre of the buildings. With langor, Alex imagined having that man in bed, and tracing his hands over those masculine contours.

But then, that man didn't know Alex was trans.

Light drained from those fantasies and the wine glass had hard, cold lines.

It was for the best. Alex was used to picking up men, back home in the U.S. But those men knew he was trans. Picking up a man who didn't know could just end in being killed.

So Alex ate and drank. The daylight waned. Lights strung from balconies and umbrellas glowed, their butter color winking back from the cobblestones. A band set up in the middle of the piazza and began to play, and the early gloaming had an air of enchantment to it which made Alex relax. He sank down into his bones and flesh, feeling every centimeter of who he had been, who he had become, and who he was, right now, drinking wine, having dinner in Florence, and watching a handsome stranger.

Maybe it was possible to have sex with him. Sucking his cock didn't require Alex to take his own clothes off. It was a once in a lifetime opportunity to fuck a beautiful man in Italy.

Another few gulps of wine and it was possible to approach said stranger and, very politely, very coyly, solicit him.

Alex paid his bill and began walking across the piazza.

He knew he could do it. He'd seduced men before. He was striking enough that it made it easy, but it also helped that he was small. He appealed to the masculinity in other men, particularly the kind of masculinity that liked to feel hard, coarse, and large, especially with another man. There were few things more potent, Alex had learned, than dominating and subduing another man, or being dominated and subdued. Gay, straight, bisexual, something else, it didn't matter. Only the sensation of bodies sliding together.

Halfway across the piazza, with the band blaring right in Alex's ear, the long legged man stood up and began walking away.

"Fucking *shit*," Alex said.

Follow or not?

Follow, goddammit. A once in a lifetime opportunity beckoned, in the form of a truly magnificent ass clad in brown pants.

The night was lavender now, the streets well lit and full of people. The city was alive with busy cafes and restaurants, the many languages of tourists; paintings and sculptures slumbering in locked museums; and cathedrals, great humming presences in the dark. Even the river sang with life, green and gold waters shimmering with the last rays of the sun, and first light of the moon.

Alex followed through those streets, tracking the man as the night turned from lavender to blue violet. At one point the man turned and their eyes met, and Alex thought he would simply keep walking. But he slowed, and stopped, waiting for Alex near a bridge full of light.

"Ciao," the man said. His voice reverberated through the air between them, and Alex shivered at the sound and sensation.

"Ciao," Alex said.

"Luca," the man said, and then repeated it until Alex understood it was his name and he was introducing himself.

Alex hesitated. Was this some Italian custom? Men back home did not give their names to one-night stands.

But what the hell.

"Alex," he said.

Luca said something in Italian, and Alex's hope, like a golden bauble, dropped and ruptured all over the cobbles.

"I don't speak Italian," he said.

Luca cocked his head.

"No?"

"No," Alex said, packing rather a lot of misery into that word.

Luca said something else, and then gestured. *Come on, come on.*

Alex wondered if this man had the same intentions he did, and, if he did, just how badly this could go. Alex reminded himself he only had to suck the guy's dick and it would be fine.

Luca led them. The claustrophobia of the tourist thick parts of the city ebbed, until they were but two men walking up a roomy lane between buildings. Here the windows did not glow with goods, like leather shoes or watches which cost more than three months of Alex's salary. Here the latticed windows glowed with people making dinner, washing dishes, talking to their children, watching the TV.

Luca stopped in the middle of one building, and pointed upwards, to a pair of green shuttered windows.

"Yours?" Alex asked, looking up.

Luca nodded.

"Sex?" he intoned.

He said it again before Alex really understood what he meant.

"Oh, yes. *Yes.* I mean—sì. Sex. *Sì.*"

Luca gave Alex such a lazy smile that Alex wanted to pounce on him right in the street. It was maddening, that smile. Luca must have known because he chuckled as he led Alex through the foyer, up a flight of stairs, and then to his own door. He held the door open for Alex, and after some patient and persistent insistence, took Alex's jacket and hung it on a peg near the door. Alex crossed his arms fretfully, feeling exposed.

Luca said something and held up a bottle of wine.

"N-n-no. No thanks. No, grazie."

Luca seemed not to have heard, or understood. He poured two glasses, not overly generous, nor parsimonious. Alex eyed his glass and even though he'd seen the other man open and pour the wine, he remained suspicious. And did the other man think this was a date, or something of that nature? Because one-night stands did not hold open doors, take coats, and pour wine. Decent wine, as well. A splendid white which just about quenched his palate.

They sat in a pair of old leather easy chairs, drinking, watching the night deepen through the opened windows. Alex liked it; this silence and warmth between them. It wasn't uncomfortable. The fact they didn't know each other's language wasn't pertinent in that moment. They both knew another language, where speaking was in the gaze, in the mouth and the hands; where vowels and consonants were but the grab and grind of two bodies; where punctuation was a tremor of anticipation, and a leisurely wait while drinking wine.

He was still mulling this over when Luca put his empty glass aside and stood. Alex saw him coming through the bowl of his glass, and then felt Luca's hands on his thighs, warm and heavy.

He parted Alex's legs with such calm and assurance that Alex almost groaned. Luca's hair was sand and silver over his eyes as he knelt, and his hands were big, strong, just the way Alex liked them, as he stroked between Alex's thighs.

Alex jolted, falling over the arm of the easy chair and shattering his wine glass.

Luca made noises which seemed to express concern, so Alex said: "Yes, I'm okay. Grazie."

He helped Luca pick up glass slivers from his wooden floor. Luca tried to mop up some of the wine.

"Probably I should go," Alex said. Any second, this could—would—go from just a silly story to something bad actually happening. Luca pawing at his crotch had reminded Alex of that.

Luca said something.

"I'm going to go," Alex said, pointing to the door.

Luca looked at him with some unreadable expression, and then poured Alex another glass of wine.

Don't drop this one, he seemed to be saying.

Fuck.

Alex knocked back half of it, and aware that the other man was looking him up and down, decided to do what he came here to do: suck a guy off. One very delicious, lucky Italian.

"Hey," Alex said, putting his wine glass down and going to his knees. Luca jumped before Alex had a chance to even touch his zipper, flinging more wine on his floor and wall.

"Shit," Alex said. "Sorry, I scared you."

They wiped up the wine and Alex tried to say he was sorry again. Luca said something that sounded anxious, and he shook his head. He made some kind of gesture that Alex eventually understood. Luca wanted to go down on *him*, but not the reverse. Alex shook his head and said he wanted to go down on Luca. The other man shook his head, and looked very forlorn as he did.

"What? Why can't I just suck you off?" Alex asked knowing he wouldn't get an answer. He didn't care. He should have just left. In fact, he should never have followed this man in the first place. He could at least be eating gelato and watching badly dubbed American movies at the hotel, instead of trying to negotiate sex with a stranger.

Luca mumbled something and continued to look doleful.

Finally, Alex sighed. Luca wouldn't understand him anyways.

"Look, I'm transgender. I can't let you suck me off because what I have to suck is like the size of my thumb. I mean, I'm hot, my cock is hot, but you've probably never slept with a guy like me, so please just let me blow you and then we can both be happy."

Luca cocked his head.

"Transgender?" he said.

"Yes, I am—what?" Alex said.

His stomach clenched with fear.

"Transgender."

Luca pointed at Alex.

Alex didn't move, didn't breathe.

"Transgender."

Luca patted his chest.

Alex frowned.

"What?"

"Transgender," Luca thumped his chest.

"No."

"Sì, sì," he said.

He rummaged through some boxes in a small closet, and came out with a few old photos. He pointed at the main figure in each: a tall, long-legged person, who could easily be mistaken for a girl. The person in the photos was younger, their jaw thinner and rounder, their shoulders slender, but there was no mistaking the lazy grin and the bottle brown eyes.

"Jesus fucking Christ," Alex said.

Luca smiled, his younger self the abstract image of the man he would become. The handsome, gorgeous man.

"Transgender?" Alex said.

Luca nodded.

"Transgender," Alex tapped his own chest.

"Sì?"

"Sì."

Luca began laughing first, baritone deep, and then Alex, chortling with both relief and disbelief.

Then something really peculiar happened. Alex, still laughing, kissed Luca on the corner of his mouth. *Do not kiss one-night stands* a voice in his head reprimanded. But Alex kissed Luca again, on the lips, and Luca responded in kind. Soft kisses. Frightened kisses, the both of them trembling in one another's arms, because nothing like this had happened before, and not just with a one-night stand. Alex opened his mouth and Luca did the same, drinking one another as their hands and arms wound round each other like vines.

Alex was kissing and nipping the other man's neck when Luca murmured. He pointed to a doorway and began stepping towards it. Alex knew once he crossed that threshold, he would come back different. Not wedding-day different, or the birth of a child different, but different. A quiet difference, which would make it all the more shattering, because only Alex and one other person in the world would know.

Alex let himself be guided into the bedroom. Luca turned on a lamp on the nightstand and the room was lit by a warm amber light. Alex's feet scuffed across downy rugs, and through a small window he could see Il Duomo's shadow with a backdrop of stars. Luca sat on the edge of his bed, and he looked at Alex as if to say *what do you want to do now?* It wasn't expectant so much as curious.

Alex began with his shirt. There was a lightness as the buttons came undone, as the fabric whispered over his shoulders and to the floor. It was an easy thing, to wriggle out of his pants and his underwear. He'd never felt so sure, so comfortable being naked with another person. He was free to be truly seen.

And Luca looked. His gaze swept up his slender, muscular legs, over his groin and navel. He gazed a long time at the scars on Alex's chest, before mapping the contours of his shoulders and arms. He nodded to himself and then looked at Alex's face, smiling.

Alex helped Luca out of his clothes because he could and because the other man let him. Luca was ticklish and every touch made him huff, but aside from that they were both very quiet. It felt sacred, this undressing: first Luca's pants and underwear, and then his shirt. Alex asked if he should unzip the binder and Luca hesitated before nodding.

"We don't have to," Alex said, drawing his fingers away from the zipper.

Luca grumbled and unzipped the binder himself, shrugging it off. He seemed embarrassed. He had the physique of a perfect man, the kind which might rival sculptures: slender waist and strong, broad shoulders, lean and a little muscular. Just stunning. And he had his breasts. Something about Luca's embarrassment, that he should feel embarrassed when he was so powerfully male, breasts and all, moved Alex. He kissed Luca as if to say: *you are handsome.*

They crept into bed, beneath the sheets. They drew each other closer, until Alex rested his head on Luca's chest. He ran his fingers through the other man's thick chest hair, and listened to his breathing. Luca stroked Alex's hair, and kissed the top of his head, all the while murmuring in Italian. Alex smiled. The night was dark and starry still, but soon enough it would drain away. Night's rich, deep colors, which saturated the senses, would be gone, and only daylight's wan, thin colors left. This moment would be lost. Pale as daylight, and a memory.

Alex let himself think of other possible futures: of staying in Florence instead of returning to the U.S. Of learning Luca's language. Of becoming old men together, strolling down the night streets of Florence. Of kisses that would still be sweet after years. A whole lifetime of seeing and being seen.

But it was a flicker and then gone. A lovely flicker, though.

For now, and for always, there was just this: two men lying together, waiting for the dawn, and loving one another as they were.

They had sex before the sun rose, and then they cleaned up and had some breakfast. They laughed and smiled the whole time. Luca walked Alex back to his hotel, and, while the bells of the city chimed and the doves flew out of the eaves, they kissed their goodbyes. Luca leaned in and whispered *you are the most beautiful man I have ever met*. But all Alex understood, and would remember, was the word *bello*.

BOI's Half Crown

what do I make with this mess of flowers
tansy & verbena make my mouth declare war
and prayer in one breath make my body a maze
of thorns intimacy spoiled by a lover's casual
kiss softness a memory ground into dust
my skin cold soaked with longing Black and then
what night holds is a false promise, hardened spine
& if not for the I then what else keeps the BOI whole?
the I licks Their lips and says I'm a good thing
feels for the roof of Their mouth and thinks rigid
wanting teeth, how space can be both void and
full is a trick only the BOI knows well, the I is a
hymnal unworthy of Their mother's tongue
What is the BOI if not sometimes an apology?

The BOI sometimes an apology is a wingless
bird stretching before the sun blinks a new day
into existence, BOI incapable of flight is pulled
closely into the body of a stranger, the I knows
the chicanery of night—how it cradles the moon
knowing it will always slip away, to be desired
(even temporarily) is enough to feed the I's ego
to open the BOI's mouth wide and cram Their
jaws with everything they will one day lose
sense of self, what it feels like to be touched—
how to soften, the liberty to pop and twist and
shake and move underneath flashing lights, what
it's like to be called home or called by name
a jolt causing the I to return to Their body

The I returns to Their body, see the BOI
cradling an indigo child—small fingers
wrapped around the I, a tiny squeeze—
BOI searches the infant's face for memory
asks the I, *who this body belongs to, what
is a name?* The indigo child yawns, becomes
ghost like—a dream sequence, the I was once
a parade of daffodils swaying in the sun's
crooked mouth, I, once a glimmer in Their
mother's wheat eyes—the son she always
wanted swaddled in pink garments adorned
in glitter, accidental girl dressed in ruffles.
The I wilts in the grip of Their mother's
religion. call the I unholy or call the BOI whole.

Call the BOI whole, the I holy
God said, *let there be light &* then
there was light cascading down the
I, BOI drenched in rain—a good
watering fit for a peculiar bloom
the Black BOI is not an anomaly
is instead a whisper exchanged
among bodies sitting on a wooden
pew, sweet saints sweet stain ruining
the choir robes. The I sings and no—
one applauds. Pastor says BOI take flight
so the I searches for the heaven all BOIs
belong to, where a cacophony of organ
chords praise the I praise the BOI—Their body.

NADINE MARSHALL

How to Cube a Mango

cradle the fruit/ in your palm/over a bowl/using a peeler/ strip half/ of the mango// take a knife/
slice tender yellow lengthwise ||||||| against the seed/ sweet juice/ runs the length/ of your fingers/
taste/_____ /take the knife/ cut tender yellow crosswise/once complete/ run the knife/ under/
freshly cut tender yellow/ along the seed/ watch the pieces/_____ / fall/ along the tips of/ or/
between/ your fingers //

turn and repeat

/ until /tender/
yellow falls

clean/

suck what remains/ until the
seed/ is bare

until the seed is bare

i find myself/breast in the hands/ of a lover, i tell them/using a knife, strip/
the front half of my body/ the first layer/beyond blemished/ black skin glistens/
let them praise/ what runs the length/of their fingers, allow/their temptations to taste/
hand them the knife/ask them to cut lengthwise/ tender plump protruding flesh/
tell them to run the knife/along the breastplate, clean/
& watch the pieces/

fall/

along the tips of/

or between/
their fingers/

my body sculpted in the palms of their hands.

Holy Awakening

Mom drives to church, irritated that I look like a displaced person in my favourite grey threadbare t-shirt. I deep-sigh while my little brothers kick the back of my seat. I thank God I'm getting away. Mom eyes me in the rearview mirror, giving me a speech about being an upstanding young woman in a single glance. I exit with a sleeping bag, and a giant bag of Doritos, Cool Ranch, the kind everyone knows are the best but give a person the worst breath.

These sleepovers are anything but scandalous, without music or dancing. Pastor Trenton, a sweaty man too old and balding to be a youth pastor, is always there. I envy friends who go to Menno churches with young, zippy youth pastors who are real-life rebels, like Jesus. They wear goatees and printed t-shirts that say things like *Jesus was a Refugee*. Not like Pastor Trenton, who recently gave us a creepy speech about how "ahhh-mazing" it was to do it with his wife and just how great the *do it* will be when we're wed. Married *do-it* seems to float his boat. The other kids and I shared sideways glances that said, gross me green, picturing him on top of his wife. Pastor Trenton's wife, Linda is spindly with translucent skin and is the church Organist. Bored in service recently, I wondered if it flips her self-esteem to have her back to an audience for her job because Linda is off. So is Trenton, but the poor guy thinks he's cool.

Pastor Trenton leads a prayer with the 12 of us gathered in the basement, then we're free to do as we wish. I beg everyone to play Hide-and-Seek in the cemetery, but there are no takers. They're a bunch of baby wimps. I brush it off, saying it's okay, who wants to hide or seek where spirits condemned to purgatory linger. We sit around on overly padded event chairs. I stare at a wall that is the saddest shade of beige. I'm mad at myself for not bringing candy, as a sugar rush could liven this party. I can't stand another conversation that starts with, "So, what are you doing for the summer?" I motion to this kid David to follow me to the kitchen. We eat spoonfuls of sugar from the Sunday Coffee-Time cupboard, and David drinks half-and-half from the fridge. His thick, chugging noises are so guttural that I gag, and he chokes and spits up a mouthful of cream. We laugh, gripping our bellies until they ache, trying to silence ourselves. We wipe up the cream with good napkins reserved for special events like the Father-Daughter Banquet.

We give up trying to find treats and head back to the central area where the fluorescent lights are howling. One kid suggests cards. To avoid gambling, we play Go Fish. I get pretty into it until, around 11, my stomach hurts from eating half the bag of Doritos. I notice Pastor Trenton has fallen asleep. He's in the back of the basement on his camping mat and sleeping bag, wearing an eye mask with a water bottle, travel alarm clock, and Bible set up beside him. This isn't his first sleepover rodeo.

This girl Tabitha, who has the shiniest black hair, has the idea to play Strip-Go-Fish. I think it's the dumbest, but soon I'm down to my fluorescent pink sports bra and flamingo boxers. Tabitha, who has dressed to impress, strips to a black lace bra and underwear duo that she obviously purchased as a set from a real underwear store. She's eating a giant rope of red licorice in a way that would make Pastor Trenton call up Pastor Jonathan, the full church pastor. The game won't go further than underwear, but the others look side-to-side like they wish it could.

I suggest that we play Sardines in the dark. Tabitha hides first. I know she'll be up in the second-floor nursery where there are boxes of digestive cookies. The sanctuary would be too obvious. I'm the first to find her behind a pair of cribs in the darkened yellow room, making the cemetery seem like child's play. A pile of stuffed bears is staring at me, and I avoid their polished eyes. I lie a few feet from Tabitha, who tells me to move closer to make room for the others. She's bossy and not in a fun way. I don't know how anyone can stand her. She didn't grow up going to our church or any church for that matter. She doesn't have verses memorized, not even John or Psalms, which even babies that spit up all over the nursery know. "For God so loved the world…" I say, thinking it isn't her fault that no one taught her. She puts her hand roughly over my mouth, and I freeze, tasting licorice and salt on her fingers. When she takes her hand off my mouth, I have the world's stupidest grin stuck to my face, like I've stuffed my mouth full of Winegums and can't move my jaw.

We scare the living Jesus out of David, who finds us. He yips like a T-rex jumped out of his birthday cake as he's blowing out the candles. David lies next to me, and me against Tabitha, whose boobs feel like balloons filled with warm jello. David smells so strongly of cheese puffs that I may as well have snorted a line of processed cheese dust. We lay there in silence for what must have been hours but was probably minutes. I've never been that close to other human bodies before, other than my siblings.

I can hear kids running around trying to find us. I feel a hand on my butt. As I'm still in my boxers, so this is the first time someone is touching my underwear. I try to decide if this is something that I want, but it's hard to say as I don't know who's doing it to me. So I leave the hand there and tell myself it was an accident, it landing there. We hear Pastor Trenton yelling downstairs, "Everyone to the basement. You know the rules, kids!" The three of us stay piled together because we're surely busted. Then things quiet downstairs like maybe the Pastor is too spent to do a headcount.

Tabitha says it isn't safe to get up yet. I mention following the rules, and she slides her hand onto my face. She puts her mouth on me and sucks my bottom lip for a second. Not like a kiss exactly, but to get me to shut up. I feel like I've drunk a giant purple Slurpee and am riding a roller coaster. I'm suspended in that split second before plunging, the purple in my belly sloshing, trying to decide if it wants to come up.

Tabitha gets up and turns on the light. The hand is still on my butt, so I know whose it is: Cheesy-mouth David's. David looks shocked and takes his hand away, saying, "Oh my goodness, was my hand there? I thought it was on your back," which is the dumbest because who doesn't know the difference between a butt and a back. I notice I'm the only one still in my bra and boxers. Tabitha stands in the doorway, looking like a full-grown woman, shaking her head at us.

She says, "Good thing, I won't tell Pastor Trenton what you two have done." I gulp, suddenly overwhelmed by the scent of David and my mouth that tastes musty like the moldy, ancient cheese that my dad eats.

Tabitha, standing there, is not a kid like the rest of us. Maybe because she never came to church until she was 13. Two years at church can't wipe away the sins committed before then. Plus, she doesn't believe in anything, she just shows up. Jenny, one girl too pious to come to sleepovers, said once that Tabitha only comes to church for the snacks. But I don't think so because the only treats are dry cookies that sit in a tin week to week. Once I bruised David in the cheek by throwing one at him when Pastor Trenton stepped out to use the bathroom. David didn't believe the cookies were as hard as hockey pucks.

In the basement, Tabitha pulls me into the women's bathroom. I stare while she fixes her hair and makeup. "Aren't we going to bed?" I ask.

"You never know," she says.

"Do you even believe in God?" I ask her face in the mirror.

"I dunno," she says, "do you?"

"Yeah, I do," I slide out in one breath.

"Do you think Dave would go for me?" She shimmies her boobs into place. I figure they are already sitting correctly.

I try not to stare into her cleavage and say, "David? Yes, I believe he would."

"How should I kiss him?" She asks.

"Ummm...I don't know about that," I say and look towards the door.

"Obviously. Come here." She pulls me close, right up to her, and draws red lipstick on my lips. "Hasn't anyone ever taught you how to pucker?" I shake my head and feel like a clown. "You'd be pretty if you put in a little effort," she says, seeming insulted by the blank canvas of my face.

"Thank you?" I say. It's hard for my mom that I don't do pretty. The fact that I could drives her crazier than anything.

Tabitha brushes blush into her jutty cheekbones and says, "I know a trick that can bring a man to his knees."

I shake my head again. "I should be getting back."

"You're not curious?" Her eyebrows raise like thin, arched worms crawling across her face.

"Why would you want a man on his knees?" I ask, and she laughs with her head thrown back.

"I might let him, you know..." she says.

"What? Who? Pastor Trenton?" I ask, thinking he's the only man there. My face folds with concern, and she laughs garishly.

"Gawd no," she says and punches me so hard I fall into the toilet stall. I put my hand over my arm, that's undoubtedly going to bruise. I don't mind the pain, and for the slightest split second, an uninvited thought crosses my mind of pushing Tabitha up against the bathroom stall and kissing her. By the time I gather my thoughts, she grabs her purse and curls away from me, out of there.

I lay awake in my little brother's Ninja Turtles sleeping bag that is kid's size and only comes up to my bra line. Tabitha and David disappear for a long time. I figure they went back to the nursery or are doing it in the choir loft. I worry my heart is beating so loudly that I'll wake Pastor Trenton. Pathetic Pastor, all he ever wanted was for us to not do that until then, and right now, it's happening right under his nose. It's hard to breathe, and my face is hot like I've done something wrong.

Like the time when I was little and ate three cupcakes that mom had made for my brother's birthday. I had to watch everybody share the remaining cakes, my siblings giving me the evil eye, an empty plate sitting in front of me. That's what it's like, laying flat on my back on the cold basement floor. I put my hand on my chest to calm myself and realize I'm still wearing my bra. I throw on my t-shirt, so I don't give the Pastor a heart attack. I hate my stupid pink bra. Black would be so much better, I decide. Pink is like unicorn puke. Nobody will ever take you seriously.

In the morning, Pastor Trenton hands out granola bars. He says, glowing, "Another successful sleepover!" I smile and don't mention that what makes a sleepover successful to a bunch of teenagers and a middle-aged pastor is certainly not the same. Tabitha and David have foolish smiles on their faces, and they can't look at each other. Tabitha squeezes my hand and winks at me as we head out the door, mascara thick and goopy in her lashes. I feel the same heat from last night rise into my chest. I force a smile.

Outside, Mom is waiting with the kids in the minivan. She eyes me up and down like she's looking for proof that I'm still her girl. Something inside me knows I'm not. At home, I scamper to my room to change. I carefully fold my Good News Bible into my pink boxers and bra and slide them between my mattress and box spring. I lay on top of my comforter, spent. I swear I can feel the outline of the package hidden under the layers of my bed.

CATHERINE CHEN

My mother points out mango trees by the river

There are so many words I can't explain despite my more influential memories pointing to the obvious legacy, an imperfect seemly truth

Memory on the whole offers anatomy less telling than its fossilized amber honestly it's too bad I love reminiscing when we're together

Burying ourselves in holes then digging ourselves out of holes then lowering our vulnerable bodies into holes then leveraging one leg up and over ground zero then returning the same leg below ground then burying ourselves in holes then digging ourselves out of holes then lowering our vulnerable bodies into holes then leveraging one leg up and over ground zero then returning the same leg below ground then burying ourselves in holes then digging ourselves out of holes then lowering our vulnerable bodies into holes then leveraging one leg up and over ground zero then returning the same leg below ground

Whatever you think to say next don't confuse our silence for emotional impoverishment

CATHERINE CHEN

Classification Only

I enter a contest of names for historically robust neighborhoods, or: equity

On the nightly news a war criminal is sentenced over and over to renounce her nationality

To engage in motions of writing *I disavow the following subjects* in one's non-dominant hand in one's non-native language

These are not state-sanctioned lies nor are they anything short of my pursuit of political perfection

In an offshore hangar vultures thrive

The road trip, the salmon nests

Only you'd think to note the corpses who have masked their odor with lilac potpourri

Staccato

"Sorry to bug you, but you wouldn't happen to have a stick of gum?" It is the girl in the seat beside her. Stephanie notices her heavy boots and grey wool socks.

"For the pressure," the girl explains, and Stephanie offers her a crumpled pack of Excel. The sun flashes off the wing and across the girl's face, stealing all her colour and painting her in light. "So, where are you going?"

"Cancun."

The girl's dark fingers are long and calloused where they meet the soft flesh of her palm, and the muscles are tight below the skin. Stephanie almost asks her what instrument she plays but swallows the question, afraid that if she starts to speak she won't be able to stop until she has told the girl everything about the last five hours: about buying the bottle of Wiser's and putting on Pablo Casals' 1939 recording of the Cello Suites. About how she gave in and let the music cut her open. She might tell her that when it was over, she remained on the floor of her bedroom with the bottle of whiskey half-finished and the familiar ache in her right arm, the line of heat and tension that reached from her knuckles to her elbow.

The idea was there when the room stopped its wild spinning. Stephanie put the ticket on her credit card and packed a change of clothes and left three post-dated rent cheques under the building manager's door. She smoked two Du Mauriers on the fire escape, trying unsuccessfully to steady her shaking hands. Then she called a taxi to the airport and bought a pack of gum from the newspaper stand to hide the whiskey on her breath.

They sit in silence during take-off and Stephanie flips the heavy pages of the safety booklet, focusing on hypothetical disaster. She tries to feel reassured that there is an inflatable slide to assist passengers on their descent into treacherous, shark infested waters should the aircraft be forced to land on a large body of water. They are flying through clouds but every now and then the plane breaks free into a clear patch of sky and through the window behind the girl Stephanie sees blue so intense that she wonders if it is real.

The girl pulls the window cover shut and says, "wake me up if they come around with juice" before closing her eyes. Stephanie reads an article in the in-flight magazine about the top-six snorkeling hot-spots on Mexico's Caribbean coast. It would be pleasant to lose herself where there was no gravity and no sound.

Several nights later, there is a carnival in the street with a small, dangerous looking carousel and cotton candy and vendors selling hand-made jewelry, clothes, and art. Stephanie swims in Spanish conversation and the beat of drums. She passes a group of children in paper hats as they roll across the grass, their hats coming apart and tossed away by the breeze. Blue and purple and orange paper tumble through the square and stick to Stephanie's shoes. All around her is the heat of bodies and the smell of sunscreen, sweat, and alcohol.

From an open window, she catches a thread of sound. Someone is practicing Bach's cello suite and she stops to listen, remembering what Allison told her once, red nails shining, piercing her heart so cleanly she hardly felt the wound: a single, solo cello can conjure the whole world.

The callouses that have been part of Stephanie's fingers since she was a child are slowly beginning to peel away. She leaves behind curls of dry, hard flesh wherever she goes like a snake, slipping out of its skin. She buys cigarettes, a road map of the Yucatan peninsula, and three Modelo Especial from the Oxxo across the street from the hotel. The heat has settled on her skin. It is eleven in the morning. She sits in a hammock in the open courtyard of the hotel and opens a beer, then she unfolds the map across her knees.

The highways of pink and black yank at her organs.

She wishes that she could hop in one of those beat-up Volkswagens that she sees parked on every street corner and roll down the windows and feel the sun scorched upholstery of the driver's seat. Just drive until she caught the scent of Allison's perfume on the breeze.

Her fingers are tender and pink and new in the places where the callouses once were. Against her skin: the rough fabric of the hammock and the condensation that trickles down the neck of her beer. Foil label. Hot earth. Her hands are vulnerable now and they feel everything more acutely. The next bus to Oaxaca leaves that evening. Stephanie packs her belongings in a dusty backpack and leaves her room key with the man at the front desk.

She smokes Marlboros while she waits for the rusted collectivo that will take her to the bus station. Hair unkept and sweat trickling slowly down the back of her neck, she lights one after another, clenching and unclenching her fist, working the muscle in her bad arm. She crushes the butts into the dusty earth with the heel of her sandal and breathes Allison's name out into the hot, dusty afternoon.

Stephanie was eight years old, but Allison shook her hand as though she were a grown-up.

"Would you play for me, please?"

"Right now?"

"Yes."

She lifted the cello from its stand and sat with the instrument between her knees. It was three-quarter size and Stephanie had to strain to reach the fingerboard. As she played, she could smell her father's workshop, the sweet, warm scent of wood. She felt the rough, unfinished texture of a piece of furniture still waiting to be born. She drew the bow across the string. Behind closed eyes, Stephanie saw her father in denim and steel toe boots with the white paper mask he wore over his nose and mouth when he was sanding pulled down around his neck, lifting the needle on the recording of Antonio Jangiro's 1954 performance of the Cello Suites.

She played from memory because the music was the memory. She didn't yet have the words to explain the way that music made time and space collapse. When she reached the end of the prelude, Stephanie played it over again from the beginning without pause. She could have kept going forever, immersing herself over and over in the sensations of the workshop until she collapsed from exhaustion, but Allison put her hand on Stephanie's shoulder and the touch broke through her concentration like daylight.

"And you haven't taken lessons?"

Stephanie shook her head. Allison squatted down until her face was level with Stephanie's.

"You play well, but your form is incorrect. Here." Allison reached for Stephanie's hand and moved her fingers on the bow, adjusting her grip. "If you want to study with me, you will have to work very hard. You will practice everyday, even the days that you don't want to."

Stephanie looked at her, eyes wide, and nodded.

"Deal."

Twice a week, Stephanie's father drove her and the cello over the bridge that reached out its long arm high above the narrows of Burrard inlet. Allison's classroom was on the ground floor of an old house in the East End, in what had once, in another of the house's many lifetimes, been a grand dining room. A large bay window overlooked the green lawn and the gnarled branches of an apple tree that never seemed to bear fruit. If Allison had other students, Stephanie never knew of them. The only other person she ever saw in the studio was Allison's husband, Mo, who could be glimpsed occasionally in some corner, fixing a broken curtain rod or installing shelves.

Stephanie's father scrounged flea markets for recordings that were different than the ones Stephanie had been listening to in the workshop for years, but he couldn't keep up with Allison's influence. Through her, Stephanie was introduced to Yo Yo Ma, Stravinsky, Cassado, Pablo Casals. Over breakfast each morning, she tapped out four-four time on the kitchen table between mouthfuls of Honey Nut Cheerios.

Her mother quit her job as an assistant in a legal office in Richmond and homeschooled Stephanie so that she could devote herself to the music full-time. Music became the force that determined the direction of her mornings, afternoons, and nights. She sat on her father's workbench, watching the shaving of pine or oak or mahogany fall to the concrete floor, and listened to the scratch and pop of the record player as though she were hearing Jangiro play for the first time.

Stephanie left the world behind. Music locked her away and wrapped her tightly in strips cut out from sonatas and concertos. It was Allison who took the music Stephanie felt and smelled and showed her how to press it like clay into a recognizable form.

It was late September and Stephanie's thirteenth birthday was in five days. She could see her mother through the window, the back of her head as she bent over the dark earth of her flowerbeds, pulling weeds. The living room was alive with warm sunlight. Stephanie felt her body being wrapped in soft ribbons of heat. She had told her mother that she didn't want a party. There was no one to invite, but Stephanie didn't mind. Her birthday was on a Friday. On Fridays her father drove her to her lesson after lunch. She would spend three hours in the studio that smelled of cut flowers and Allison's perfume.

She watched her mother stand and brush the soil from her jeans, lift the half-empty sac at her feet and place it in the plastic wheel barrow. Her mother pushed the wheel barrow around the side of the house and disappeared. Through the window Stephanie saw the garden, the lawn and the trees and the flash of blue sky that broke now and then between the clouds.

She felt the sunlight on the back of her neck and the vibrations that rolled through the body of the cello between her thighs. She saw the small pencil marks that Allison had left on the page of the sonata in front of her, and they made her remember the smell of perfume. Suddenly uncomfortable, she paused, leaning her ear against the cello's neck, and closed her eyes.

The warmth had moved from the sunlight on the back of her neck down her shoulders and chest to rest at the very base of her belly like a hot stone. She imagined that Allison was beside her, leg next to hers, the way they often sat during class.

Stephanie's hip pressed painfully against the back of the cello. She thought of Allison's blond hair. Her jaw. The hollow at the base of her throat. The shining red nails. Stephanie let out a soft moan.

Another September: Stephanie waited, tapping her fingers absently against the neck of the cello and looking up at the lights, while Allison went nervously from the registration table, to the lady's room, to the row where the invigilators sat stiffly in their velvet-covered seats, and then back to Stephanie's side. Stephanie was seventeen. Beneath the vaulted ceiling of the theatre, Allison reached out to touch the course silk of Stephanie's tie.

"Leave it alone, would you? It's fine." She pushed Allison's hand away and then a voice was calling her name. She stood and let Allison smooth the invisible wrinkles from her shirt, before stepping onto the stage.

Across town, while Allison stood in the wings watching Stephanie's freshly polished shoes against the waxed floor, her husband, Mo, stood in the driveway with his right hand on the driver's side door of their sedan.

Stephanie lifted her bow while Mo placed the key in the ignition.

Mo put the sedan into drive and backed out onto the cul-de-sac as Stephanie drew the bow across the string.

He drove. Stephanie played.

The invigilator's faces were expressionless when Allison glanced at them out of the corner of her eye, but she knew it didn't matter. She felt her cells responding to the music.

Mo put his foot on the brake as he came to the stop sign; he looked both ways and then turned on the radio. Allison had driven the car last. Mo scrolled through the stations until he found one that was playing country.

The sheet music was set up on the stand in front of Stephanie, but Allison could tell she wasn't reading it. As always, she played from memory. Allison closed her eyes and listened with her whole body, not just her ears but her skin and her lungs and her tongue.

Mo rolled down the driver's side window, but the storm-smell of the clouds made him roll it back up again a moment later. The main street was long and largely deserted. Mo sang along to the radio under his breath. Fat raindrops hit the windshield and he turned the wipers on. Mo put his foot to the gas hard when the light turned green.

A pain in his chest.

His heart shuddered. Allison felt the swell of the vibrato as Stephanie's fingers shook against the strings.

Mo collapsed onto the steering wheel and the sedan skidded on the wet pavement. The windshield wipers: back and forth and back and forth. The headlights of an oncoming pickup truck. The sound of breaking glass and crunching metal drowned out the rain, but Mo had lost consciousness and didn't hear a thing.

The sirens screamed as the last note of the music died. Allison watched with pride as Stephanie took her bow.

"Can I give you a ride home?" Stephanie wasn't sure why she said it, surely there were other people that could drive her. People who would know what to say. Stephanie was wearing the same tie that she had worn for her audition. Allison reached out and touched it gently.

They were among the last people left. She had waited until the women from Mo's church had finished packing up what was left of the deviled eggs and cucumber sandwiches before coming over to offer her condolences. Now she listened to her own voice echo in the empty hall.

"Sure," Allison said.

Stephanie loaded the flowers with their delicate cards of sympathy into the back of her mother's station wagon. Out of the corner of her eye, as she drove, she saw Allison's hair coming loose from its bun, the freed strands whispering against her neck and shoulders.

There had been an open casket, but Stephanie hadn't had the courage to get close enough to see inside. Instead, she slipped into one of the back pews and tried to stay out of everyone's way as the church filled with mourners, many of them Mo's relations from Mexico.

She recalled the few times over the years that she had met Mo: infrequent glimpses of him in some corner of Allison's studio, fixing a broken curtain rod or installing shelves. Once, years ago, she had gone to Allison's house with her mother to pick up some sheet music. They hadn't ventured beyond the front hall, but Stephanie remembered how Mo had appeared and pressed a peppermint candy into her palm.

They drove in silence, not speaking until Stephanie turned into Allison's driveway. Together, they carried the flowers into the living room.

"Thank you," Allison said, when the last of the arrangements had been placed to rest on her coffee table. "You've been very kind."

Stephanie thought of telling her again how sorry she was for her loss, but it seemed stupid and redundant. She knew that she should say goodbye, but the thought of leaving Allison all alone made the pit of her stomach ache.

She made a move toward the front hall, where she had left her shoes.

"Have you heard back from the orchestra?" Allison asked suddenly.

Stephanie hesitated.

"They called on Thursday," she replied.

"And?"

"They offered me a permanent position in their string section. Second cello."

"Stephanie, that's wonderful news." Allison took off her coat and tossed it over the arm of the chesterfield. "We must celebrate."

"Celebrate?"

She watched Allison slip out of the shoes she had worn to the funeral and cross the living room in stocking feet. Stephanie was still holding keys to the station wagon as Allison disappeared into the kitchen. She heard cupboards opening and closing and the sound of glasses being set down on a granite counter.

When Allison reappeared in the living room, she held two glasses of red wine.

"To a brilliant career."

Stephanie felt the wine, cool and sharp, fill her mouth. Allison vanished back into the kitchen and returned with the bottle.

Later, they lay together on the carpet of Allison's living room with the empty glasses and wine bottle lost somewhere among the vases of flowers. The whole room stank of sweetness.

Stephanie had given herself to someone else's grief and now she took the cigarette that Allison offered her, the bitter smoke filling her mouth as Allison's cherry-red nails drew complicated patterns across her chest. Allison had not been young when Stephanie's parents first gave her to her, almost a decade ago. Now, there were fine lines around her mouth and a softness to her belly and thighs.

"They got the name of the town wrong," Allison told her. "In Mo's obituary. They said he was born in Oaxaca, but really it was a town along the coast. La Manzanilla."

"What is it like there?" Stephanie asked.

"Where?"

"La Manzanilla."

"I don't know." Allison's flesh was shining in the tender places where Stephanie had kissed it: the top of her shoulder, the base of her neck, the hard nipples of her small breasts. "I've never been."

The second time it happened, Allison called it a mistake.

"You should go," she said, and Stephanie didn't argue.

After Allison shut the studio door behind her, Stephanie stood on the wooden step for what seemed like a long time, letting the scent of the dead apple tree wash over her.

Six days later, Allison was gone.

It began in Stephanie's right arm. A sharp, quick jolt that struck when she held her wrist at certain angles. When she closed her fingers around the bow. When she tilted her head to hear the French horns. Sometimes for no reason at all.

She kept practicing: eight hours a day, every day. She sat with the body of the cello between her thighs and felt the tension of the strings against her fingers. She tried to separate herself from the pain: gathering it into a ball in her mind. Containing it. Pushing it away. The more persistent it became, the further she tried to distance herself.

At night, she lay awake and stretched the muscles in the hands the way that Allison had taught her years ago. Bending each finger back and rotating her wrist until she felt the agony that she could not acknowledge.

"Keeping your fingers strong will prevent injury," Allison had told her.

She remembered the first time Allison had shown her how to hold the bow properly. She remembered her long, hard fingers with their silver rings. The nails painted cherry-red.

The orchestra flew to New York for a concert series that would last six weeks. On opening night, Stephanie was already fighting against her own body. She tried to play the way she had a thousand times before. She focused on the conductor's hands: on the twitch of his wrist and the perfect whiteness of his shirt. It should have been as natural as breathing, but with every movement of the bow Stephanie felt like she was drowning, gasping for air.

A wrong note. Then again.

She closed her eyes. Clenched her teeth.

She didn't feel anything at all when the bow fell to the floor, her hand and arm were numb. She heard the clatter of the wood as it hit the stage and felt the confusion of the musicians around her, but no one stopped. No one even looked. She pressed on her tendon with her good hand and sat in silence, listening, as the orchestra continued playing all around her.

It was everything that she had been afraid of for months but now that it was real she couldn't feel it. She listened to the tissue paper on the examination table crinkle as she shifted her weight. The doctor asked her if she had ever felt pain in her arm before. Stephanie looked straight ahead at the green curtain.

"Yes."

The affected areas were primarily in the wrist and forearm. Months ago, it had begun as acute tendonitis that had gone untreated. Without rest or ice or painkillers or physiotherapy, it had persisted.

In the doctor's expression there was no trace of judgment, or sympathy. He placed a finger lightly on Stephanie's arm and traced the length of the injured tendon. The spasms indicated that the damage was severe. Surgery offered some hope. Combined with regular steroid injections, they may see some progress. Either way, she wouldn't be able to play for months. And the pain would return eventually. There was no doubt about that.

The next morning, Stephanie went to the airport in a yellow checkered cab, certain she would never play again.

The bus swings along narrow highways, twisting around sand-coloured hills. Stephanie falls asleep in the morning and wakes to a sun that hangs low on the horizon. She is finding it more and more difficult to hang onto the days and place them in a row. They slide together and then break apart again, fracturing in the most inconvenient places.

The bus passes through the outskirts of a town and she watches the sky change from purple to deep blue to a blackness that seems to press itself against the glass. Outside the window, the lights whirl by, shoving the darkness aside and forcing pin pricks of life into the desert night. The lamps of a gas station. A kitchen light on and the front door wide. The silhouette of a stray dog. The headlight of a motorcycle going in the opposite direction. Stephanie focuses on each one, trying to take it in and store it inside of her somewhere safe.

A street sign emerges from the darkness, lit up in the headlights of a passing transport truck: La Manzanilla. 37 kilometers.

Finding her was easier than it should have been. Stephanie sits on the front porch, watching the lines around Allison's mouth, the threads of age tangling and untangling as she places a cigarette between her lips. Stephanie's hand shakes slightly as she lights it for her. They both cup their hands together over the flame and she is reminded of that first cigarette: the one that Allison had passed her after they had finished, lying on the carpet of the living room in a jungle of funeral bouquets.

Stephanie eases back into the cushions of the wicker couch and watches Allison exhale smoke through her nose.

"You were only a girl," Allison says, finally. "It was wrong of me to do what I did."

"You mean what we did," Stephanie says. "I was there too."

The loose skin on Allison's arms and neck embarrasses her. It hangs like overripe fruit and sways when she lifts her hand to shield her eyes from the evening sun that is settling gold and low over the palms. Stephanie looks away.

"I was seventeen." Stephanie doesn't know whether she is coming to her own defense or to Allison's.

The wrinkles around Allison's mouth fold into something like a smile. She lifts the cigarette to her lips.

"I was old enough to know better," she says.

"Mrs. Garcia—"

"Please, Stephanie. I told you to call me Allison years ago." She puts out her cigarette in the crystal ashtray and pushes it toward Stephanie. Then she stands up slowly, tugging her straw sunhat straight. "I think this conversation would go better with a drink, don't you?"

Stephanie follows her as she shuffles across the tiled patio through the French doors. When she grasps the handle of the refrigerator door, Stephanie notices that Allison's nails are no longer cherry-red but unpainted, dull, and brittle.

Allison passes her a Corona and she has begun to ask if there is any lime when the pain sears from her fingertips to her shoulder. Something about the movement of her wrist and fingers as she went to grab the beer.

She lets the bottle fall and shatter on the kitchen floor, shards of glass showering both their sandaled feet.

"Shit." The pain gnaws at her wrist like sharp, hot teeth. "Allison, I'm so sorry."

Allison's hand is still on the refrigerator door. She looks from the mess on the floor to Stephanie's outstretched arm and lets out a small sigh.

"You certainly aren't the first," she says, reaching for a kitchen rag to wipe up the mess. Stephanie stands and watches her, gripping her injured wrist with her good hand. "You should have gone looking for a surgeon that can work miracles, not for an old woman in the middle of nowhere."

"I suppose it was natural," Allison says later as they sit in the wicker furniture on her patio, drinking the Coronas and listening to the croaking of geckos and the snap and click of nocturnal insects that have no names in their language. "After Mo died, it felt right to go to the country where he was born."

She looks out into the darkness for a long time exhaling thin ribbons of smoke into the night.

"When we are lost, we always go in search of the beginning of things," she says at last as she places a comforting hand on Stephanie's knee.

Allison pauses and for a moment they are both silent.

Then: "Stay here."

Putting out her cigarette, Allison raises herself to her feet and goes back into the house, leaving Stephanie alone on the porch with the echoes of pain still running up and down her arm. When Allison returns a few moments later, she is carrying a slip of paper folded carefully in half. She sets the paper down on the table, beside Stephanie's beer. Stephanie unfolds the paper with her good hand.

"What's this?" Stephanie recognizes the looping tendrils of Allison's handwriting. A name and phone number.

"A surgeon who's been known to work a miracle or two." Allison smiles. "I can't promise he'll be able to help."

There is nothing to say. She wraps her arms, good and bad, around the woman who was once her teacher. The best gift anyone ever gave her. Allison lets her stay that way for a moment or two, before gently removing herself from the embrace.

"How about a swim?"

Allison lays her shawl out on the sand. She sits and smokes and watches as Stephanie wades out into the ocean, back and shoulders pale in the moonlight.

The waves remind Stephanie of Bach. She inhales the trumpets, the spray of piccolo, and, as she raises her arms above her head, she tastes the salty strings of a cello. The phosphorescence blinks and the wind changes and she finds herself conducting a whole orchestra. Waist-deep she sways, her blood and heartbeat alter to match the rhythm of the water that heaves around her belly and thighs. The sea rises and then falls again, leaving droplets of sound and moisture clinging to the fine hairs on her stomach and arms. When she stretches her fingers toward the stars, the pain pulses through her arm, a terrible and necessary part of the song.

Stephanie sees her again, several weeks later, in a Metro station in Mexico City. It is the girl. The one with the boots.

"How was Cancun?" the girl asks. Then, eyeing Stephanie's backpack: "Are you going home?"

She remembers the way the girl sat cross-legged in the seat beside her on the airplane and the desire she felt to confess everything to her. The openness of her face. The callouses she thought she saw on the girl's fingers.

Reaching a sweaty hand into the pocket of her jeans, Stephanie withdraws the slip of paper with Allison's handwriting. The ink is smudged: a week of the humidity and her body heat have rendered the address and phone number illegible.

When she first noticed, several days ago on the bus from La Manzanilla, she had braced herself for the sinking disappointment. But it never came. Instead, she thought of the last few weeks, of the sun and the beer and the taste of the ocean and the possibilities that seemed to unfold before her in every direction.

"No," says Stephanie.

The girl is smiling at her.

"You want to get a coffee?" she asks. "I know a good place around the corner."

The train pulls up to the platform and she feels the crowd shuffling forward together. She crumples the promise of a miracle in her fist and stands in the rush of human life, twitching her fingers just to make sure that the pain is still there.

"Sure."

She once believed, because Allison told her so, that music of a single cello was the whole world. But all around her, she hears it: the footsteps and the voices and the wheels of suitcases. The girl takes her by the hand. Around them, the crowd swells, a thousand people all moving and breathing as one organism. Stephanie doesn't resist; she lets herself be jostled and pulled. She shifts with the heat of the bodies around her and breathes the station smells and hums along to the symphony that is everywhere until she vanishes into the crowd.

CYRUS STUVLAND

Lake Coeur d'Alene

We walk slowly down the gravel road behind her house, my mother and I, looking for cedar bows. It's 20 degrees but no snow today, just cold trees, laced with frost. We gather white pine, grand fir, doug fir, and my favorite, hemlock—iced over. We take turns carrying our findings in a plastic tub. She is talking about her church friends.

I cannot understand my mother outside of her Idaho. I return often to this one image of her, some summer years ago: She's standing up driving the boat, leaning into the wind and pointing out all the good Kokanee fishing spots to whoever will listen. Her short curly hair has gone grey and white. Her face is reddish tan. She has seen a lot of sun, been in a lot of weather—the skin above her eyes sinking. I remember her saying she didn't mind wrinkles as long as they were from smiling and not frowning, but she has some from both. She grits her teeth a little, her chin jutting out—it's the same face she makes when she's scrubbing something particularly dirty and finding joy in the process. But here in the boat she grits her teeth with the satisfaction of wind and sun and a day on the lake, people to show it to. I know I make this face too, know I look just like her. I am both fascinated and horrified by this. I am so tethered to her at times, so hers. "I am writing you from inside a body that used to be yours," says Ocean Vuong to his mother, "Which is to say, I am writing as a son."

Perhaps she is the reason I have any love left in me for this state—it's a senseless sentimental attachment. I am queer and trans, a vegetarian now. This is a deeply red state. And yet. Idaho is both the woman who raised me to love and care for the earth and everyone on it and the woman who tells me that my friends and I are all going to hell, set against a backdrop of ponderosa and hay fields, a smoky sunset.

I once sat through a sermon at her church that blamed 9/11 on us gays. I watched the full pew of my family members nod along, saw the crescent moon of my mother's pursed lips and knew she was blaming herself. "All women become like their mothers," says Oscar Wilde. "That is their tragedy. No man does, and that is his." And what about those of us in between? Since I was a kid she has often cupped my hands in hers, examined them closely, and marveled that I ended up with "hands just like your dad's, such thick knuckles." But it is always her anxiety I see in the mirror, her eyes that look back at me, her words I hear coming from my mouth.

I haven't seen Idaho or my mother in the winter in a long time. Both are beautiful and painful to look at for too long—it's hard not to see them through the way things might have been. My mom fills me in on my childhood friend: "married a logger from St. Maries," she says, "real nice guy." A pause and then, "I think they have four kids now." Shortly after I was forced out of the closet, my mom asked me if I still wanted kids. My dad responded before I could, from the other side of the house: "Gay people can't have kids, that's disgusting." We have not talked about it since.

Here in these woods I feel like I'm 14 again, going on long walks with Mom. There's something about her that feels the loneliness inside of you, especially when you're trying to hide it. I know she feels it in me now, but it is something we cannot talk about directly—both of us products of rural Idaho: too tough, too passive aggressive, which is to say too white. And so she gossips about people I don't remember, talks about nothing, interrupts herself, keeps going. And then she comes up with projects for us—wreaths tonight, cookies tomorrow.

Sometimes she sends me packages full of herbal remedies she's made from local plants, always accompanied by a letter full of bible verses, pleas to come back to Jesus. She says that I should marry the farmer who lives out by Uncle Jeff's old place and is "such a nice Christian man." Other times, she'll say something surprising, like: "I'm praying God helps you find the right *person*."

We do eventually find some cedar bows, which are the most fragrant of the local evergreens. I prune as she holds the branches back—it's still automatic, after all these years. She breathes in deeply and sighs, looking out across the frozen lake. "I never really understood her," she says. "She could be so mean. But I sure miss her this time of year." I look too, across the steely white lake and sky at the little logging town on the other side and remember my grandma is dead now and this is my mom's first Christmas without her.

Later, by the fire, my mom sighs and says she just can't remember anything anymore. Her head in her hand, her bible on her knees. She's not crying, just defeated, exhausted. She can't remember if she's told me this story; she has, but I can feel the loneliness inside of her, so I say no and ask, "Can you help me mend my pants?"

"Of course, honey."

◆ MINYING HUANG ◆

Accession #02.18.329

                              the armlet nephrite like
              I sight you into *O* into the   soft paper
              O of your (now) mouth   like
         how the *O* tilts always in   jaded
           from my shut mouth tilts   diaspora
         unsightly this vision falters   concret-
          my *O* of contortion against   ising
          bird's eye view if   illusory
         we have to tilt why not   tilt and
         make what lies on edges   shift
        outsides rims skins shells appear   cautious
       we sight around and   somehow
       not around curious two   splintering
       dimensions it   is a coming together it
       occurs to me you're not quite   an absence maybe you aren't
       here this mouth not yours if   not here where and you say warrior
       we have to tilt why not   fixity hasn't worked so
        make this clear how   displacement latches
        can I register the you of the   harder
         O I seek a mouth speaks   sometimes
          to me does it speak who   is speaking
         what is seeking really   just groundless
            should I sempitern(us) is   this belief is
          this a trace and can we trace   a tremor or
           the *O* for what it isn't   immaterial
           really and really the word   maybe
            shakes me as I think I sight a   hollow
            mouth not infinite yours   grasping
           not around an ancestor's arm it occurs
           to me this tilting stretch of movement
           does not roll you onto your sides
           the way I'd like you
               are too hard flat for that the way
                I like though somewhere always
               you are bent out of shape
             and still motion still
           life still a ways
           from the
            always O (infinitely) we   un-
              sliding arms into 0   clasp
               the armlet nephrite
                              like

CYRÉE JARELLE JOHNSON

Eight of Spades
-for NLN

Hot boys go to heaven and you're headed soon.

A shark stunted by the fishbowl
that raised it, no second body in sight
for days, I'm sure. No food or light
for days, I'm sure. Smaller than
even my bathroom, you say
and I trust you on that, I guess.

If I write this poem, you can never die.
If I write this poem, you will always be
the body unwinding around my fist.

*

You said *(not promised)* you would stop drinking
after the surgery two doctors forbade.

Autistic child of addicts—I believed.
            Stupid, like waiting for the crunch
            of my father's ghostly car to crush
            the gravel of my three year-old front yard.

Now each drink is prolific in your shrunk gut.
You wake to delirium.
            You tremor my dreaming.

*

Since you've been gone, I watch
local news—waiting for the stomped can
of your two-stripe car.

The morning-drunk men open me.
My sadness turns sickness   that's who I am

some fem   writing elegies
               for familiar men.

*

When you die, I hope you'll visit.
I know no one
knows about your gay
lover, no one will tell me
you're dead. You are the last man
who can claim I was his   who never
claimed me.

I know I deserve better, but what of my desire? Can't I have
the life I imagine? Can't someone
always do the driving and never complain? Can't
your arms stay lemniscate around my neck? Oh, can't you just try
the A.A. meeting at The Center? Why won't you
come home? Why won't you come home and stay?

*

Now I draw the Ace of Spades. I pull again, insulting the deck.
Now I draw the Ace of Spades, and the noose circles your neck.
Now I draw the Ace of Spades; your wrecked car on the highway.
Ace of Spades, Ace of Spades worst sight in the deck.

CYRÉE JARELLE JOHNSON

a review of *Hamilton: An American Musical*

If I could go back in time, which is a game
I am sometimes forced to play I would lynch
george washington Standing there in step
with slaves whose teeth he yanked out & wore
for oil paintings & public appearances
Also auctions, to be sure My boyfriend & I
won the *Hamilton* lottery last week $10
of course Every beige actor singing on a wheel
Oh New York! Oh New York! GREATEST CITY!
Over a field of black bones scraped clean
The subway is also a boneyard The papers
won't tell me where so I say everywhere, except
nobody but nobodies care what I think I joined
The Organization because I wanted to practice
holding America hostage *Huckleberry Finn* stage
coach robbers 219 times the nigger That's the hardest
part of the whole thing: nobody cares what I think
Unless I frighten them Nothing ever resolves
itself in America No incentive, you see All
fireworks are just replicas of some foreign
bomb They drop bombs & bronze sculptures
for every genocide anyway Somebody says
we bouta bomb North Korea Nobody cares
what I think America is an experiment lit up
by sparking wires Oh please Oh please
let it burn down this time

Binkybonkychonkytown

We decided on the name as a measure of protection, a last line of defense. Horrors were happening all over the country in places with names all but begging for provocation:

Bakersfield.

Huntsville.

Florida City.

Together we joined in the democratic process, had ourselves a vote, then it was settled. We figured nothing so bad could happen in a place called Binkybonkychonkytown. The name was simply too playful. Tongue-plucky. Honey-glazed. Too pure.

"Twelve-year-old gang member arrested, charged following a streak of deadly bludgeonings in Binkybonkychonky—"

No. Media outlets would never allow it. Their audience would never believe it, and rightfully so. Given that we citizens of Binkybonkychonkytown are merely too gentle and kindhearted to be capable of such evil. Which is why it came as no surprise when the first reported crime in town revealed the culprit to be not, in fact, one of our own.

"This criminal was an outsider!" announced our Mayor. "And thus does not, by any means, represent the good citizens of our law-abiding town! This man's first name, Ronald —as is generally known—is a name given at birth to persons inherently deficient in moral, outstanding qualities. Indeed, as has been demonstrated historically time and time again by Rons and Ronalds alike: Reagan, Jeremy, Dio, McDonald…the list goes on! Rest assured, my good people," continued our Mayor, "this man was no true Binkybonkychonkytownian!"

Countermeasures were taken. Security forces were placed at all entry points leading into town. All outsiders were rigorously vetted prior to admittance, according to a comprehensive list of first names banned due to their innately dangerous nature, including any and all Frankies, Tommys, Justins, Roberts, Donalds, Ethans, Stevens, Jacobs, Davids, Trevors, Dylans, Dillons, Bretts, Brents, Gregs, Brads or Teds.

Following the removal of a few dozen criminals harbored in town under nicknames, once more we citizens of Binkybonkychonkytown were permitted to live on, at ease—that is, until a second crime was committed, bringing yet another blatant oversight to the public eye.

"This lowlife felon has been a chameleon amongst us!" declared our Mayor at a press conference. "As is common knowledge, adults of short stature—as was this grown man, at a mere five feet, four inches tall—are genetically predisposed to disobey societal law! This is due to a subconscious urge to revolt against one's own physical law of always being so close to the ground. Tiny adults have never been allowed in Binkybonkychonkytown for this express reason! They are an elusive breed, small yet domineering as a germ.

That being said, we suspect this miniature adult has been wearing protracted footwear such as high heels, or even stilts, to bypass detection. It is because of this I ask of you, my good people, as your own civil and moral duty," rallied our Mayor, "to stay vigilant for other small fries still in our midst!"

Afterwards, it became common practice in town to greet each other with a firm kick in the shins. No one took offense to this—such was merely out of patriotism, communal safety and care. The gesture also sought to expose though who, in violation of the max. allotted height of six foot, three inches tall—an outrageous size, posing a constant precarious risk—had managed to remain in lawful range by walking on their knees.

Gradually, with each subsequent crime committed, the factors in predicting, and therefore warding off, all potential criminals were calculated down to a science:

Wearers of socks with flip-flops (Loitering; Internet Piracy)

Plastic straw users / A fondness for reality TV (Unattended Campfires)

Cat owners, in direct correlation to # of cats owned (Bad Tipping Habits)

Mustaches—as was the case with our ex-Mayor—(Failure to Return Shopping Cart)

Now there is only a handful of us left in Binkybonkychonkytown: Jamie B., whose inability to roll his R's has been called into question by Jamie O., whose own credibility took a hit after revelations concerning his favorite ice cream flavor (lemon), which is to say nothing about Jamie G., whose choice in kitchen décor is atrocious, and yet has the nerve to raise doubts about my own habit of sleeping with a fan on, even during the winter.

But who am I to complain? Every day, we become that much safer. We keep an eye out on each other, for each other, and will stop at nothing to protect our little town.

D.M. RICE

Tabula Rasa, Innit?

THIS IS HOW THE WORLD ENDS. One is the singular. Deception, re unity, a coherence clearly lacking in the concept of god, not one form but many. The very concept of multiplicity, form as such, even a conceptual form that hangs like mist over the moors of imagination. I dearly miss my homeland but do not accept the state of its union. Exile is the truest form of martyrdom. Clash of the titans with calloused hands to crush the golden bough. Roots in the idle vine of bigotry, advancement without merit, constancy without vision. Boxcars filled with tears, libraries of inertia. Kill the pulse of instinct, tire your conspiracy with truth.

THIS IS HOW THE WORLD ENDS. In the realm of dream and fancy, ivy league after parties and masqued balls, a parade through this love letter to capital. Bodies floating in the hudson good to eat a thousand years. Angel pasta sold as authentic cultural stock. Painted canvas with the crimson organ. My beautiful house, beautiful lawn, manicured wife and two point five kids. My inevitable status as a renter. Suicide blonde screaming venus in the starry trap house of contemporary poem, a nude picture taken tastefully with no art. Hold my hair, Eloise, this is the pier of restitution. Sick words by the streetlight, manifestos of pixie cut demurral. We take a litter of kittens and throw it into the Mississippi then we all convert to veganism. Hashtag millenial. Hashtag unfiltered. Hashtag death. I wonder how she feels about being left to burn in paris while the rest of us kept balls, divided into houses when she meant us to protect, defend, regard collectives through the very dissolution of ego that keeps us held over the pit. Mother, queen of the meta-tomb, let off your wig and speak to me in your chosen name. Everyday the optimists are covered in flies. Everyday there is another tweet that buries us. Forget the weight of destiny, it is freedom that you taught us, not fate. Fortune favours the survivor's guilty conscience. I meet you in the cellar speakeasy good to drink a thousand beers. I follow you to Boulder good to live my clever fears. Delta resonances your vocal latency, epistle of high-speed wifi. Tiresias detransitioned so that I could live as my authentic self. I have much to tell you, Caesar, if only you had the grace to see me as I have seen you. Bacchanals and private islands. More to skeletons in form of stranger things. Nodes of greek christiandom, roman inquisition. Constantine holding a field mouse in his servant's hand. Titus Andronicus. Make haste, countrymen, for the fire of apollo's chariot severs at the quick. Journey with orpheus, with the wife of lot, with your unspeakable tragedy. Look behind you at the headlight in the rear-view mirror and learn all you need about god. Distending little trickster, albion of oblivion. Confer with your fates, a poor tailor, the greater hypocrisy of THEM. I will change without being changed and call it peace. I call this providence, a glimpse of truth. To the gallows of common law, marriage of limbo and purgatory. Kiss me in the bathroom of the loudest ecstasy, my crude concealer bothers not with taste. Ego all, ego quick, ego plain. Disappear like sandtracks over the nile. Another bed, estradiol night-terrors. Listen to the revolution on vinyl, order curry to your disposable person, eat it in your car. Who hallowed the asylums with intricate matters of foreign policy and new historical criticism. Horsemen of election fraud, selling fake news for free. Leopold sitting in his palace, discussing the delicate passes of succession. Fragile world, Xi Jinping. Mao swimming in the Yangtze River. Pol Pot picking mute-colored ties from the department store. Jersey girls sold out at the hollywood bowl, trending housewives, mansions and irreverent crossover episodes. Touch the border, wash your hands of this. Starve the Wet'suwet'en into honest negotiations. Bushfires in the royal blood of earth.

THIS IS HOW THE WORLD ENDS. Mass migration into machine gun, Kellyanne. Nature with a broken muzzle three degrees off kilter. In faith, pray tell, what have you done with Madonna? Kabbalah rock. Freudian lampshade, Jungian mirror. Shadow of the colossus. Miles davis tyrant, dizzy birds in spain letting blood to halt the inquisition. There may be none of me to give, my lightning is unwieldy as corruption, set loose in a china cabinet. A loaded gun, to never leave the house. Constellations of queer affection. Hazy neighbor, do not burden me with your nom de plume. To her death's quite romantic, her sin is her lifelessness. Kafka drank milk and wrote. Capote sipped martinis. Hemingway drank anything he could get his hands on. I was there. I saw it. Microtransactions, automated intelligence, all serve to bring to machines the a priori complexity we dare not know. Experience, in virtual terms, is replicable through zeroes and ones. Which brings us to our port of call. The infinite space between nothing and uni-ty. The unbreachable gap of theory cuts me in the name of medicine, a witch doctor in a plague mask, so they call me fairy, elf, otherworldly, other. Miss me when I'm gone, or all of this is all for naught. I miss you already, you can't even figure. When I write I drink despair, or else your hidden countenance. Facial expression, qu'est que c'est. Omnis dei spiritus. Sing me to sleep. For in that sleep of death, what dreams may come. What dreams may come. What dreams may just yet come.

 Milo Todd

excerpt from *Snuff*

TUESDAY
June 24th, 1969

I woke up too beautiful for this world: cotton-mouthed, hungry, and naked from the waist down. I was so tired last night upon my return to Trannyville that I forgot to take my bulge off. Apparently Nighttime Freddie wasn't deft enough to unpin it, and so I'd taken off my underwear in full and chucked them across the room. I wish I could say this was an uncommon occurrence.

I rubbed my eyes, which felt like that part of the matchbook you strike, and I reached for my cigs. Only then did I remember that Radio had given the rest away to the kids.

I groaned and tried to turn over to a dry spot on the mattress, me already sweating in the heat of the day. My arm and leg flopped off the old springs to the cement floor right beneath me. At least that still felt cool to the touch.

I only lifted my head from my pillow when I heard the Mister Rogers theme song downstairs. I cursed, realizing I'd forgotten to reset my useless clamshell of a clock again. Mister Rogers was just reruns in the summer, but shit, man.

I tripped over some of my busted textbooks as I shuffled out to our main room. Radio was sitting at the counter, hunched over a mess of her electronics in a frown. Her face looked worse than last night, but that's kinda how healing goes.

"How're you feeling?"

"Mmh."

I leaned closer. "What're you doing, anyway?"

"Computer."

"The hell is that?" But when she didn't answer, I chewed on a hangnail and went about my way. When I opened our door, I nearly fell backward trying to avoid the stuff on the floor. The kids had left gifts for Radio overnight since she'd been beat: a couple of cigarettes, a single-serving bag of chips, a fifth of a bottle of Jack, a tattered copy of *Rat*. Someone even made some sort of art piece, a cracked mirror the size of my own hand, a heart fastened to it with what looked like chewing gum and pieces of broken bottles. I brought it all in and placed it on the counter. Morning light hit the deco, bouncing little shards of greens and blues onto the wall as if they were no longer sharp enough to cut. I saw Radio glance at it and soften. But when she caught me eying the Jack, she sighed and returned to her work.

"Just take it."

I snatched the bottle up in a swipe and removed the cap, bringing it to my lips.

"Easy. You haven't even had breakfast yet."

I pulled the bottle away in a gasp. A drop lost its grip on the corner of my mouth and began to roll, but I caught it with a swipe of my arm. "This is breakfast."

"That joke will get old the second you stagger your stupid white ass into traffic."

I screwed the cap back on to save the rest for later. I looked at Radio a moment, her head bowed to her work, me feeling the Jack start to work through my veins. I suddenly wanted to choose my words carefully. "One day, I'm gonna get us outta here."

She looked up at me a second before giving a small smile, but her eyes didn't change. "I know, sweetness."

I put the bottle on the counter and went down to the first floor, Mister Rogers getting clearer with each industrial stair. I saw the blue glow before I saw the box, the flickering shadows of the kids. Nearly all of them were sitting around the little screen in a circle, cross-legged, hunched over just enough to not miss a word, but not so much that it might give away that they actually cared.

Most of them were teenagers of any sort of range, the youngest kids ten or eleven, all of them riddled with some sort of mark or another. Old blisters on their faces, branded asses, knife marks and stab wounds. Boiling water, hot irons, cigarettes. These were the marks of families with only conditional love to give. A shame we were all they could find for replacement.

I stood behind them all for a moment, staring at the screen. It was all snowy again, but you could still hear most of the words.

As I continued to watch them, every last eager back to my face, I felt the hurt trying to sharpen itself against the edges the Jack had dulled. I wished I could take them on field trips. Museums, national parks, even libraries where they could get any book they wanted, to drink up everything and anything life had to offer. Their world was so fucking small. And I was useless in prying off the padlocks. All me and Radio could do was what we did so they wouldn't have to, but that only prolonged their suffering instead of helping them out of this mess. Because once there was opportunity to get them somewhere better, to give them something that might lift them up, the money was already gone. Living was too expensive to concern ourselves with thriving.

There was a knock at the door behind me, real soft. So soft none of the kids heard it. I turned to it, already on edge. Knocking wasn't something that happened around the piers.

I slunk to the door, my heels off the floor in a fox step, ready to scare off fags looking for a place to fuck. I grazed my hand across the top of the weapons basket and came up with a pair of scissors. I held them at my side, in plain view as I opened the door. I blinked in the morning sun, felt that sharp pain behind my eyes as they worked to be human. And for a moment, I couldn't see anything at all.

"What," I barked, yanking the noise up from my stomach. I flashed the scissors limp by my hip in the sharp sunlight.

But then I held still. The newcomer in front of me shrank back, some kid the age I hated most, though that wasn't their fault. The bruising around my vision left me fast as my eyes adjusted. Blue-eyed, golden-haired. Petite and fine-boned. The kid looked fluffed in the cheeks, as if it was the part of their body that decided to grow first. Storing nuts for winter or something. Their mouth was messed up in some way.

I whipped the scissors behind my back, returning them to the basket. The clank of metal seemed to relax the kid's shoulders. I opened the door wider and held my breath. To say I was looking in a mirror is kind of a lot, but man, it felt like that. Like, a real smudgy mirror. That was teeny tiny. And just before I went off my rocker.

"You're like me." I said it so quietly that I wasn't sure they'd heard me. They weren't supposed to hear me. But then their wet blue eyes got big. Their words were like marbles and it seemed to take effort to work their tongue. Something was definitely wrong with their mouth.

"This lady Marsha said to say Cupid could help me."

I opened the door the rest of the way. I began to wonder if somebody had slipped stuff into the Jack. "I'm Cupid." I stepped aside and that little chickabiddy came in.

The door closed us back off into darkness, the kid almost invisible as my eyes fought again. The black and white flashes of the television were making me wince.

"My mouth hurts." They pointed to their face as if I wouldn't be able to locate it myself, and their eyes began to go wet again. They blinked in a flurry.

I looked at them better now as my eyes ratcheted back down, seeing the one cheek much more swollen than the other. I knew better than to touch it. And that I shouldn't presume a damn thing. "You a tranny?"

They picked at their sleeve, words still mumbled. Their mouth barely moved when they spoke and I had to lean in to hear them properly over the royal bitching of King Friday. "...I don't like that word."

I nodded. I tried again. "You a transvestite?"

"And a boy." He picked at the hole in his sleeve, the size of a cigarette burn. He sniffed once before his voice cracked like a bad note. "My mouth really hurts." He said it loud enough that a few of the kids turned.

I was already heading for the stairs. "Come with me."

He followed me up, silent. I hoped to get some information out of him.

"Where you from?"

His voice was small behind me, whisking around in the dark like a ghost. "Jersey. Got kicked out. Hitchhiked here."

"How long you been in New York?"

"Just last night."

I didn't say anything to that. His story, in the end, wasn't unlike anybody else's. He was rejected love, left to rot. I'd thought waste was supposed to be a sin.

We hit the end of the stairs and I placed my hand on me and Radio's door. It was then I heard him speak again, as quiet as the first time.

"I thought I was the only one, too."

I couldn't handle the tone in his voice, so I opened the door and let us both on in. "Nurse Radio. I've found a stray in need of care."

Radio looked up from her work, ready to give her usual small smile, to welcome a new baby chick into her fold. But then she saw the boy, saw me, and stopped halfway. We only got girls around here, nearly all of them black or brown. She caught herself and pushed her smile out farther than usual. "You're lucky. Dr. Cupid is the best around."

I scoffed at this, leading the chickabiddy to the good chair. I reclined him a couple clicks and put on some gloves from my med drawer. The morning light came in through the smeared window upon his face, motes drifting lazy about us as if we were some happy little suburban home and not an abandoned warehouse in the Meatpacking District. Motes are brainless. "Open your mouth, please."

He did as told, but it took me all of two seconds to see what was going on. I realized then he might be older than twelve. He definitely had the tranny boy curse. Baby face for life.

"Abscess," I muttered, standing back upright. "Bet it hurts like hell, too. But the good news is it's just a wisdom tooth. You don't need it."

He shrank in the chair. "You're gonna pull it?"

I was already fishing out a vial and dental syringe from my med drawer. "It'll be over quick and you'll feel so much better in just a couple days. I promise. You'll never miss it." I began filling the syringe. It was just a bit of lidocaine—or maybe it was procaine, who can remember—with a vasoconstrictor I'd added to help control bleeding.

He looked at the needle and I could see him getting pale in the face. "You sure you know what you're doing?"

I smiled with half of my mouth, looking him dead in the eye. "If I could do it backwards in a mirror on myself, I can do it to you."

"He knows what he's doing, baby." Radio took a moment to put her screwdriver down and hook a finger into the corner of her mouth, the unripped side, showing the gap of a missing molar. "Just about everybody here's missing teeth."

"It's all the starch," I said simply. "We can't afford dentists and they wouldn't take us even if we could. But we got toothpaste here to share and we'll make sure to get you a toothbrush, okay?" I leaned toward him with the needle, but he failed to open his mouth as wide as I needed. "Though in your case, the situation was unavoidable. Wisdom teeth abscess all the time. You're gonna be just fine."

He still wasn't opening his mouth properly and I knew I needed to calm him down. "You can stay with us as long as you need, you know. We can be your family."

"I have family." He said it so abruptly that I felt insulted, then jealous, then possibly a third thing I didn't have time to think because he kept rapping. "An uncle in San Fran. Gonna get myself there soon as I can."

"Ah. And how do you plan to do that?"

"Hitchhike."

I was suddenly very aware of how closely Rade was listening to us. I shook my head. "You need to get a bus ticket. You're lucky you hitchhiked even here in one piece. Across the country, you'll be toast."

"I'll earn some money, then."

"And how will you earn money?"

"Well…" He shrugged and glanced around the room, as if that said it all. My own eye caught my work outfits lined up far behind the arc of him, hanging on a wheeled closet pole.

I knew how easily he'd get snapped up, and how quickly he'd be destroyed. "No." I cut him off as he began to protest. "Open your mouth. We need to take care of this."

I felt bad the moment I plunged that needle in, how he gave a sharp cry and then tried to cover it up. He'd already started that thing where he was trying to prove his manhood in all the wrong ways, the only chance to convince others he was one. I ignored the tears that sprang up in his eyes, as if begging me to stop, as if I was the bad guy. I had hold of his cheek, wiggling it to help the anesthesia spread.

"You're doing great," I said. I pulled the needle out, giving him a tissue for his silent tears as we waited. He kept his mouth open as he wiped them away.

"You know why we got wisdom teeth?" I asked. He looked up at me, curiosity poking out from beneath his anxiety. "It's because our jaws used to be bigger. We had these extra teeth to help us grind up plants so we could digest them better, but now we don't need them anymore. We're always evolving. But a lot of times in evolution you get stuck in these periods of still-evolving-into-something-else. Humans are constantly playing catchup, and to resist it just results in problems."

I watched him as I babbled until I saw his face slacken with the relief of going numb. I tapped a finger against his first molar. Then his second molar. Then the wisdom tooth itself. When he didn't jump, I went ahead and pushed my nail into his swollen gum line. Nothing.

"Looks like we're ready to go, then." Keeping it from his line of sight, I rounded over a scalpel and put it to his mouth, easing gently into the tissue until it pierced. The blood started to seep and I knew by this point I'd have to be quick. I cut through the first layer or two of gum, now at a better pace knowing for sure he couldn't feel it.

The payphone down the hall suddenly sounded, crisp and offensive as it pummeled straight through our door. There was only one reason that shit would ever ring, and that was for a job. To keep a number here otherwise was too dangerous.

"Fuck," I muttered. The high ring of the bell felt like it was trying to shove ice into my ear, raising the nodes of my spine through my skin. "Radio, could you?"

"I'm kinda in the middle of something."

"Oh come on, Rade."

Radio huffed and clattered down her screwdriver. But when her eye fell to the blood smeared on my gloved fingers, she went out into the hall, leaving the door open. I heard her heavy footfalls until the ringing stopped.

"Somebody wants to make an appointment," she called out.

I was already cutting through the next layer of tissue. I didn't look away, though I felt bad for pretty much shouting in the kid's face. "Who?"

"Someone new, I think."

I needed to get this done fast as I could for the boy's own sake. It wasn't like I had suction in the room and I couldn't exactly let him choke on his own blood. I eyed the rate it trickled. "When?"

There was a pause, a murmur I couldn't hear. "Tomorrow."

"Tomorrow?" I groaned. I didn't want to pull a triple, if only because it was a higher risk of bringing one cat's scent to another's nose. But then I had a thought, the only thought I had to help the kid. I huffed again. Worst case scenario, I'd have to shower twice in the same day at the hotels.

"Shit." I tried to run Wednesday's schedule through my head as I finished cutting through his gum. With the bone exposed so deep, I switched my scalpel over to some pliers. I quickly wiped down his exposed tooth with gauze to help get a better grip. The blood kept trickling. "Not until tomorrow evening," I called back out. "I got some earlier in the day. Tell them nine and please write down what hotel they want to meet at. Must be somewhere within Manhattan."

I grabbed onto the tooth and started to wiggle. I calmed my voice back down again and smiled. "You're going to feel some pressure here, but it won't hurt. Almost done." I could feel it already starting to give, the abscess helping push it.

Radio's voice called out once more. "You like licorice?"

"Jesus fucking Christ," I breathed. I resisted the urge to drop my head a moment in a groan, keeping my eye instead on the tooth, my hand steady. Almost there. "Shit, Rade, I dunno." The blood was starting to slick my grip and I had no way of drying him off again without losing my momentum. It was pooling in his mouth so deep it looked like the piers at night. What a way to drown. "Sure, I dig licorice. Just say yes."

I could feel the pliers starting to slip in the blood, but goddammit, I wasn't about to let that happen. I put a palm on the boy's head as gently as I could, making my voice soft. "One last pull and we'll be all done and you'll feel lots better. I promise. You're doing great."

"Twizzlers or Red Vines?"

"Fuck, Radio, I dunno, okay? Twizzlers. Just say Twizzlers. Nobody fucking digs Red Vines." I was pulling with all I had now, keeping the kid's head down with my hand. He whimpered, but I think he was just scared. That was my fault. But if I couldn't get this tooth, I was gonna have to smash it and dig out all the little pieces. Please don't make me smash it and dig out all the little pieces.

"I fucking dig Red Vines!" Radio barked back.

"They're not even licorice!"

"Fuck you!"

"Fuck you, too!"

The tooth suddenly gave so fast that I fell backward. I threw the pliers to the floor and stuffed gauze up the boy's mouth. I held it there a minute, firm. I counted how many pads he bled through, and when I saw it was thankfully few in number before it slowed, I smiled at him again. "See? Nothing to it."

Radio came back in, closing the door and handing me over a scrap of white bakery bag. "Static's acting up on the line again. I'll go out soon as it's dark and tighten the wire." She gave me a not-so-light smack on the shoulder before returning to her work. Her voice softened, though she still eyed the newcomer with some amount of skepticism. "You got a name, baby?"

That chickabiddy shook his head beneath my hand. I was beginning to soak up the blood that'd pooled in his mouth with extra gauze, careful to hold it tight so he didn't choke. I kept slinking the chunks of dripping massacre away from his vision and into the trashcan. They each gave a distinctly heavy thunk when they landed.

"Well," I said, "you better think one up soon or it'll be made for you." I left the gauze stuffed to the hole of his mouth, seeing it was staying fairly white now, and picked up the pliers. The tooth was now latched between its jaws with drying blood, and I examined it in a full rotation. "Word association, you know? Like, tooth...wisdom. Wisdom Tooth—shit, no."

Radio looked up from her work with a smirk. "You're bad at this game."

I shrugged and looked at the nameless kid, keeping my hands out of his sight as I plucked the tooth free from the pliers and tossed it in the trash. "Welcome to Trannyville. You can just call us The Castle, if you want."

He leaned back in the chair, giving a sigh that it was over. I brought the chair back up in a sitting position.

I looked over my shoulder to Radio, who was still making poor work of looking interested in her electronic doodads. She glanced at me without moving her head. I turned back around, blocking both me and the kid from her with my back. I moved so close to him that all I could see were his eyes.

"Look," I whispered. "I'm gonna get you that dough, okay? We'll get you on that bus as soon as possible."

He frowned and tried to mumble something past the gauze, but I stopped him. "You can't do anything for at least three days, anyway. Nobody will want you." That wasn't true, but he didn't have to know that. "You need to recover."

I didn't know how I was going to do it. I didn't know even if I could do it. All I knew is that I'd give it everything I had. I could feel Radio's gaze hot on my neck now, knew that she'd just heard me when I hoped she wouldn't, knew exactly what it was about this situation now that was putting her off me, of who I was willing to help out more and why, and that she was right, and that I was nonetheless willing to risk our immovable friendship to do it anyway. I realized my voice was shaking. I turned my face slightly away from the kid, suddenly, for the first time in a long time, self-conscious about the Jack on my breath. "Just give me three days."

Sometimes you want to do good in the world even when you know this isn't it.

 CHING-IN CHEN

En Route Family
December Haibun

No longer ask me who keeps my family in the thin
The whole grey day, the sky came down in slips of snake and skin.
who returns to that shrub of a short house
We shielded our eyes from what dropped into air.
a distant cousin sweeper paid to cry over a grandmother's bones
We stopped to ingest hot pepper and bits of unrisen bread.
uncle with a thrown voice booming over a table full of crab we throw up for days

At first, you didn't want any liquid, but regretted it when you saw that there was none left in the bowl.

weak untrained stomachs not used to the storming of our bowels
keeping warm through layers of tea steepings
All the sop had gone running, all the mouths had closed down.

CHING-IN CHEN

No

She says. Don't
      show me any more words for water.
                    For your mess.
                        Say No. I'm waling
               home alone, under the rain.
                  Says, there's not much left
             in my mouth for you. I've finished
                    my lesson. Stayed in the hall.
             Bit my puppy. Tumbled with the afterschool kids.

There's only a length left. Bolt of a pushed down girl. She's a hard time coming.
                      You don't know what she's got in her but
             sand. Don't know
                what else keeps her flying.

                    No, she's not coming here. She doesn't
want to hear any more
      stories. She's a thin line come down
             the street. You don't know her name.

◆◆◆ CHING-IN CHEN ◆◆◆◆◆◆

"Registration Marks" or
"a kind of breathing vocabulary on a daily level"

Young child has a complaint about weather.

> Weather is hot.
> Air crumbles in mouth.
> The mouth an oven where metal sits enamel.

We are on boat in hot weather.

> Child and her attached humans.
> The air a layer I watch.

We float by discarded bodies of small plastics, decorating surface.

> The plastics a focal point, transformed colors along waterway.
> I cannot define these unnatural
> colors. Our boat guide narrates the bayou.
> Plastics gathering like mob.
> The plastics wait.

> We watch the water.
> Tugboat in path. Floating structure
> with job to transport metal mountain. Giant
> claw grabs and transfers.
> We watch claw working in heat.

Hot and child wants water.

> No one on board thought to bring clean water.

We wind down passageway.

> Story of narrower days, trees of the past form tunnel.

> Now we unfortunates baking in sun.

> I am also very hot.

Industrial docks float by. Company structures. Our guide points forward and says "Look at the view! You forget we are in Houston!"

> Neighbor jostles another, nodding towards industrial building. Guide amends statement: "If you look forward, you forget we are in Houston!"

The boat a complaint.

We see a heron. Long legs and queer tuft, waiting.
See little burps of fish.
A trestle, a stopped train, waiting for its transformed garbage.

Child goes up to stern.
Testing metal not advised. Sometimes the metal swings out and away into water. Fall in and a dragging under boat.

Don't complain to hot boat.

We edge to turning point. Instructed to wave at cameras.
Child can't see cameras. If we cross and can't see cameras, will
Homeland Security wave?
We are bending the point. We wait and look forward.

Note: "Registration Marks" and "a kind of breathing vocabulary on a daily level" are phrases taken from Roni Horn's 'When I Breathe I Draw.'

Our Apocalypse: A Disaster in Three Movements

1.) Music

Midway through removing her brain tumor, surgeons wake the violinist to hand her the bow, then the body, of the violin. With her skull exposed to the surgery suite, she picks up the instrument and begins to play. This is the only way to ensure that the crucial areas controlling delicate movement in her left hand haven't suffered significant damage.

A team of surgeons, therapists, and anesthetists consult the map they made of her pre-surgery brain, monitoring the active areas.

What does she play?
Gustav Mahler, Julio Iglesias.
George Gershwin's "Summertime."

The team successfully removes ninety percent of the tumor "including all areas of aggressive activity."

I return to this video in which she plays with her eyes closed. The surgeons, gathered at her crown, lit like angels in a renaissance painting, continue their methodical carving, unmoved.

I return because I want to know what it's like to love anything that much.

I want to know, in the moment the scalpel moves through the right frontal cortex, whether or not I would know you that way, with so much intimacy.
I want to know whether I remain attuned to you, whether your body would be rote memory for me.

2.) Migration

In another life, I rose early to feed you each morning, and made food for the hummingbirds. And we would smoke and drink coffee and marvel at the hummingbird's ferocity, and the fact that at the end of migration they'd return, inevitably, to the same branch of the same tree. Having been in love since we were thirteen, I think we found comfort in this, the ferocity of the hummingbird and the notion that his returning home was a skill and a miracle of evolution, rather than a default or disappointing choice.

I recently learned of the Arctic tern, a bird born in Arctic spring when the sun shines twenty-four hours a day. The way this bird, addicted to daylight, leaves every fall when the sun grows thin, cleaving the globe to reach the Antarctic where the endless day is replicated.

You were always so terrified of my darkness. When the light grew thin, some part of you would leave, your body tense beside me, your eyes filled with the rush of all you hoped to outrun.

To be fair, I saw your sunshine obsession, your belief in heaven, as weakness, though I never stopped you from praying. Did you ever consider that "Maybe we pray on our knees because god / only listens when we're this close / to the devil."[1]

Or did you forgo that thought, and others like it, because it's enough for you just to be on your knees?

3.) Maw

The only thing of consequence at the moment is the virus, initially indicated on the map by a few red freckles scattered across the face of China. The virus is wildfire now—it is global, doubling on itself daily, spreading beyond our capacity for containment.

I'll admit that the breadth and depth of my apocalypse research was conducted via zombie flicks and action films in which everyone stares at the sky, waiting for the asteroid to obliterate. The hero's a hot guy, or has-been with a gun, or asshole in a space suit. From underneath the tepid dialogue swells Aerosmith's "I Don't Wanna Miss A Thing." People learn in these films to be fearless, to liberate themselves from the scars that stood between them and love.

No one ever wonders what they're worth—our lives, these tiny offerings—if the virus is coming in waves to take it back.

I wanted our love to be as remarkable as our love story.
We could've been a movie, you and me.

I don't know where you are tonight, and it wouldn't matter anyway, as you are no longer mine to touch.

---

[1] Ocean Vuong

You told me once that I was beautiful. That each time I entered a room, I changed it the way a cello would.

I left when your brutality became a secret I was incapable of keeping from myself.

Three days later, the virus came.

The bodies are carried through back doors, deposited into refrigerated trucks that hum down back alleyways.

"We have been drawn into a new calculus," writes Ariana Reines.

In two short months, we've all become strangers on this planet, staring out at the empty streets from the relentless room where we have sheltered in place.

And here it is at last, as warned: the way the abyss gazes back.

GABRIELLE GRACE HOGAN

the hedges are burning / no, they are just on fire

the cardinal mimics a suicide against the glass
       & after disposing of him, i wash until my hands

are each a cardinal, making passionate bird love—
       praise be to the cloaca—over the drain's humble *O*.

the sink leaks with me, both of us clogged with
       blood & hair. there are some things that exist

only in water—coral reefs, the sex life
       of dolphins, the human brain. did you know

we are only one protein away
       from bioluminescence? this is how i know

in god's image swarm the fish, cyan globules
       haloing the bright dark, canonized in chemicals.

if birds could luminesce, oh!—
       teal-feathered orbs flying low,

bright ghost of an ambulance siren,
       how it hollows out the ears.

(i am walking past the hospital,
       which means i am almost home.

forgive the brainstem
       from which my spine

dangles like a hooked trout.
       forgive my desire to become a noun.)

if humans could luminesce, i can only ask:
       what massacre would we make in the name

of which blue?

summer's belly swells with black children but never births

teaches womb-rot dance routine
hemorrhages funeral pamphlets
mommas over open caskets
mourning sickness, wails in back bending contractions
brown baby body bag fingers found in concrete outlines

this country gave pigs chalk,
                              tracing every meal in bullet seasoned
4-hour sunglaze sweet sweat

summer's belly swells with black children but never births

sun kissed death body waits
decays warm and tattoo needle fresh pain sweetens branches from which it hangs, wonder what
exactly the tree is thinking

what apology is owed her

sun kissed death body is worn on the airbrushed t-shirts of gospel choirs
worn by the box braided balding blondes single file, waiting bleached for burned butt surgery
visits and rat lip injections
sold, now, with a foundation that's 6 shades too light for her skin
auction block spring/summer collection in the nearest designer store

summer's belly swells with black children

                              never births
sliced open
invaded for playtime plundering
drained plasma renamed winner on another's skin
be consumed by heat
swallowed with nails

summer's belly swells with black children but never births

the next black thing doing their style for them
full term fashion spat linguistic gentrified once it leaves black lips

summer's lips drip bullets,
drool teargas,
handcuffed,
suffocated
growing belly
feeding pigs

TREVOR KETNER

[Weary with toil, I haste me to my bed,]

desire: i'm a they-boy / welt / thaw—omit
throb-eel (limp) / red star (fisted)—a river: to hew
/ hue (honeying bay)—adjust rib—net men—
does kink word by word—wet sphinx memory /
high bath hem—doe ferns rare fur—my tit
so petaled i mouthe gin tang—realize
i periwinkle, peony, pansy, edge—odd dome
(do bite)—dew's holiness and elk horn—choking
men as hag (might slay)—suit: vary it so
a host, empty stylish ghost, views—red-sewn
she-thigh (ink)—hung claw lay jeweling hit—
lube breakfast / doe haunch—i acknowledge stamen—
my manly thumbs (dying symbol / hid by it)—
men feed off liquid / thorn any forest.

TREVOR KETNER

[When, in disgrace with fortune and men's eyes]

sweetened fang / runic ram / honeyed hiss—twin
witness—to pale tea / to blue lace—*may
i eat chub beef* (nods heavy)—trans slime / welt /
fur—neon sand / pale fate (my lucky sodom)—
ripe omens: wool, chime, heron—i keg—i thin
—a mere needle kiss—if i fist them lush i'd work hips—
neat shade imprints—damn stars / hag tonics—
wettest hilt—my coat / jeans (wind)—to hone
teeth, sing (homo yelps)—styles gut (is famed)—thins
thin the hand (mistakenly) to pet hyena—
a dirty folk song—a lake: i (heart)break it—
gyrate: manflesh hangs—she-son (me): salt, vein, rut—
severe butch bowl (terf hair)—messy gown melt—
heathen act (oystering)—night swatch / mist knot.

◆◇ TREVOR KETNER

[Let those who are in favour with their stars]

teahouse thirst (oval)—freshwater with iron
tip / a dual blood rush cups to bonfire—not
house, room—hips fit / warm flush—witch
tooth / hoof—do i not ruin joy—*man* lurks
in *i* / i refract *vase* (further reversal)—to gape / piss,
taste me—blush at us / a honeyed grit—
i hit / mend / build—naive dress—eels rip there
and there (withering)—oil for toy / fray—
mouthful of tide / war hair—finger for sap—
i heft / cloud—i savor *son* refaced to a tin
hook, to queer orb—i harmonize *stud* (off /
deflection / shift)—gather or hold— howl / tar—
a phantom by the path (doe / divan-level
moon)—we boat home: rim every red nerve.

Joey, When She Knew Him

A cold day in January, in the middle of a snowstorm. The store bell tinkled, Sid looked up, and there was Joey, shivering, big flakes clumped on his wispy long blonde hair, starting to melt down his face. There was something endearing about his bedraggledness, his shy smile—she could tell right away he was family. He pulled an application out of his coat where he had been keeping it pressed flat against his chest and presented it like it was a birthday present. His fingers were icy, the paper damp at the edges.

Sid looked it over, noting he lived only a few blocks away, not far from her own apartment. Then she cleared her throat and, trying to sound authoritative, asked, "You have much experience in this line of work?"

Joey was earnestly giving the life story of each family pet and explaining his expertise in pet-sitting when Olivier, the actual Pets R Us manager, came out of the back office. He shot Sid an exasperated look. "Go clean the parakeet cages, Sidney."

At the time, Joey was attending the Traditional Chinese Medicine college out in New West. He'd ride the train there most days, rushing back to the West End to make it to his late afternoon shifts at the store. Sometimes Sid would cover weekends for him so that he could do his hours at the student clinic, practicing acupuncture on the poor volunteers. One slow Saturday at the shop he suggested that Sid come to the next week's clinic.

"Needles? No thank you." She was arranging the plastic toys by color and size on a hanging rack and squeaked one at him. "Do I look like someone who would enjoy having needles stuck in her arm?"

"It's not painful. And anyway, how would I know what kind of pain you like?" He gave her a sultry look and licked his lips. They had taken to flirting with each other to pass the time.

"Can you say butt plug?" She held up a particularly suggestive toy and made a humping motion. Just then Olivier come out of the back office and she quickly put her head down and started hanging up the toys.

But Olivier wasn't there to reprimand them—turned out he just wanted to chat. "You guys are both gay, right?" he asked, and then he launched into his spiel before either of them could answer. "My sister—she's, I guess, 'coming out'—I mean, she's still married, happily married, until recently, I guess and now she has this 'girlfriend,' she says...my mom isn't happy. Really isn't happy." He looked from Sid to Joey. "What should I do? My mom and sister are trying to get me to take sides."

Only in his early forties, Olivier seemed ancient, though he had an air of sophistication that Sid and Joey admired—savvy fashion sense, a French accent. Even though he rarely joked and could be an outright asshole at times, they felt sorry for him. Being the manager of a pet store did not seem the appropriate vocation for a man who had such long dark eyelashes, wore such nice shoes, and often greeted people with a soft "Bonjour." He had never talked to them so informally before and this breaking of the unspoken code of conduct between manager and employee was too much for either Joey or Sid to make sense of. They stared at him silently.

After an awkward pause in which Sid and Joey pretended to busy themselves with the plastic toys, Olivier said, "I guess I'll figure it out." He looked embarrassed and shrugged defensively as he headed back to his office.

Joey looked after him and licked his lips. "I wish."

"Really? Come on. He's way too old."

"He's hot."

"You think anything with two legs and a penis is hot."

Recently Joey had been cultivating a new persona, acting like he was at all times sexually voracious, constantly on the make, like every man was a potential fuck-mate. It was an act common to young gay men his age, but it didn't really fit Joey. Sid had only recently started to notice it, and still found it a bit jarring. Where had he picked it up? His roommates?

Joey tossed his hair dramatically and went behind the counter to get a box of fish food which he started to unpack, lining the small canisters up on the shelf. "Want to come to the club with me tonight?"

"The club? You never go out."

"I know. I haven't been dancing forever. I really want to dance."

At eight Joey was standing on Sid's doorstep with a backpack full of clothes and a bottle of vodka. They tried on four or five outfits each as they sipped on tumblers of a drink that, at twenty, they still considered a cocktail: Sprite, vodka, a big slice of lemon and a big slice of lime. They hair-sprayed each other's hair, curled their eyelashes, painted their nails white. Later Joey would grind on boys, Sid would grind on boys and any girls who happened to be around. They would drink more, they would wait in long bathroom lines or go into the alley to piss, they would flirt, they would squeal and laugh. But before all that they were with only each other. Joey squeezed into a gold lamé half-shirt, Sid in an oversized men's button-up and black tie, in front of the big bathroom mirror, catching each other's eyes as they put on black eyeliner.

Sid still calls him Joey, even though it's not his name anymore and Ian doesn't like it. Joey goes by Richard now—his middle name, the name of his grandfather, who was once rich (lawyer-turned-real-estate-investor) but lost the family fortune through incautious investments and so Joey had to put himself through college by working at the pet store. The whole family was bitter about the lost money ever after and rarely visited the old man in his stuffy retirement home as he slid slowly toward his death.

Joey's husband Ian doesn't have to work. His grandfather made a killing investing in steel and coal during the Second World War—something the family tries to keep hush-hush—and all of his descendents have been living off the proceeds ever since. But Ian is prideful and, unlike the rest of his family (to hear him tell it), has a decent work ethic, so after trying law school and dropping out and trying medical school and failing out, he became a successful interior designer.

It is a cliché for a gay man, the career, but in this case, it is apt. Ian has the eye; he knows how to make a room look good, bright and airy or cozy and full of dark wood, depending on the client's wishes. He knows the best shops, the nicest fabrics, has an impeccable sense of color. He once counseled Joey to buy Sid a pair of navy and red striped throw pillows, silk, for her couch—that was ten years ago, and she still gets compliments on them.

And Joey? After dropping out of college, he quit the pet store and started working at an upscale pet daycare. Later, he opened his own doggy spa (backed by Ian's family money) just a few blocks from their condo in the West End.

Every August, Ian and Joey throw a big party after the Pride parade. Their building has a pool on the roof, and they commandeer it from early evening until three or four in the morning— people dancing, drinking, smoking weed and doing lines until they finally have enough and stumble home. Sid is always there—sometimes with a date but more often between girlfriends and in search of effervescent cocktails, fresh cantaloupe slices, hors d'oeuvres featuring expensive goat cheese from Salt Spring Island. She hasn't been to a party in weeks and is excited to be out of the house. Finally back in school for her Masters, she spends most of her days studying.

This year, they've hired go-go dancers. The two boys gyrate around the pool in silver shorts, a glazed look in their eyes. One is beautiful—a round, shiny belly and lots of dark curly hair everywhere. Sid tries to talk to him when she first arrives but he only drops a few words her way before turning to his wiggling partner and imitating his movements. She watches as he pulls a joint from his tiny shorts to share with the other dancer—they barely slow down to light the thing. What was the deal Ian struck with them? Dance, dance as if your life depends on it, and don't stop for anything or you won't get your hundred dollars? (Ian, like most rich people, has a cheap streak.)

There's something mesmerizing about watching the boys twirl around each other, bathed in the turquoise glow from the pool lights, like two seals circling each other in a luminescent sea. They are covered in silver glitter, and they are young—a decade or two younger than most people at the party. Although their movements are smooth, they look tired, and Sid wonders if Ian has hired them for the entire night, or just for a few hours. She sips her margarita, looking around for faces she recognizes. Everyone is beautiful but also a little grimy from the day's festivities, fake eyelashes askew, lipstick smudged, smelling of chlorine and sunscreen and sweat. She looks back at the dancers; they're grinding on each other but neither looks very into it. She hopes Ian is paying them decently, at least.

The prettier one with the belly reminds her of Michael, her best friend in high school, her "boyfriend" for a semester—they were each other's beards in grade 11 until they both came out spectacularly—in drag, no less—during an open mic night in the cafeteria. She still remembers some of the lines from Michael's spoken word piece—she's pretty sure he rhymed "trust" with "lust."

Michael's birth name is Miguel, and his Peruvian mother was pretty pissed when he changed it in grade 9. He and Sid worked at Dairy Queen together for two years. They'd clown with the hot dogs, make weird sculptures out of the tasty freeze and share makeup. Their manager, a worn woman who smoked two packs a day, had feathered greying hair and a tough edge that made them think she was a closeted dyke, loved them, loved (they thought) their eager adolescent gayness. She laughed when they camped it up, gave them the best shifts and free cigarettes to smoke on their breaks.

The last Sid heard Michael had changed his name back to Miguel and was in Toronto, working in a cafe in the gay village. She takes a sip of her margarita. The bartender—a friend of Joey's—poured her a double and she's starting to feel it. She closes her eyes, leaning into the sensation. But then a hand touches her shoulder—it's Ian, proffering a joint.

She takes a big drag and blows out a question with the smoke. "Where did you find these guys?" She motions at the dancers. "They're gems."

"At the Rodeo," Ian says. "They dance there on Sundays. I asked them if they ever did private parties. They said maybe."

"Are they brothers?" This question makes no sense; the two look nothing alike. The other dancer is skinny and blonde. But something about the way they move together reminds her of siblings practicing a carefully choreographed dance in their living room.

Ian looks at her like she's stupid.

She takes another drag and hands the joint back to him. The weed is super skunky and she starts to cough, trying to explain, "One of them reminds me of a friend from high school— from the Dairy Queen. You ever work fast food?" This question makes even less sense.

"Uh...no." Ian stretches out the "no" in what seems a parody of bitchy TV show queenness, except she's not sure it's a parody. But then he looks at Sid with affection. "Are you high already, girl?"

She fashions her face into what she hopes is a charming expression. "I certainly hope so." Around the pool deck, people are dancing and chatting, waving at people they know, clutching champagne flutes half-full of sparkling pink, weaving through the crowd to get another drink. Ian's friend DJ Lulu is on decks, set up in a corner by the bar. She's one of only a few women at the party, and one of maybe three other lesbians. Sternly handsome, she's wearing a black ball cap with "LULU" in silver letters pulled down low over her dark face. She concentrates on the music, head down, bobbing slightly to the beat.

The song makes the air throb and there's a feeling of heaviness, as if there might be a storm later, and suddenly Sid feels sexy, feels like dancing, but she doesn't have anyone to dance with. She sways a bit, holding her drink up so it doesn't slosh. Everything is wavy, subterranean. And where is Joey, her beloved Joey?

There he is—across the pool, ridiculous and retro-stylish in a tangerine caftan, laughing and vamping it up with his well-dressed friends. Even though the sun has dropped, he's wearing black cat-eyed sunglasses with rhinestones circling the frames.

Sunglasses at night, like that dumb eighties song Michael and Sid used to sing to each other as they mopped the floors with bleach water after close—using the mops as microphones, whipping their wash rags in the air like feathered boas. Michael in Sid's garish makeup—blue eye shadow, orange lipstick—and Sid's hair slicked back with his astringent-smelling gel, blobby like the bacteria that lives in dirty aquariums, the color of mouthwash and slimy to the touch.

Was it one of those nights that they kissed? What a mess. Tongues mashed against each other's teeth, neither of them having any idea of what they were doing, saliva dribbling down their chins—they gave up pretty quickly.

Pulling away, Michael had made a weird face.

Hurt, Sid quickly said, "Let's just be friends."

"Agreed," he had said, patting her cheek tenderly. "We're definitely friend material."

Ian waves over some friends, a group of guys Sid has met at their parties over the years. She remembers a few names—Sergio, Cole, Leonard. They hug her and tell her she's looking fabulous, trim—both are lies. She's put on weight and as usual couldn't find a nice enough outfit for the party so is in cut-offs and not-white-enough high tops. But right now she's high and doesn't care. She's drifting in and out of the conversation, watching the dancers, one eye on Joey's theatrics, one ear listening to Ian tell a story about his uncle who owns a beach-side villa in Mexico. "He says, 'the gays are okay, and the Jews, but not these god-damned Indians, and those Mexicans...'" Everyone laughs, even Sergio and Leonard, two brown men in a party of mostly whites. Is Sergio's smile strained? He lifts up his glass. "Those damned Mexicans, eh?" he says, using an exaggerated Mexican accent.

Everyone laughs. Leonard sniffs, "Wonder what he has to say about the blacks—oh wait, don't tell me, don't tell me—I really don't want to know." He takes a big sip of his drink and lifts his eyebrows at the other men.

Ian smiles. "Who knows what he says about the gays when I'm not around. But the man's so rich—everywhere he goes, he sees money, makes money. He says it's like there are these endless streams of money floating in the sky. All you have to do is scoop your dipper in, get a dipperful."

"Insane," Sergio says. "Truly bizarre. Only a super-rich dude could have such mystical ideas about money. The rest of us just have to hustle along with everybody else."

"Yeah, down here on the *ground*. No scooping from the heavens for this man," Leonard says.

"Yeah," Sid chimes in weakly.

Cole, a rainbow heart painted in watercolors on his pasty chest, twirls his glittering pride beads around his neck and flutters his fake eyelashes. Everyone laughs and clinks their glasses. Ian sparks up another lethal-smelling joint and passes it around. Sid refuses this time, wondering if they're all as high as she is—she can't tell if the conversation they've just had was intensely uncomfortable or whether she's just being paranoid. She decides to sneak away to refill her drink and to find Joey, who has disappeared in the crowd on the other side of the pool, in the darkening dusk.

Back in the pet shop days, when they called each other the Pet Shop Boys, she'd take her Women's Studies textbooks to work, try to study when the shop was slow. She'd read to Joey, paragraphs of Audre Lorde, Judith Butler. Back then, Joey would listen. Back then, he called himself a feminist. Sometimes, when she was feeling particularly tender, she'd call him "Joey Boy," "Joey Joy," or "My Joy." When she was feeling snarky, it was "Bitch" or "Whiny Bitch." He called her "Mr. Sidney" or "Repent Sinner." When the store was empty and Olivier wasn't around, they'd yell, "God hates fags!" across the aisles at each other, mocking the preacher in the States who protested soldiers' funerals to say that God hates America because America loves gays. The preacher's convoluted logic always made Joey and Sid laugh. "America loves gays," Joey would scoff. "That's news to me."

The store had a particular smell, as all pet stores do—close, humid, musky. The smell was also comforting, familiar—similar, Sid imagined, to what barn smell must be like for a kid who grew up on a farm. Whenever she opened the door, she breathed it in—cedar shavings in the bottom of cages, fish food flaky as Brewer's yeast, mouse and bird droppings, new carpet on the scratching posts, chemicals for the aquariums.

And the animals—she loved them all, but especially the hamsters, each of whom she had given a name. Pebbles. Mousy. My Girlfriend. And the prettiest one, who she called Joey.

Ian loves to call Joey "Richard," caresses the name, stretches out the syllables. Sid often has to remind herself that Ian can be generous, kind even. He flew to California to be with his parents when his mom got sick. He helped pay his friend's art school tuition. He gives money to gay charities. And he often buys her dinner, fills her up with cocktails, gives her free weed. Yet she somehow still feels judged by him—she isn't sure why. Her weight? Her clothes? She dresses mostly from thrift stores, and even her shoes, which she buys new, never stay bright--even the whitest sneakers seem to dim the minute she walks out of Sports Chek.

Ian is very finicky about his clothing, but he is too rich to dress too nicely, so goes for casual—a pair of new sneakers in some surprising color, like orange, and chinos or designer jeans. A puffy gray jacket in winter, a crisp jean jacket in spring.

Joey, on the other hand, always dresses to impress. Ironed shirt and skinny tie even if he's just meeting a friend for brunch, haircut so fresh you can see the skin above his ears, at the base of his neck. He must carry one of those drugstore quick shine kits in his bag because his shoes always gleam, and Sid has more than once seen him pull out a small mirror to check for bits of salad in his teeth.

Sid's friends will remind her, when she complains about Ian, that he turned Joey's life around.

And they are right. But—

When Ian met Joey, he was in a deep depression, struggling through school, questioning if he would make a good doctor, taking extra shifts at the pet shop to pay rent. He barely went to his beloved yoga anymore because he couldn't afford it, and he even had to give up the free chanting sessions at the studio because he had to work Friday nights. He started sleeping in instead of doing his homework, blowing off the weekend clinics to smoke dope with his flighty roommates. Sid tried to talk to him about it, but he shrugged off her concern, saying he just needed a release.

But sometimes he would call her late at night, when she was already asleep. He would ask her things like am I going to make it, am I going to be okay. Sometimes his breath would catch, he would say his chest hurt and he couldn't breathe, or he'd be on the verge of hyperventilating, in the grips of a panic attack, and she would talk him down, soothing him with phrases she'd read in self-help books, telling him she was with him even now, holding his hands. Sometimes he would list all the people he knew who loved him, his mom, his brother, his dead grandfather, his old guru. Sometimes he'd even list random people, people he didn't know very well, like Olivier or one of his yoga teachers. She would never interrupt, would just wait until the litany ended, nodding, saying softly yes, it's okay, they do, yes.

But more often Joey would sit on the ratty couch with his roommates, doing bong hits and telling borrowed stories full of bitchy exaggerations, or go out dancing and drink until he threw up or passed out. It was on one of these high-as-a-kite nights when he was out at Ponyboy—the club of the hour—that he met Ian, who was on E, single and ready to mingle. They went home together that night and within a month they were exclusive. Exclusive but semi-open, Joey explained, which meant they could still have sex with guys they met online or at the club, as long as they were safe, discreet, didn't tell the each other about it, and didn't boast to their friends.

Joey used to tell her all the time that he loved her. He'd also call her "lover." "Don't worry, lover, I'll be there," he'd say, promising to stop by her place on his way home from school. Sid misses those days before cell phones, when they'd make plans at work to meet up and actually would meet up a few days later, or when they'd just show up on each other's doorstep with a new CD or a tip about some cool-sounding party in the neighborhood. Back then, it seemed like people bumped into each other more often. There are people she used to run into all the time, people who still live just a few blocks from her, who she sees now only once a year, at Joey and Ian's big party.

Michael also used to tell her he loved her. "Love you, girl," he'd call over his shoulder, as he rode his bike away from Dairy Queen after a late-night shift. But he never called her "lover" and he stopped saying he loved her after the one time they slept together.

There was a person who used to come through the Dairy Queen drive-through all the time in a banged-up blue truck. The person's name was Mitch, and Sid thought she was a woman; Michael thought he was a man. They vied over who would get to work the drive-thru when Mitch came through, and the lucky one tried to prolong the interaction for as long as they could, bringing Mitch extra salt and ketchup packets, saying they were sorry the kitchen was slow again, asking how Mitch's day was going.

One night Mitch came through late, much later than their usual hour, and Michael happened to be on the headset. After Mitch roared away, Michael came beaming to where Sid was cleaning the milkshake machine.

"What?"

He pulled a little baggy out of the pocket of his brown work slacks and waved it in front of her face. "Want to come back to my place tonight? Mom's at her boyfriend's."

"For real?" She felt a nervous electric excitement start up in her legs.

"Mitch is going to come over."

"Oh my god. Really?"

Michael nodded. Although he was trying to play it cool, he couldn't stop smiling.

This many years later Sid remembers only a few things about that night. The lead-up is still fairly clear—asking Sherry to buy them peach coolers, going home to take a shower and change her clothes. Mitch came by, she remembers that. And they drank the coolers, and some whiskey from Mitch's flask, and they popped the pills. And there were jokes, and kissing, and fumbling. After awhile, everyone was naked in Michael's mom's king-size bed. She remembers wishing she had a dick—she didn't own a strap-on yet—so that she could do something with it. She remembers putting her hand down the front of Mitch's jeans and her triumphant gasp when she encountered wetness. "I knew it," she said.

"Knew what?" Mitch had countered, and she had felt embarrassed, even through the fuzzy warm haze of the drug.

She remembers Michael kissing the back of her neck, and thinking it felt so soft, so good. And she has a clear image of the two of them fucking, Michael on Mitch's back, both of them groaning.

Then it was very late, almost morning, and Mitch drove away in his truck and Michael was tearing the sheets off of his mom's bed, saying he had to wash them before she got home, and that Sid better go too.

They had a shift together two days later but they didn't talk about it. A week passed and they still didn't talk about it. Mitch stopped coming through the drive-thru, but one night after work Sid saw his truck idling in the parking lot as she unlocked her bike and she knew he was waiting for Michael. She biked home crying.

The next day as she and Michael were smoking in the parking lot after their shift she gathered up her courage. "I saw Mitch's truck last night."

"So?" Michael's voice was immediately defensive.

"I guess, I just...we never talked about it. I mean, are you dating?"

He sighed. "I don't know what we're doing. We're figuring it out. It's just—fun, okay?"

"It was fun for me too," she said quietly.

"Yeah, well, he likes me, okay? He chose me. I'm sorry. But he did."

Sid looked down at the cigarette burning away between her fingers. She realized she was holding her breath.

Michael distanced himself after that. He no longer joked with her, he no longer invited her over for Friday movie nights or asked to borrow her makeup. After Dairy Queen closed, he would clean like a demon and hurry to get out of there as fast as he could, saying he had plans. A few weeks later he quit and started working at the McDonald's across the street. At school, he avoided her. She'd see him sometimes biking home after work, or she'd see Mitch's truck in the parking lot waiting for him, but they rarely spoke and they never hung out again.

When Sid finally makes it through the crowd to Joey, she can see that he is half-lit, and in full-on entertainer mode. She stops a couple of feet away, sipping on her re-filled margarita, even stronger than the last pour, and watches him. He's laughing, tipping back his head to show off his long neck, gesturing extravagantly with a gold (real gold? It can't be) cigarette holder that holds an unlit cigarette. He doesn't notice her, he's telling one of his stories, lapping his tongue like a little dog as his friends lean in, smiling. One of them asks, "Your new puppy?"

"No." He takes a fake-drag of the unlit cigarette and pauses for dramatic effect. "Ian's mother."

The group breaks into peals of laughter. Sid notices that one of them sounds like a barking dog.

She has the sudden desire to slip away before she's noticed, but just then one of Joey's former roommates, a gorgeous old queen who used to host a popular drag night—Pringles, everyone calls him, for reasons she's never understood—sees her and waves her over. "Dear!"

A big hug from Pringles, a round of greetings and gropings, glasses clinking, and Joey has his arm around her, she can smell the gin on his breath. He pushes his sunglasses up on his head. "I've missed you," he whispers into her ear, but she can't feel there's any way this can be sincere. They haven't seen each other in months. Their last hangout was supposed to be just the two of them, but it turned into a dinner with Ian, some Italian-Japanese fusion place in what used to be Chinatown. As usual, they had suggested a restaurant she couldn't afford and she'd been too embarrassed to tell them that. She stared for a long time at the menu of small plates, things like homemade chickpea tofu with pesto for twenty-seven dollars, and finally ordered miso soup and the least expensive beer. Ian had spent the night complaining about how it wasn't fair that his parents had to pay extra taxes on their two empty investment condos, and Joey had spent the night complaining about the silk trousers he had hand-sewn for their wedding, how he had to take them back three times, how the tailor just couldn't get it right. He hadn't even asked her about school, just carried on about himself while he and Ian devoured small plates of roast duck, parsley meatballs, gnocci wrapped in seaweed. She left early, rode her bike home in the rain feeling alienated and alone.

"I've missed you too," she says, and as the words come out she realizes it's true. But the moment doesn't have a chance to land—Joey is already distracted, flirting with his friend Bernard, talking about the last time they went to Rodeo, all the hot bears in chaps, and who might be going to the club tonight when the party starts to die down. DJ Lulu has put on another dangerously sexy tune, an undulating stretched-out beat that makes Sid think of swimming underwater, of slow kissing, and it's as if everyone's popped a Molly all of a sudden, pupils dilated, slithering and prancing around the pool. Maybe they have all popped a Molly, come to think of it, maybe that's why Joey's entourage seems so spacey and touchy, although no one's offered her any. This brings up a wave of loneliness. Why does she keep coming to these things? She doesn't even have a girlfriend this year to hide behind. She should be home, alone with her books. She takes a big gulp of her drink and tries to look insouciant.

Around the pool people are using exaggerated gestures to tell each other stories, lifting their arms up to capture it all in another blurry selfie. Someone pushes one of the drag queens into the pool and she shrieks, reaching for her hair. A couple is slow dancing and making out—one misstep and they'll fall into the pool as well. The music thrums; the bar is buzzing.

And suddenly Ian is there beside them. Someone has slipped a lei around his neck; its bright colors are echoed in the flowers decorating his designer shirt. He holds Joey's elbow and says something in his ear. Joey leans in, sliding his arm around Ian's waist, and his usual slightly dissatisfied expression softens as he listens, slowly nodding his head. For a moment Sid remembers his gentleness, the way his mouth used to quiver when he was nervous or about to share something important, how open his eyes used to be. He kisses Ian's cheek tenderly. Then they both turn to the group and smile, as if they are on their honeymoon, bare feet in white sand, waves rising behind them as they pose for a photo.

Ian raises his glass. "To Richard! Ten years!"

"Of sobriety?" cracks Pringles, and everyone laughs.

"Ten years of the spa! Still going strong!" Ian turns to Joey and kisses him on the mouth. "I'm so proud of you, lover."

Everyone clinks their glasses and calls out, "To Richard! Ten years! To Richard!"

And Sid joins in, "To Richard!" But she can barely hear her own voice in the choir of congratulations. Above her head are strings of lights and further up, stars she can't see. She feels the crowd of bodies encircling the pool, the throb of their energy, and beyond, the thrum of the city. Her greenish drink glows luminescent as she holds it up against the deepening blue night. "To Richard," she says again.

preface

erasure from Leslie Feinberg's Transgender Warriors

I've heard the question   the answer
the history   hero   the rub   battles
the words woman and man
the bodies and styles   of living struggles
in language   I heard language
yelled   screeching   words that made us
catalogue the heat of struggle

I come from wounds   chosen
language in movement
butch   bulldagger   cross-dresser
I reassign   I have crossed the line
of socially acceptable   being transed
I have shaped my life   from limitations

TR BRADY

index
erasure from Leslie Feinberg's Transgender Warriors

a mis   a saint (
action is   trans in revolution
Armstrong Artemis a bright gall
over   all   all ash
all mar   ash   a river gender
a star a start   *See also*
a line a then   an attic son
a fault e   saint   a Nancy
ana sex   double-edged
see us

back cover

erasure from Leslie Feinberg's Transgender Warriors

personal
[leaves sense concept
                fully   whole both valid
nothing new.

                        Report

[Trans
gender   delves   the transgender experience, inviting
consider a spectrum

and hold well   become art   become transform

become   versal

challenge   forth – complex   multi – take up

a ground

        large   *Synapse*

                        trans

body

        / /   /
                        Butch

AHIMSA TIMOTEO BODHRÁN

Plume Protocol (Post-Penance, Peri-Pandemic)

Each bead falls in alignment,
bones pulled tight, taut,
enough room to breathe
through each lesson.

Each jingle is a prayer sung
upon a milkened mouth, then
danced, passed hide-hooved to
hide-hooved, metals bent
bright, bent backwards, birch-
bitten, moved forward, shells
slotted, shaking in the
distance, remnants of
sweetness in each canonical,
tin-harped step, we pull.

You, two of six, meet one of
six. There is an exchange. You
do not have enough
credentials to carry quills,
drape plumes from your rear-
view, but this stone, close to
your heart, you do carry,
lacing and enlacing again
leather someone might tie for
you another day.

Until you know songs, this is
what you'll carry to protect
throats, something more than
padded pensioned priests and
candles crossed, ancient altar
boys before you, can offer.

A brown bone blessing for
each outstretched neck. Sweet
songs to carry each of you,
antlered, arisen, and shaking
in sweat, through your days
each lenten week.

Contributors

Ahimsa Timoteo Bodhrán is a multimedia artist, activist, critic, and educator. Bodhrán is the author of *Antes y después del Bronx: Lenapehoking* and *South Bronx Breathing Lessons*; editor of the international queer Indigenous issue of *Yellow Medicine Review: A Journal of Indigenous Literature, Art, and Thought*; and co-editor of the Native dance, movement, and performance issue of *Movement Research Performance Journal*. A 2019 Tulsa Artist Fellow, Bodhrán has received scholarships/fellowships from the Voices of Our Nations Arts Foundation, CantoMundo, Radius of Arab American Writers, Inc., Macondo Foundation, and Lambda Literary Foundation. His work appears in 190 publications. **TR Brady**'s work has recently appeared in *Colorado Review, Copper Nickel, Denver Quarterly, The Adroit Journal*, and *Tin House*. TR is a graduate of the Iowa Writers' Workshop and co-edits the journal *Afternoon Visitor*. Find more of TR's work here: www.trbradypoet.com. **Kayleb Rae Candrilli** is a 2019 Whiting Award Winner in Poetry and the author of *Water I Won't Touch* (Copper Canyon 2021), *All the Gay Saints* (Saturnalia 2020), and *What Runs Over* (YesYes Books 2017). Their work is published or forthcoming in *POETRY, American Poetry Review, Boston Review* and many others. Follow them on IG @kayleb_rae. **Catherine Chen** is a poet, performer, and author of the chapbook *Manifesto, or: Hysteria* (Big Lucks). Their writing has appeared in *Slate, The Rumpus, Apogee, Anomaly*, and *Nat. Brut*, among others. A recipient of fellowships from Poets House, Lambda Literary, and Sundress Academy for the Arts, they're currently working on a libretto. Website: www.aluutte.com. Twitter/Instagram: aluutte **Ching-In Chen** (www.chinginchen.com) is author of T*he Heart's Traffic, recombinant* (2018 Lambda Literary Award for Transgender Poetry), *how to make black paper sing* and *Kundiman for Kin :: Information Retrieval for Monsters*. Chen is also co-editor of *The Revolution Starts at Home: Confronting Intimate Violence Within Activist Communities*. **Diana Clark** is a 2019 alumni of the University of North Carolina Wilmington, where they graduated with their MFA in fiction. They are the recipient of the LGBTQ+ writer scholarship for The Muse & The Marketplace 2019, a partial scholarship recipient to Sundress Academy for the Arts, and a 2020 candidate for the Kenyon Review Writers Workshop. Their work has appeared in *Portland Review, BULL, The Indianapolis Review, Lunch Ticket*, and more. They currently live in Wilmington, North Carolina with their adopted cat, Emily D. **S. Brook Corfman** is the author of the poetry collections *My Daily Actions, or The Meteorites* (Fordham University Press 2020, chosen by Cathy Park Hong for their poetry prize) and *Luxury, Blue Lace* (chosen by Richard Siken for the 2018 Autumn House Rising Writer Prize), as well as three chapbooks including *Frames* (Belladonna* Books). sbrookcorfman.com & @sbrookcorfman. **David Antonio Cruz** is a multidisciplinary artist and a Professor of the Practice in Painting and Drawing at the School of the Museum of Fine Arts at Tufts University. Cruz fuses painting and performance to explore the visibility and intersectionality of brown, black, and queer bodies. Cruz received a BFA in painting from Pratt Institute and an MFA from Yale University. He attended Skowhegan School of Painting and Sculpture and completed the AIM Program at the Bronx Museum. Recent residencies include the LMCC Workspace Residency, Project for Empty Space's Social Impact Residency, and BRICworkspace. Cruz's work has been included in notable group exhibitions at the Smithsonian National Portrait Gallery, Brooklyn Museum, El Museo del Barrio, Performa 13, and the McNay Art Museum. Most recently, at Monique Meloche Gallery. His fellowships and awards include the Joan Mitchell Foundation Painters & Sculptors Award, the Franklin Furnace Fund Award, the Urban Artist Initiative Award, the Queer Mentorship Fellowship, and the Neubauer Faculty Fellowship at Tufts University. Recent press includes *The New York Times, Art In America, Document Journal, Wall Street Journal, WhiteHot Magazine, W Magazine, Bomb Magazine*, and *El Centro Journal.* **Jen Currin** is the author of *Hider/Seeker: Stories*, which was named a Globe and Mail top 100 book of 2018. Jen has also published four poetry collections, including *The Inquisition Yours*, winner of the 2011 Audre Lorde Award for Lesbian Poetry. Jen lives on the unceded territories of the Qayqayt and Kwantlen Nations (New Westminster, BC), and teaches writing for a living. **Piper J. Daniels** (she/ her) is a queer antiracist intersectional feminist and mother to an extraordinary chihuahua mix. Her debut essay collection, *Ladies Lazarus*, won the Tarpaulin Sky Book Award, was longlisted for the PEN Diamonstein-Spielvogel Award For the Art of the Essay, and was a finalist for the Lambda Literary Award in LGBTQ Nonfiction. She is founder and HBIC of Creative Consultation Collective, an instructional platform and manuscript consulting service dedicated to the support and proliferation of LGBTQ / POC voices. **Chekwube Danladi** is the author of *Semiotics* (UGA Press, September 2020), selected by Evie Shockley as the winner of the 2019 Cave Canem Poetry Prize. From Lagos by way of West Baltimore, she currently lives in Chicago. www. codanladi.com. **Dez Deshaies** is a writer and game designer from Chicago. His work, which focuses on the intersections of fiction, games, and queerness, has appeared or is forthcoming in *Menacing Hedge* and *The Heartland Review.* His work has also been exhibited at The Adler Planetarium and Orlando Museum of Art. His website is binch.biz, and he is on Instagram and Twitter @dezdeshaies. **Jai Dulani** is a trans writer and artist who spent most of his life in New York City by way of Pittsburgh, PA and Chandigarh, India. His work has appeared in *Waxwing, Open City*, the anthology *Experiments in a Jazz Aesthetic*, and elsewhere. A former BCAT/ Rotunda Gallery Multi-media Artist-in-Residence, Dulani has received fellowships from Kundiman, VONA/Voices, and the Asian American Writers' Workshop. **Cody Dunn** is a poet living and working in Washington DC. More of his work is forthcoming in *Indiana Review.* **Hazem Fahmy** is a Pushcart-nominated poet and critic from Cairo. He is currently pursuing his MA in Middle Eastern Studies and Film Studies from the University of Texas at Austin. His debut chapbook, *Red//Jild//Prayer* won the 2017 Diode Editions Contest. A Kundiman and Watering Hole Fellow, his poetry has appeared or is forthcoming in *Apogee, AAWW, The Boston Review* and *The Offing.* **Andrew Sean Greer** is the Pulitzer Prize winning author of six works of fiction, including the bestsellers *The Confessions of Max Tivoli* and *Less.* He is the recipient of a NEA grant, a Guggenheim Fellowship, and the 2018 Pulitzer Prize for Fiction. He lives in San Francisco. **Lyd Havens** is the author of the chapbook *I Gave Birth to All the Ghosts Here* (Nostrovia! 2018). The winner of the 2018 ellipsis… Poetry Prize, their work has been published in *Ploughshares, The Shallow Ends*, and *Tinderbox Poetry Journal*, among others. Lyd is currently an undergraduate at Boise State University, where they are studying creative writing and history. **HR Hegnauer** is the author of *When the Bird is Not a Human* and *Sir*. She is a book designer specializing in working with independent publishers as well as individual artists and writers. She received an MFA in Writing & Poetics from Naropa University, and an MBA in Business from the University of Denver. **Shira Hereld** is a writer, activist, trail worker, and soon-to-be lawyer. She hopes all survivors find and trust their own voice. Her writing has been published in *The Baltimore Review, plain china, Impossible Archetype, Lilith, Almond Press, Outrageous Fortune, Assisi: An Online Journal of Arts and Letters, F-Bomb*, and *Control Lit.* **Gabrielle Grace Hogan** is a poet from St. Louis, Missouri. She resides in Austin, Texas while she pursues her MFA from the University of Texas as Austin as part of the New Writers Project. Her work has been published by *The Academy of American Poets, Sonora Review, the Chicago Review of Books' Arcturus*, and others. Her micro-chap *Sentimental Violence: Some Poems About Tonya Harding* is available in a free PDF from Ghost City Press. She is the Poetry Editor of *Bat City Review* and Co-Editor of *You Flower / You Feast*, an anthology of works inspired by Harry Styles. Her social media and projects can be found on her website gabriellegracehogan.com. **Minying Huang** (she/they) grew up in Cambridge, UK. Her work appears in *PANK Magazine, Electric Literature, Tinderbox Poetry Journal, the Shade Journal, Nat. Brut*, and elsewhere. She is studying for a PhD in Medieval and Modern Languages at the University of Oxford. She tweets @minyingh. **Cyrée Jarelle Johnson** is a poet and writer from Piscataway, NJ. He earned his MFA in Creative Writing from Columbia University. *SLINGSHOT*, his debut collection of poetry, was published by Nightboat Books, and won a 2020 Lambda Literary Award in Gay Poetry. **Trevor Ketner** (they/them), is the author of *White Combine, Negative of a Photo of Fire*, and *Major Arcana: Minneapolis* and has been published in the *Academy of American Poets' Poem-a-Day, Best New Poets, New England Review, Ninth Letter*, and elsewhere. A former Poets House Emerging Poets Fellow, they are the publisher for Skull + Wind Press. Twitter handle: @TKetner; Website: trevorketner.com. **Mihee Kim** (she/they) is an artist and community organizer working at Kearny Street Workshop, an Asian Pacific American arts nonprofit based on Ramaytush Ohlone land. She earned a B.A. from UC Berkeley and is in the MFA program for Writing at CCA. Mihee lives on Chochenyo Ohlone land, called Oakland, California. **J.S. Kuiken** is a queer American writer. He earned his MA in Creative Writing at the University of East Anglia. In 2013, he was a Lambda Literary Fellow. Most recently he was a winner of Project Outbreak's audio play competition. He likes to take naps with his cat Beatrice. **t. tran le** is a poet from Texas. They've received fellowships from Brooklyn Poets & Kundiman. You can find more of their work in *8 Poems, Breakwater Review, Apogee, Kweli Journal* & elsewhere. They live in Brooklyn with their spouse & three cats: Piaf, Freddie Mercury, & birdie. **Sarah Lord** is a writer of introspective prose themed around queer becoming, healing, and resilience. She writes professionally for an online publication. She is published in *Malahat Review, Minola Review* and *Black Bear Review*. She was long-listed for the 2020 CBC Short Story Prize. Living in the Kootenays of British Columbia, Canada, she is writing a novel. @SLordAlmighty sarahlord.ca **Francisco Márquez** is a poet from Maracaibo, Venezuela, born in Miami, Florida. He has received support from The Fine Arts Work Center in Provincetown, Breadloaf Writers Conference, Tin House, and The Poetry Project. His work can be found in *The Brooklyn Rail, Bennington Review, The Common*, and elsewhere. He lives in Brooklyn. **Nadine Marshall** is a Black NBTrans writer and organizer living in Detroit, MI. Their words have reached the audiences of TEDxUofM, Gertrude Press, *Shade Journal*, and *Freezeray Poetry Journal*. Nadine is a 2019 Lambda Literary Fellow in Poetry and is currently working on a manuscript exploring *BOIHood*. You can say hello to them on Instagram @WriteMindDET **Wryly T. McCutchen** is a hybrid writer, interdisciplinary performer, community educator, & 2018 LAMBDA Fellow in poetry. Their work has appeared in *Papeachu Review* & *Nat. Brut*. Their debut poetry collection, *My Ugly and Other Love Snarls*, was published in 2017 by University of Hell press. Wryly resides in the unceded Coast Salish territories where they cast spells in text & flesh & sweat. **Breena Nuñez** (they/she) is a cartoonist and educator based in the Peninsula of the Bay Area. They enjoy creating autobiographical comics and zines that center the nuances of existing as an Afrodescendiente with Central American roots in El Salvador and Guatemala. **Shannon Page**'s essays and short stories have appeared in *Untethered Magazine, The Scattered Pelican*, and elsewhere. She lives in Vancouver, but you can find her online at shannonpagewrites.wordpress. com or on Twitter (@ShannonEvePage). **heidi andrea restrepo rhodes** is a queer, Colombian/ Latinx, poet, artist, scholar, & activist. Her poetry collection *The Inheritance of Haunting* (University of Notre Dame 2019) was selected by Ada Limón for the 2018 Andrés Montoya Poetry Prize. A 2019 CantoMundo Fellow, and 2018 VONA alum, her poems have been published in *Poetry, Academy of American Poets, Raspa, Feminist Studies*, & *Huizache*, among other places. **D.M. Rice** was born in Dallas, Tx, and studies Creative Writing at the University of Essex. They have recently completed a course in the Avant Garde, generating full-length redactions of foundational queer theory texts, and are working on a PhD studying canonicity in contemporary literature. D.M. tweets @quizlemon and is co-EIC @sybiljournal. **Kimani Rose** has spent her time writing works where she could see herself and her experiences represented. Focused primarily on self-publishing, she works to make her art as accessible as possible. When describing her work, she says "Poetry is my first language. Everything I write feels like bleeding, feels like ripping myself apart and sewing myself back together with literal thread. I find myself in the darkness through poetry. I can move between this realm and the ancestral realm with my poetry, it seems. It's the thing that makes me free." **Martha Ryan** (she/ her) is a queer poet living in Los Angeles. She was the recipient of a Fulbright Fellowship (2016-2017) to India. **Zak Salih** lives in Washington, DC. His writing has appeared in *Crazyhorse, The Rumpus, The Millions, The Chattahoochee Review, The Florida Review, the Los Angeles Review of Books*, and other publications. His debut novel, *Let's Get Back to the Party*, is forthcoming in February 2021 by Algonquin Books. Twitter: @ZMSalih1982; Instagram: @ zakigrams; Website: zaksalih.com **Natalie Sharp** is a Black queer writer, dancer, and educator hailing from Savannah, GA and based in Denver, CO. She completed her MFA in poetry at the University of Colorado Boulder. Her poetry and nonfiction have previously appeared or are forthcoming in *Cosmonauts Avenue, The Shade Journal*, and elsewhere. If you propose to her in a Waffle House, she will probably say yes. You can follow her on Instagram at @short_sharp_shock. **Duncan Slagle** is a Queer poet studying Ancient Greek, Latin, and Creative Writing at the University of Wisconsin-Madison as a First Wave scholar. Duncan has won poetry prizes from the *Crab Creek Review, Mikrokosmos Journal*, and *Epiphany Magazine*. Duncan's work can be found in *BOAAT, Vinyl, The Shallow Ends*, and *The Adroit Journal*, among other publications. Duncan has more work online at duncanslagle.com & tweets / practices vanity @ssscurvy. **Emma Stough** (she/her) is a bisexual Midwestern writer living in Charleston, South Carolina. She has work out in *Quarterly West, Third Coast*, and *SmokeLong Quarterly*. **Cyrus Stuvland** is beginning their MFA in creative nonfiction this fall at the University of New Mexico. Their poetry and nonfiction has appeared in *Crab Orchard Review, The Lindenwood Review*, and *Broad Magazine*. **Lehua M. Taitano** is a queer CHamoru writer and interdisciplinary artist from Yigu, Guåhan (Guam) and co-founder of the artist collective Art 25: Art in the Twenty-fifth Century. She is the author of *Inside Me an Island* and *A Bell Made of Stones*. Taitano's work investigates modern indigeneity, decolonization, and cultural identity in the context of diaspora. She hustles her way through the capitalist labyrinth as a bicycle mechanic in Sonoma County, California. **Mimi Tempestt** is a daughter of California. She is an artist, writer, and academic whose works are aimed at disrupting negative and stereotypical narratives around the iconography and constructions of black and queer people. She is the 2019 winner of the Mary Merritt Henry Prize for a group of poems, and her debut book of poetry, *The Monumental Misrememberings*, is scheduled to be published in the Fall of 2020. **Milo Todd** was a Pechet Fellow in GrubStreet's Novel Incubator Program, received a scholarship as a Lambda Literary Fellow in Fiction, and is a regular presenter at the Muse and the Marketplace and the Boston Book Festival. His writing has appeared in *Writer Unboxed, Dead Darlings, GrubWrites, Everyday Feminism, Emerge: 2019 Lambda Fellows Anthology*, and more. You can follow him @todd_milo or on milotodd.com. **Stephen Wack** is an Atlanta-based writer. His work has previously appeared or is forthcoming in *Salt Hill Journal, Maudlin House, Cleaver Magazine*, and *The Woven Tale Press*. To get in touch: @stephen_wack / stephenjwack@gmail.com